DEAD
REVELATIONS

THE LIFE AFTER SERIES

DEAD REVELATIONS

AMANDA FASCIANO

4 Horsemen
Publications, Inc.

4 Horsemen Publications, Inc.
1497 Main St. Suite 169
Dunedin, FL 34698
4horsemenpublications.com
info@4horsemenpublications.com

Cover and Typeset by Autumn Skye
Editor Kristine Cotter

Library of Congress Control Number: 2022952160

Print ISBN: 978-1-64450-800-8
Hardcover ISBN: 978-1-64450-972-2
Audio ISBN: 978-1-64450-802-2
E-Book ISBN: 978-1-64450-801-5

This Book Is Dedicated To

This book is dedicated to all those out there who go searching for the truth about the paranormal. As always, it is dedicated to my loving and supportive family.

In particular, this book is dedicated to Tim and Dianna McKenney in memory of their son Erik, who passed away at the age of 3 from Acute Lymphoblastic Leukemia.

AUTHOR'S NOTE: If you have the means, please consider donating to the Saint Baldrick's Foundation for childhood cancer research. Thank you.

Table of Contents

CHAPTER 1

Of Injuries and Information

Ramon felt a little tingle on the back of his neck, and he knew Cadence and Snow were there. He wasn't sure whether that was an effect of his having been a monitor at Lexington Hills. Because of that job, he had always been attuned to when the officers or anyone else came into the building. It also could be an effect of having worked so closely with them over the last several months. Even more, it could be a side effect of his relationship with Cadence. Whatever it was, he knew they were there, in the spirit version of a hospital, and that filled him with dread.

"What have you done this time?" Ramon asked as he saw Cadence and Snow coming toward him. The handsome Cuban doctor with short brown hair watched them approach with a mix of concern and humor in his blue eyes. Neither seemed too bad off; they were both conscious and walking, so he relaxed a little. The dread that had filled him at the knowledge of their presence receded a little, but not entirely.

"It isn't me this time. I swear," Cadence said, holding up one hand in a defensive gesture as she guided Snow with her other hand. Ramon could tell the night had been rough. Cade's usual sleek ponytail in which she kept her dark blonde hair was messy now, hair falling out of it to frame her face. Her jade eyes had dark, dusky circles beneath them, evidence of how much energy they had been slinging around.

"This isn't necessary, Cadence," Snow said, even though he was cradling one of his arms against his chest. His British accent always got sharper when he was annoyed, and it was sharp enough to cut through shoe leather. He also bore the same dark circles under his ice-blue eyes that Cadence showed.

"Yeah, well, let Ramon tell you that," Cadence retorted. She never let Snow's bad moods bother her much.

"Right in here." Ramon guided them through a doorway and into an exam room. He gestured for Snow to get up on the exam table.

Snow shook himself free of Cade's guiding hand and managed to get onto the cushioned table. "Cadence is simply trying to get back at me for all the time she's spent in this infernal place," he argued, irritation plain on his face and in his voice.

"Someone has their cranky pants on," Cadence said with an apologetic look at Ramon. "It's been a hellish night."

"What happened?" Ramon looked between the two of them as he asked the question.

"You're the injured one, you tell him," Cadence said, prodding Snow to talk instead of sitting there looking sullen.

Snow began with a deep sigh. "Fine, I'll skip the preliminary details. I ended up caught in a force field made to trap spirits. I thought I could perhaps use force to get out of it. To that end, I attempted to punch my way through. I was mistaken. The action was foolish and did nothing but injure the arm I used to punch with. However, I fail to see how an injured arm requires a trip here."

"Ozzie, you are a worse patient than I am," Cadence said, shaking her head.

"I need to look at your arm." Ramon cut off whatever retort Snow had opened his mouth to say. "Please remove the jacket and change your shirt to something with short sleeves."

"Do you want me to leave?" Cadence asked because she didn't want Snow to feel uncomfortable.

Snow thought about it for a moment, then shook his head. "No, I've seen you injured. I suppose it's only fair." It didn't take long for his jacket to disappear and his long sleeve, button-down shirt to change into a plain white T-shirt.

"Oh my God," Cadence said, her voice quiet and her eyes wide as she saw his arm. She moved to a chair in the corner of the room and sat down heavily. She had not been prepared for how bad it looked.

Ramon glanced back at her. "If you're going to stay, you need to keep the comments to yourself, Cade," he warned.

Cadence nodded, but her eyes remained glued to Snow's right arm. The entire arm was a mottled mix of angry red and brilliant yellow. It was like his arm had been painted in splotches and lines. Cadence had never seen anything like it.

"I'm going to have to touch your arm and manipulate it a little," Ramon said. "I'm not going to lie; it is going to hurt."

Snow grimaced as he nodded, bracing himself. Ramon tested the motion of Snow's arm and joints while watching the man's face intently for signs of pain. There wasn't much movement before Snow's eyes narrowed, and not much beyond that before he hissed at the pain. Ramon stopped moving Snow's arm and began prodding at the skin. This elicited grunts of pain from Snow as he shifted a bit on the table. Ramon released the arm and sat back, thinking.

"Rest it. Let it heal, right?" Snow asked, his words beginning to slur a little. Both he and Cadence had spent a good deal of energy on the evening's events. That expenditure was beginning to take its toll on both, as evidenced by the fact that Cadence had nodded off in the chair she was occupying.

"No, this looks like something a little more complicated than that," Ramon said, keeping his voice quiet so as not to wake Cadence and to keep the conversation between himself and Snow private. "I want to keep you here while you sleep, so I can monitor how your arm is doing."

"That's not necessary," Snow argued, trying to slip down off the table. Ramon's firm hand on his chest stopped him.

"It is necessary," Ramon stated, giving Snow a look that brooked no arguments.

"Just do it, Ozzie," Cadence said. Her voice was thick with sleepiness as she spoke, having awoken with a little bit of a start at Snow's raised voice as he attempted to argue with Ramon. "He wins all the arguments about this kind of stuff anyway."

Snow sighed and looked at Ramon. "Fine, but I assure you that it will all be well and good, and this fuss will be about nothing. This is all silliness."

Ramon helped Snow off the exam table, ignoring Snow's show of temper, and called over a nurse. "Please get Inspector Snow settled in a room. I must consult with someone, but I won't be too long." The nurse nodded to Ramon and took Snow from him, walking him across the hall and into a room.

"Who're you consulting with?" Cadence had been nearly asleep in the chair again, but Ramon's voice had woken her.

"Well, first, I am going to take you to consult with your bed," Ramon said, his smile soft.

Cadence giggled, acting a bit drunk at having used far too much energy. "Why, Ramon, what kind of girl do you think I am?"

"A tired one," Ramon said with a chuckle. He scooped her up into his arms and teleported the two of them to her living room. Sam was there on the couch, fast asleep. Ramon turned and made his way to Cade's bedroom and laid her on the bed. She made a murmuring noise and turned onto her side.

Ramon took the opportunity to remove her shoes and socks and examine the silvery skin of her feet. With the stress of the investigation tonight, he had been afraid that she would have re-injured herself. He was relieved to see that the bottoms of her feet were intact. No skin had broken. He traced the silver scars as they ran up her legs, moving her pant legs as carefully as he could to mid-calf. Everything looked fine, much to his relief. Her feet were a little pink and swollen where the silver scars hadn't stretched the skin tight, but all in all, the healing burns had held up, much to Ramon's relief.

He pulled her pant legs back down and covered her with the soft, fluffy throw blanket she had at the foot of her bed. He leaned down and kissed her cheek as he gently caressed her honey-gold hair away from her face.

"Sleep well, mi amore," he said.

He still had one more stop to make before he went back to the medical center. Teleporting out of Cadence's room, he found himself in the waiting room at Croft's office. His secretary was not there, which was under-standable as it was late. Or early, depending on how you looked at it. He moved toward the secretary's desk but paused as he thought, *What the hell? The man is either in or he isn't.* Ramon moved to the door to Croft's office and knocked.

"Enter," a deep, commanding voice said from the other side of the door.

Ramon opened the door and entered the office. Croft looked up from the papers he had been going over and offered a smile and nod to Ramon. Ambient light in the office shone off the dark skin of Croft's bald pate, and his large muscular build made the desk he sat at seem too small.

The office was much like Ramon had anticipated. The shelves to Ramon's right were filled not only with books and tomes, but many scrolls. A great deal of plant life grew in pots near the desk. Centered above Croft was a breathtaking painting of an Ibis in shallow water. On Croft's desk, to the right, was an antique scale, the kind with two bowls, one on either side of the center, that must be equal. A white feather was resting in one of those bowls.

"Ah, the good doctor," Croft said in greeting. "How can I help you?" Croft put his papers to one side, gestured for Ramon to have a seat, then folded his hands together on the desk.

"I have Inspector Snow in a room of the hospital," Ramon said without preamble as he took the offered chair. "I'm not sure what to make of his condition."

A deep baritone chuckle emerged from Croft. "I'm not a doctor. Why would you want to seek me for answers?"

"Because doctor or not, you are the one who trained Snow," Ramon said in reply. "I think part of his injury may be due to using a particular power, and only you would know if he had the ability in question, as you would have had to teach it to him."

"As spirits, most of our gifts are innate, doctor," Croft said.

"Knowledge of this one isn't innate," Ramon countered. "I've kept my mouth shut in regard to what I suspect about you, Director Croft. It isn't my business or my secret to tell. But I need confirmation because I need to know how best to treat Snow. I'm not even asking for your secrets. I'm asking you to come and look at his arm and verify if my theory about the injury is correct."

Croft was silent for a moment, regarding Ramon from behind steepled hands. After a heavy moment of silence between them, it was Croft who finally said, "And what is it you suspect?"

"It doesn't matter," Ramon said. "Who or what you are isn't the point. The point is that I have every available piece of information in order to treat my patient." Ramon leaned forward, cupping his hands together as he eyed the ancient-looking set of scales on Croft's desk. "I would appreciate it if you could meet me in the morning, once Snow has had a chance to rest."

Ramon rose and held out his hand. In it lay a red paper heart, like one might see on Valentine's Day. He then set the paper heart lightly on the empty bowl of the scale opposite the bowl that held the white feather. The scales remained balanced. He bowed his head to Croft and then turned, closing the door to the office as he exited. He left Croft staring at the scales in contemplation.

Liam

Teeny was exhausted. They had investigated the prison until roughly 3:30 in the morning. That was when Detective Halleran had burst into the prison, running like hell for the gallows room. She had followed and had been completely unprepared for the sight of Liam, surrounded by broken glass and blood, one leg broken beyond recognition, covered in cuts and bruises. The ambulance ride to the hospital had been torturous as she sat there watching the EMT work Liam over.

The emergency room had been no better. Nurses and staff peppered her with questions about Liam's health history, blood type, the last time he had eaten, and a million other questions she only sometimes had the answers to. The emergency room doctor called in an orthopedic surgeon. By five in the morning, Liam was heading up for surgery, and she was in the waiting room of the surgery suite. She had dozed off on the vinyl-covered couch in the waiting room.

"Ms. DeLucca?" Teeny opened her eyes as a woman called her name.

"Yeah?" she said as she sat up, trying to push the grogginess from her brain. The sterile smell of the hospital invaded her nose. She glanced at the standard issue, white, round wall clock. It was almost 8:30 in the morning.

"Dr. Michaels will be out here to talk to you in a minute, but after that, you can go to room 424 if you want. That's the room Mr. McIntire has been admitted to," the nurse said.

"How is Liam?" Teeny felt the anxiety and panic creep back in as she thought of what he had looked like when they found him.

"He's in recovery. The doctor will be able to tell you more, but he's not going to ICU if that helps," the nurse reassured. She could see the familiar worry in Teeny's eyes that most friends and family members had in this waiting room. She hoped she could ease it by assuring her that the ICU was not necessary.

"Thank you," Teeny said. She ran her hands through her black hair. She knew she looked a mess and didn't really care much, but she also didn't want to look like a completely insane person to the doctor.

It took about five more minutes for Dr. Michaels to come out. He wore simple light blue scrubs and one of those light blue, paper, shower cap type hats. His dark brown hair was beginning to grey on both his head and his goatee. Glasses were dark-rimmed and worn over warm brown eyes.

"Ms. DeLucca?" he asked as he approached her.

"Yes, Dr. Michaels, right?" Teeny knew it had to be, but still, it seemed the appropriate response. She stood to greet him.

"Yes, ma'am. Mr. McIntire is out of surgery and in recovery. He may be there a couple of hours, depending on how long it takes for him to come out of the anesthesia sufficiently," the doctor said.

"How is he? I mean, obviously not great since he had surgery, but what all happened? What did you do? Will he walk again?" A dozen more questions tumbled through Teeny's mind, but those were the most important to her. Dr. Michaels gestured for her to have a seat on the sofa as he took a seat on a chair facing her, pulling it a bit closer.

"He had three compound fractures to his right leg. Two broken ribs and a possible spinal cord injury. There is swelling from his fall, which is to be expected. Tomorrow, I will run more tests to see what we can find out about that. He also has a concussion and a fractured skull, but he got lucky in that the skull fracture is simple and linear, so it didn't break the skin, and it shows no sign of vascular or brain damage," the doctor finished.

Teeny had gone ice cold the moment he had mentioned the spinal injury, and his words on the skull fracture were not as comforting as the doctor had intended them to be. She took a minute to go over everything he had said, and he sat there patiently as she processed it.

"Do you mind if I go through this with you one by one?" Teeny asked because she knew surgeons were in demand and often stingy with their time. To his credit, Dr. Michaels shook his head.

"Not at all. I want to make sure you understand. I'm sure you have friends and family to report this to," he said.

"Okay, the leg. Were you able to put it back together?" To Teeny, it had looked as though Liam's leg had been trying to play Humpty Dumpty and had taken the full impact of the fall.

"Yes. He is likely going to have nightmares with airport security from now on, though," Dr. Michaels explained. "He has a couple of rods in place, and we had to do complete ankle and knee replacements as both of those were shattered beyond repair. There are some screws in there to hold the rods in place, too."

Teeny took a deep breath and moved to the question that was bothering her the most. "What about the spine?"

"The trauma of the fall injured his lumbar spine, which is the part of the spine in the lower section of your back. We won't know yet if it is a complete injury or an incomplete injury," the doctor said.

"What's the difference?"

"A complete injury means paralysis. An incomplete injury could mean anything from difficult mobility or sporadic pain to partial paralysis. We will be able to tell more once the anesthesia has worn off completely, which is why I will run more tests tomorrow."

"Okay," Teeny said with a sigh, trying to wrap her brain around all of this. "I know about broken ribs. I know about concussions. What about the skull fracture?"

"It's not as horrific as I know it sounds," Dr. Michaels said with an understanding smile. "It will take time to heal, but it didn't break the skin, it didn't web out, meaning multiple fracture lines, and it didn't dent inward to damage the brain or to cause any issues with the veins there."

Teeny nodded with a sigh. "Okay. Is there anything else I should expect?"

"Currently, he is catheterized. We've cleaned up the cuts, but a few did require stitches. Most of his bruises are on his back and legs. He is going to be on serious pain meds for a couple of days that will likely make him sleepy and perhaps a little loopy." Dr. Michaels leaned forward a bit. "Now, I have a couple of questions for you."

"Shoot," Teeny said.

"I understand that you and he are part of a TV production that goes around investigating haunted places. That an accident while investigating is what caused the injury. Is that true?"

"Yeah," Teeny said, rubbing her face to try to wake herself up a bit. "Yeah, he was on his own, and it looks like the gallows trap fell open while he was on it."

"Then I assume you will need to let someone in your production company know. This would fall under Worker's Compensation. They are also going to need to know that he is going to need to stay in town for a while. I expect at least five days in the hospital. Then, some time in a physical rehabilitation center if the spinal injury is less serious, which is what I am hoping for. Best case scenario, you are looking at about seven weeks in town."

Teeny's jaw dropped. "Seven weeks? Here? Can he go to physical therapy at home instead?"

"He could," Dr. Michaels said. "However, he would then be switching to a different doctor who wasn't there at the beginning of the injuries and treatment. That's something most doctors don't recommend. If you do decide to do that, however, I will gladly send his next doctor the records and consult with them over the phone. What's important is Mr. McIntire's recovery."

"Right," Teeny said with a nod. She saw it that way and was glad the surgeon did. She only hoped their producer would as well.

"Did the nurse give you his room number?"

"Yeah, 424," Teeny said.

"He's likely going to sleep for a few hours, even after recovery. Why don't you go back to where you are staying, grab a shower, some food, and some rest? Doctor's orders," he said with a smile.

Teeny managed to smile in return and nodded. "Thank you, Doctor."

"I'm sure I will see you tomorrow," Dr. Michaels said. He stood and offered a hand to Teeny. She shook it as she rose from the couch.

"See you tomorrow," she said in return.

She watched him leave then headed off while ordering an Uber from her phone since the van was still at the prison. She was going to go back to the hotel and shower and change. She might grab some food if she could convince herself to be hungry and then go get the van. She wanted to be back in the room by the time they brought Liam in. She didn't want him to be alone when he woke up.

CHAPTER 3

What the Cat Dragged In

Cadence sat at her desk, filling out the paperwork for the prison case. Her mind wasn't on the task, however. She was furious. She had only stopped pacing and turned to work when she realized that pacing was only making her angrier. She was alone in the office, and she shouldn't have been.

She had checked in on Snow at the medical center. He was sleeping, but his arm still didn't look good. She had also checked in with Sam on the phone. Things seemed to be fine on his end, but he was still wondering what had happened to Whitfield. And that was the question that was the crux of her anger. *What had happened to Whitfield last night? Why didn't he go where he was supposed to go? Why didn't he contact them, return calls, or be in touch at all?*

Cadence shook her head and huffed, trying to clear the questions and anger from her head. She couldn't do anything until Whitfield showed up, and she could talk to him. Being angry was doing nothing except winding her up, and she knew that. She tried to refocus herself and concentrate on the paperwork at hand, and there was plenty of it to do. Between the case itself, the arrest of spirits, not to mention the arrest of the monitor of the location, there was a metric ton of paperwork to be filled out and filed—not all of which she knew how to do.

Cade looked up sharply as the door to the office opened. Snow walked in, closing it behind him. He was impeccably dressed, as always, in a dark gray suit with a light blue tie that matched his eyes. He still looked tired and pained, but waved her down as she started to get up.

"I'm fine, I'm fine," he said, trying to assure his partner.

"Yeah, you look it," she said sarcastically.

He sat down at his desk, sighing. "Already started on the paperwork. I'm impressed. How are your legs doing after last night?"

Cadence laughed bitterly and shook her head. "My legs? You just got out of the hospital after brawling with both some weird machine and with inmates of a prison, and yet you're worried about my legs?"

"I went into last night healthy. You went into it already wounded and having just returned after over a month's recuperation. So yes, I am worried about the health of my partner," he said with a small smile.

"Were you even released, or did you just dodge Ramon and leave? And I'm doing okay, thanks," she said the last part almost as an afterthought. "You were asleep when I checked on you a couple of hours ago."

"I healed a bit. It's going to take time," he said with a shrug. "But I'll be fine. I just need to learn to not try to punch my way out of electromagnetic fields. And yes, your Ramon did release me."

"He's not *my* Ramon," Cadence said with a roll of her eyes at Snow's little taunt.

"Oh please," Snow chuckled. "Be honest, I can see how the two of you feel about each other. It's nothing to be defensive about."

Cadence scowled at him in response, but the dark expression didn't last long. "Well, I'm glad you're feeling well enough to be released. Though you still look as if you ought to go home and get a little more rest," she said.

"Not a chance," Snow said. "We have work to do. Besides which, I am not about to miss you dressing down Whitfield."

"Oh?" Cadence laughed.

"It should be quite the fireworks show," Snow said with a nod.

"Well, since you are here and he isn't, maybe you can help me out with some of this paperwork. We haven't done a case together where we've brought in spirits. I'm not quite sure what needs to be done."

"Just standard paperwork for the inmates we brought in. The former monitor, however..." Snow paused for a moment as he thought of how to phrase it. "Paperwork regarding the former monitor will be different. We will have to interview him before we can finish it."

"Interview him?" Cadence was surprised. She had thought that once they hauled him in, it would be done.

"There are questions to be asked, Cadence," Snow said. "Who he was working with? How the portal system came to be? How long it had been going on? And most importantly, why?"

"Good point," Cade said with a nod.

"Plus, a new monitor is going to have to be assigned. What did you think of that Roland fellow?" Snow asked as he looked over at Cadence.

For her part, Cade shrugged. "There's not a ton left to choose from there, but yeah. He seemed alright. He at least had the balls to come talk to us after everything that had happened."

The office door opened, cutting off the conversation. Whitfield made his way in, looking sheepish. His wild ginger hair seemed more unruly than usual, and he looked tired.

"My, my, my," Cadence said slowly as Whitfield sat down at his desk. "Look what the cat dragged in."

"Sorry," Whitfield apologized.

"Sorry?" Cadence rose from her seat as she parroted his one-word reply. Meanwhile, Snow leaned back in his chair, crossing his arms over his chest to watch. "Sorry for what? Sorry for being completely out of contact last night? Sorry for not being where you were supposed to be when you were supposed to be there? Something which left an investigation completely unattended except for the psychic's guardian spirit. Sorry for being late today? Sorry for completely ditching your responsibilities here to go do whatever it is you have been doing with the NHD?"

For each question Cadence hurled at him, Whitfield shrank down into his chair a little more. His hands were clasped tightly in his lap, and he was staring at them with intensity.

"Alright, Cadence," Snow said. "Let the man answer."

Whitfield gave a quick, thankful glance to Snow and then looked back down at his hands. He couldn't bring himself to look at Cadence. "I'm sorry for all of that," he said, his voice quiet and small. "The NHD had me working on a project before you got back," he said, lifting his head toward Cadence but only chancing a look at her chin before dropping his eyes again. "I thought I could finish it up before the investigations. I was so deep into what I was doing to finish it up that I lost track of time."

"And when Sam called, you didn't answer," Cadence said. She was still angry but saw how defeated and miserable Whitfield looked and couldn't help but take her anger down a bit when she spoke.

"I forgot to take my phone off silent from when we were at the prison the other day. It was in the pocket of my jacket, which I had put on the chair behind me," Whitfield said.

"Regardless," Snow said, piping up, "you are supposed to be available to them only when you don't have responsibilities here. You knew damned well that you had responsibilities to us. To those investigations. What happened last night should not have happened."

"Are you okay?" Whitfield asked Snow, realizing that he wasn't the only one looking rough around the edges.

"No, he was injured last night. He spent the rest of the night under Ramon's care in the hospital after we got back from the prison," Cadence said, her voice venomous as her fury riled up again. "Which you would have known about ages ago had you been doing your goddamned job. Or at least answered the fucking phone!"

"Cadence, enough," Snow said. "It's obvious Whitfield feels bad about what happened."

It was true. Whitfield was still staring at his hands, eyes cast down in shame. He had shrunk in on himself and sank back into the chair as much as he could. "I'm sorry," Whitfield said. "I know I screwed up; I know I owe Sam an apology, too. It won't happen again."

Cadence sat back down in her chair and sighed. She let the heavy silence hang in the room for a minute before relenting. "Fine," she said. "I accept your apology." His acknowledgment that he owed Sam an apology, too, seemed to placate her ire at the situation and calm her down.

Snow nodded in agreement. "As do I," the Englishman said. "But do see that it doesn't happen again. Last night could have turned out very badly for all of us. We're just lucky that it didn't."

"What did end up happening?" Whitfield asked with cautious curiosity. "Sam left me two messages. There was one message asking where I was and one message saying that the night was done, but nothing more."

"There is a really long and convoluted answer to that question," Cadence said.

"Oh?" Whitfield's eyebrows raised, his forehead crinkling with the movement.

"It turns out the ghosts of the girls were summoned by our favorite cult leader," Cadence said with a sour note in her voice.

"Why?" Whitfield's surprise at this news was obvious.

"To split the ghost hunters up," Cadence said with a shrug. "Make them split their team into two for the night, which would then make chances lower that anyone would find out what was really going on at the prison."

"The prison? Are you saying the two investigations were connected?" It was plain to see that Whitfield couldn't believe what he was hearing as he asked the questions.

"We have to confirm a few things first," Snow said, rising from his seat. "But it does look that way. Now, may I suggest that you find Sam and get the full details from him about his side of last night's events? Cadence and I have a couple more loose ends to tie up, and then we can fill you in on our adventures."

"Sure," Whitfield said, getting up from his chair. "I'll see you two later. Call if you need me; I have the ringer on," he added with a small smile.

Snow nodded to Whitfield, and Whitfield left the office, teleporting away.

"Ozzy?"

Snow sighed in response. "Cadence, I've asked you not to call me that."

"No, you told me not to call you that. And by now, you know that telling me not to do something pretty much makes it mandatory that I do it," she said with a grin. "You sent him off on purpose, didn't you?"

"I simply wanted your brother to receive the apology he deserves as soon as possible," Snow said, spreading his hands out as if to say he held nothing else.

"Uh-huh. And?" Cadence prompted.

"And I see no need for him to be involved in our questioning of Mr. Pruitt. Whitfield's absence from the other case aside, he was not involved in the prison investigation and has no need to be involved in this. He would end up asking us questions and likely derail the entire interrogation."

"Yeah, you're right," Cadence said with a nod.

"So, shall we go speak with Mr. Pruitt?" Snow smiled at his partner, doing his best to ignore the continued ache in his arm.

"Yes, let's," she replied, matching his smile with hers.

CHAPTER 4

The Interrogation

Cadence had only been to the "jail" a couple of times, and both times had been early in her afterlife. Because of that, her memory of the place was blurred in with all the other places that had been shown to her as part of her training. Stepping into it now, she recalled that she didn't like the vibe of the place.

The most obvious reason for her dislike was the fact that the walls, floor, and ceiling of the area were all solid white. It just reinforced her opinion that nothing good ever happened in an all-white room because here were the worst of the worst of spirits. The blackness of their hearts, or auras, or whatever it was that made them so evil contrasted against the pure white walls. It made the hairs on the back of her neck stand on end, and she was hyper-aware of every little noise and motion. Despite being dead and having no pulse, she could swear she felt her heart beat faster in her chest. Her mouth also suddenly dried out. She wasn't to the point of having leukophobia, a phobia of the color white, but she wasn't too far off from it either.

Snow was aware of his partner's aversion to all-white rooms, but this was one place where the walls could not be changed for her comfort. Nothing could be changed here; it was purposefully designed that way. That way, a prisoner couldn't make their cell into something more comfortable for them, a place darker so they could hide, or a place more akin to where they wanted to be. Overton had been able to change the prison he had been in over the course of time, with the use of a lot of energy. Here they were unable to hide in a dark corner or make fire pits or booby-trapped tunnels. They were unable to be anything but what they were for the rest of eternity.

"Snow! Riley! Good to see you both," the uniformed man at the desk said, standing to greet the two of them. He was a hefty middle-aged man with a thick mustache and a cheery demeanor.

"Officer Garrett," Snow said with a smile as he shook the hand offered to him by Garrett.

"I had a feeling I would be seeing you two today. Brackett told me during shift change that you had brought some in last night." Garrett shook Cade's hand while he was talking. "So, which one are you here for?"

"Pruitt," the two said in unison.

"This way," Garrett said with a nod.

Garrett led them down a hallway that was one white wall panel after another. Some panels had plaques with names on them. Snow had once told Cadence that behind those walls were the actual cells. The ones with the name plaques had been judged by the council, and it had been decided the worst punishment they could receive was to stay in the jail cell in perpetuity.

Cadence shuddered a bit at the memory of that conversation. The thought of forever spent in a small, bare, all-white room was something she knew would end in her going insane. She followed Snow and Garrett past the wall panels with name plaques, staying close to them. As usual, she was unable to shake the feeling that something bad would happen. The unease was like a tightly clenched fist in her core that refused to relax. They stopped in front of a wall panel that had a sticky note with a number on it.

"Here we go, cell 638. Your Mr. Pruitt is in here." Garrett pulled a remote from his pocket that looked like a small TV remote. He pushed a few buttons, and the device gave three quick chirps. Garrett then handed it over to Snow. "Just make sure to give this back when you're done. You know the ropes."

"Indeed," Snow said as he took the remote with a nod. "Thank you, Officer Garrett."

"Welcome," he said and then turned, heading back the way they had come.

Snow pushed a button on the remote and the wall panel slid down into the floor. A wall of what looked like Plexiglas now stood between them and the errant prison monitor. He was still surrounded on all other sides by solid white walls. There was nothing else in the cell with him. No bed, no chair, nothing. His clothing had been changed. He no longer wore the uniform of a prison guard. He now was clad in what looked like loose-fitting white pajamas. He sat cross-legged on the floor, looking down at his lap, making no move to acknowledge that anyone was there.

"Mr. Pruitt, I see you've settled in," Snow said.

Roy Pruitt didn't move. He did nothing to acknowledge them. He simply sat there, staring at the floor.

"Aww," Cadence said, trying to goad him into a reaction. "Is the big bad man still angry he was beaten by a girl?"

Pruitt's expression darkened, the full mustache above his mouth twitched, and his fists clenched at his sides. He was struggling to keep still, to ignore them. When Cadence laughed in response to seeing his struggle, however, he rose to his feet and stormed toward the glass wall.

"You little bitch," he yelled out, his southern twang thick. "You got no idea who you are crossin' by keepin' me here."

"Well, really, Mr. Pruitt, that is what we are here to find out," Snow said, his voice and manner calm despite Pruitt's outburst.

"Who were you working with on the other side of that portal?" Cadence crossed her arms in front of her as she asked this.

"Portal?" Pruitt scoffed. "What portal?"

"The one that we found in the Rec Room at Barrington," Snow said. "The one you did such a good job of keeping us from all evening."

"The one you were sending prisoners through," Cadence added.

Roy looked between the two of them. "I don't know what you're talking about," he said, trying to stonewall them. "But you know what I do know? I know you two and that one ghost hunter have a working relationship. He was obviously working with the two of you. Wonder how news of that will be taken by the higher-ups at my hearing."

"Given that the working relationship we have with him is not only known by them but sanctioned as well, I would wager it will be taken just fine," Snow said. "What they will not take well is a monitor who acted in opposition to his actual job. They will not look well upon your complete and total disregard for your duty. And it is quite definite that they will show ire at your attacks on the two of us."

"You two ain't no better'n me," Roy said, looking amused. "You just got a bigger area to look after. Yer just jumped-up monitors."

"You couldn't be more wrong, Roy," Cadence said. "But something that might help them be a little kinder to you in your hearing would be answering our questions. Telling us what was going on."

"You think I care 'bout helpin' you?" Roy laughed and shook his head. "Yer barkin' up the wrong tree there."

"What about helping yourself, Mr. Pruitt?" Snow asked.

"I am helping myself," Roy said, and there was a determined fire in his eyes that said he believed what he was saying. "I'm helping myself to stay out of oblivion."

"Big word for you," Cadence said. "Who threatened you with it to make you learn it?"

"Yer mouth does an awful lot of runnin', missy," Roy said as he narrowed his eyes at Cadence. "You oughtta look to stoppin' it."

"It doesn't matter," Snow said, cutting Cadence off before she could retort. "Roland, one of your last inmates, was straightforward with us. He disclosed what you were doing. We were just giving you the chance to come clean, own what you did, and perhaps help us catch someone who is dangerous."

Roy frowned, once more looking between the two on the other side of the glass from him. "Roland don't know everything," Roy said.

"This is the only chance we're giving you, Roy," Cadence said. "We will not be back after this."

"Don't expect you'll be doing much at all if'n you keep on pokin' about in this," Roy said. "You ain't as safe as you think. That's all I'm gonna say."

"Mr. Pruitt, you were a good man. You were an honorable man," Snow said to appeal to what might be left of the good inside the guard.

"Past tense," Roy said. "Ain't the case no more. I'm done talkin'." To emphasize the point, Roy turned and walked back to the middle of the room. He sat back down on the floor, his back still to them.

Snow sighed in disappointment and shook his head. He pushed a button on the remote and the white wall panel slid up, going back into place with barely a sound made. They made their way back through the white hallways to the desk at the entrance to the cell area. Garrett was seated at his desk talking to a tall, black, bald man who both Snow and Cadence instantly recognized.

"Alistair," Snow said in greeting to his friend and boss. "What brings you down here?"

"I was looking for the two of you, and when you weren't in your office, I figured the next most likely place for you to be was here," Croft said. "How's your arm?"

"Oh, it will be fine," Snow said, waving Croft's concern away. "Why were you looking for us?"

"And how did you know about his arm?" Cadence asked.

Croft lifted an amused eyebrow and looked at Cadence. "I know when my people get hurt." He then took an envelope out of his blazer's inner pocket and handed it to Snow. "For the new monitor of Barrington Prison," Croft said. "I was hoping for you two to deliver it for me."

"At least the title is going to someone who is bit more on the up and up than Pruitt was," Cadence said, seeing Roland's name on the envelope.

"Indeed," Croft said with a nod. "I'm hoping you two can speak more to him. Try to puzzle this situation out and how it ties into what we already know."

"Of course," Snow said, pocketing the envelope in his own blazer. "Hopefully, we can find something there to put everything together. Right now, it all seems to be in a bit of a jumble."

"I'll hold off the deadline on your paperwork to give you time to get as much information as you can. No matter how this gets presented to the higher-ups, they are going to have questions. The more answers we can give them through your paperwork, the fewer questions they will come at us with."

Snow handed the remote back to Garrett and nodded to Croft. "We'll do our best."

"I have no doubt of that," Croft said with a smile. He then turned and left the cell level.

Cadence looked at Snow and gave him a half smile. "So now we're off to Barrington?"

"Yes, and here's hoping that Roland is still as forthcoming as he was last night," Snow said. Together, they then teleported back to the brick-and-mortar carcass of Barrington Prison. The afternoon was overcast as they stood at the entrance doors. The dark clouds combined with the chill in the air threatened snow later. Snow that would drift in through the broken windows and compromised roof areas to pile within the prison's brick walls, only to melt later and add to the growing water damage in the derelict building.

The two detectives passed through the closed doors of the prison. The generator that had been used by Teeny and Liam for their equipment was still in the lobby. Cables led away from it and into the prison rotunda, its walls covered with broken tiles, where their special version of a Faraday cage was. Cadence and Snow approached the special piece of equipment with caution.

"It can't do anything while it's switched off, right?" Cadence wanted to be sure they weren't in any danger.

"Don't worry. We're quite safe as long as it is off," Snow said. He didn't get any nearer to the machine, however. The memory of the pain he had felt in that cage was still acute, his arm still aching and tingling.

"Roland!" Cadence called out into the prison, hoping to rouse the attention of the man's spirit.

"We could go look for the man instead of shouting," Snow said with a tone of disapproval in his voice.

Roland appeared in the rotunda in front of them, and Cadence smiled at Snow. "Why, when shouting works so well and saves time?"

Roland looked between the two and lifted an eyebrow in curiosity. "I didn't expect you two to return so soon. Or at all." The inmate wore his prison jumpsuit and had his dark hair cut short. He was clean-shaven with dark eyes.

"We still have a few questions about what's been going on here," Cadence said.

"And we've some direct business with you," Snow said.

Roland held his hands up defensively. "I haven't done anything for you to have business with me," he said.

"You have, though it isn't something bad," Snow said. "You sought us out last night, and you were honest with us, even though you didn't have to be. You also explained to us what you knew about what was going on. Again, that was not required of you. So, you are to be elevated to location monitor." Snow produced the envelope from his jacket pocket and extended it to Roland.

Roland stood there for a moment, looking from Snow to Cadence and back again. "Are you serious?" he said, at last able to give voice to the doubts running wild in his mind.

Cadence nodded. "Yeah," she said. "Like Snow said, you were upfront and honest with us when you could have just stayed in your cell and left us alone. We appreciate your help. Someone interested in starting a life on the right side of the law is what this place needs."

Roland took the envelope and opened it. He withdrew a phone and a letter.

"The phone lets you contact us whenever people show up to investigate the place," Cadence said.

"And with our contact information comes a request," Snow said. "Keep watch on that portal. Whoever opened it from the other side may not know that Pruitt is no longer in charge. They may not be aware that things have changed on this side. If that portal opens, or if anyone contacts you about it, give us a call, please."

Roland looked at the phone and then back at Snow, nodding with understanding. "I'll let you know one way or another if anyone tries anything with the portal. I'll also see if the few who are left know anything more about what was going on. Were you able to get anything out of Pruitt about it?"

"Nah," Cadence said with a sigh. "He's determined to not say a word. He seemed afraid of whoever it is pulling the strings for that thing."

Roland nodded. "That makes sense. He always was jumpy whenever anything was going on with that portal."

"So, we'll leave this in your capable hands, then?" Snow said.

"I'll do my best," Roland said with a nod. "Wish I had more to offer you."

"Was there ever a set schedule for it? Like every Friday night the thing would be opened at 8. Anything like that?" Cadence cast a glance down at the hall that led to the rec room as she asked.

"No. If I had to hazard a guess, it happened when the person on the other side was able to get a hold of someone to be possessed by one of us," Roland said.

Both Cadence and Snow nodded, then shook Roland's hand, congratulating him on his newfound authority. They then teleported out of Barrington Prison.

CHAPTER 5

The Professor

Derrick walked into Pho-Q, his backpack slung over one shoulder. The young man had short black hair and dark circles under his eyes. After their adventure with the Owens family the previous night, he had remembered that he had a workshop class first thing this morning. He'd had little sleep and less food. Taking in a deep breath of the tangy barbecue scent in the air, he looked around. He could see the heads of Tom and Chris, the two owners, back in the kitchen as they handled the Sunday lunchtime rush with their kitchen staff. A quick scan of the room proved there were no tables to be had, but there was a spot at the counter, providing that the seat wasn't being saved. He made a beeline for it.

"Excuse me, is anyone sitting here?"

"Nope, all yours, Derrick," the man said. Close-cropped brown hair, which was graying at the temples, gave way to a face hidden behind a brown and gray goatee and glasses.

"Professor Phillips?" Derrick was surprised to see his history professor from the previous year there.

"Before you act shocked, just remember, teachers need to eat, too. We don't just survive off the souls and tears of undergrads, as much as the undergrads say otherwise," the professor said with a smile. "Besides, you always recommended this place."

Derrick settled down on the stool beside his old professor with a smile. "Yeah, it's great food."

"Hey, Derrick, what can I get for you today?" A waitress wearing a tag that identified her as "Holly" stopped in front of Derrick with her pad and pen.

"The smoked pork pho and a soda, please, Holly," Derrick said, giving his order.

"Sure thing," she said with a smile. "This for here or to go?"

"Here, thanks," Derrick said.

"Be right back with your drink," Holly said and walked away.

"So, how is your semester going so far?" Professor Phillips picked up the conversation now that Derrick had ordered.

"Good, so far, I guess," Derrick said with a shrug. "It's early in the semester still, though. There's still plenty of time to screw it up." He gave the teacher a grin as he said that.

"Please," Professor Phillips scoffed. "If there's one student who isn't going to mess up their standing, it's you."

"Unless it's math," Derrick said.

The professor shrugged and nodded. "We all have our weak areas."

Holly brought over Derrick's drink and a refill for the teacher. Both men thanked her and went back to their discussion.

"What about you? How's the semester going?" Derrick was curious as to why the professor was hanging out and engaging him in conversation. Not that it was unheard of for Derrick to get on well with his teachers, and he had taken every class Professor Phillips had taught, given that he was a history major. Still, it seemed a little off, and the professor was acting as if he had something to say but wasn't sure how to.

"Oh, fine," Phillips answered with a shrug. "I heard you had something of an eventful holiday break."

Derrick nodded and groaned. "You read it too, huh?" The local newspaper had picked up the story about the strange goings on in the notorious college dorm, and the college newspaper made an even bigger deal of it. After all, it's not every day that a cop and three civilians nearly get killed by a sitting college board member in a dorm house that had already played host to a massacre.

"It was hard not to hear about it," the older man responded.

"Yeah, it was definitely eventful," Derrick said.

"Are you still doing that ghost-hunting thing with those people after everything that happened?" The professor finished the last of his pho.

"Yeah, we just did an investigation last night," Derrick said, taking a minute to thank Holly as she set his bowl of food down in front of him and slipped the professor his check.

"What exactly do you do with them? Are you psychic?" Phillips seemed genuinely interested in how it worked.

"Oh, no, that's Lauren who is the psychic. I'm their historian. I research the property and people associated with whatever disturbance is going on before we go in. Then when we are there, I usually just fill in where they want me. I film, take pictures, do EVP work, things like that."

"What is it that fascinates you about doing that kind of work?" The professor pulled out his wallet as he asked this and put his card down on the bill.

"I like the research," Derrick answered with a shrug. "I always have. My sister used to give me crap about it, but my folks always encouraged me. I enjoy learning about the history of these places and people. Why else would I be a history major?"

"True." The professor faltered as the waitress picked up the check.

"Are you okay, Professor?" Derrick asked. "You look like something is up."

"Well, I was wondering if you and your friends might be interested in doing an investigation for me," the teacher confessed.

"Really?" Derrick's eyebrows shot up in surprise. "I can't really answer for the group, but can you tell me a little bit about what's going on?"

"I've inherited a house, property really, there's lots of land," Phillips began with some hesitation. "There have been rumors about the property for years. The house is starting to fall apart because no one in my family has wanted to live there for a few decades. I'm debating moving in and fixing the place up if the stories are just that. But if the stories are true, then I might just demolish the house and sell the land. I knew you were into this stuff from the news articles, and I know you were the best researcher in any of my classes. I figured if there was anyone who might be able to help me out, it would be you."

Derrick nodded. "Give me a sec," he said, pulling out his cell phone. He fired off a couple of texts and set his phone down by his bowl to wait for answers. "I'm honestly dying to hear the stories, but I don't want to make you repeat them. Are you free for a while?"

"I don't have anything going on this afternoon," the professor nodded.

"Okay, cool. I want Lauren and Aiden to talk to you, too. We all kind of decide together if we're taking a case," Derrick said.

"Lauren is the one who owns the shop at the end of this strip mall, right?"

"Yeah. We were out until almost dawn with an investigation last night, so I want to check that they are both up," Derrick said.

"I hope no one got hurt this time," the professor said, alluding to the dorm case again.

"A little girl stepped on a big nail, but other than that, everyone is fine," Derrick said. His phone made a video game noise as he got a text back from Lauren. "Okay, she is up and will meet us at the shop, and she is going to call Aiden." Derrick didn't bother explaining that they had actually been on two different investigations with their group split. He didn't want to get into the TV show or the fact that the dorm incident had been one in a line of moderately dangerous cases they had worked on recently.

"Thank you," the professor said. "I appreciate you arranging the meeting."

"No problem," Derrick said between mouthfuls of food. A few minutes later, the video game noise sounded from his phone again, and he checked the message. "Aiden is in; they should be here in about fifteen minutes or so."

"Pretty quick," the teacher said.

"Neither of them lives too far from here," Derrick said. He flagged down Holly and ordered two more meals to go, which was Aiden's condition for getting out of bed and coming in.

"So, can you talk about your cases, or is there some kind of confidentiality?" Professor Phillips asked.

"Depends on if it involves a person or just a place," Derrick shrugged. "Last night, there was a family involved. So, out of respect for them, I wouldn't really go into details. But if it's just stories about investigating someplace like Lexington Hills, or some other carcass of a building, that I can talk about. Well," he paused, thinking it over for a moment before adding, "maybe not some of Lexington Hills."

"That's the old asylum and hospital out off of 60, isn't it?" the professor asked.

"Yep," Derrick said with a nod, laying out cash for his bill.

"Why can't you talk about that?" Professor Phillips was curious as to why an abandoned building would fall under confidentiality.

"It's a long story, but don't even bring the place up to Lauren. Her ex-husband died around the time we investigated there, and she just doesn't like to talk about any of it," Derrick warned.

"Okay, no mention of Lexington Hills." The professor nodded.

Holly brought back Derrick's change and a bag with the two to-go meals he had ordered. "Say hi to Aiden for me." She smiled brightly.

"Uh, sure," Derrick said, faltering for a moment at the interest Holly showed in Aiden. He left his change as a tip and grabbed both his backpack and the food bags. Professor Phillips rose as well and picked up his attaché case.

They left the restaurant and its swirling aroma of barbecue behind as they walked down the strip, passing various shops. Derrick felt a little awkward about one of his teachers coming to him for help, even though Professor Phillips was technically a former teacher. They reached the door of the New Age shop as Lauren pulled into a parking space. The dark-haired woman with the Rubenesque figure got out of her car and made her way to the shop's front door.

"Oh God, Derrick, you got food? You're an angel," she said with a grateful smile, unlocking the front door of the shop. The window still boasted a sign that they were closed for a special event. The chimes by the door tinkled together as Sam followed his charge in. Derrick and his former professor followed her in. She took the bag of food from Derrick and put it on the round table in the back of the store. She then went about making a pot of coffee.

"I'm not sure how well coffee and barbecue are going to mix," Derrick called after her as he set his backpack on the floor.

"I am pretty sure neither Aiden nor I care," Lauren chuckled as she returned to the table. "You're still young enough to be able to pull all-nighters." She moved her eyes to the professor and extended her hand. "Hi, I'm Lauren Kurtz."

"Paul Phillips," he said, shaking her offered hand.

"It's nice to meet you," Lauren said. "Please have a seat. We're just waiting for Aiden to get here."

"No, you're not," Aiden said as he closed the front door of the store behind him, locking it. The tall, lanky man with shaggy hair looked bone tired. As he made his way to the table, Derrick could see the dark circles under his eyes.

"Okay, I guess we're not," Lauren corrected herself. "Aiden, this is Paul Phillips. Mr. Phillips, this is Aiden Perkins."

"Call me Paul." The teacher reached over and shook Aiden's hand. "You, too." He nodded to Derrick.

"Hi Paul, nice to meet you," Aiden said with a tired sigh. "Sorry, we were up most of the night."

"Yeah, Derrick was telling me," Paul said. "Why don't you guys get settled before I begin? Get your food and coffee and such?"

"I like this man," Aiden said, getting up to grab a cup of coffee as the aroma of the coffee battled for superiority with the aroma of the barbecue. He folded his tall, skinny form back into the chair as Lauren was passing his food over from the bag.

"How do you know Derrick?" It was Lauren who asked the question.

"I'm a history professor at the college. Derrick has taken every class I offer," Paul said.

"Is he taking one of your classes now?" Aiden asked this time.

"No, he's not," Paul said.

"Alright," Lauren said with a nod. "We just wanted to make sure that whatever is going on, our involvement wouldn't have any effect on his grades, either good or bad. Not that we think you would do that; you just have to be careful sometimes, you know?"

Paul nodded in understanding. "I get it. I've been debating for a while if I should even approach your group since he was involved. But I have zero involvement in his grades or his progress on his degree at this point. I figured it was safe."

Derrick nodded. "We're here. Tell us what's going on."

Paul took a deep breath and folded his hands in front of him. "About fifty years ago, my dad's older brother bought a piece of property on the west side of the county. According to my dad, my uncle was a very black and white man. If he couldn't see it or touch it, he didn't believe it was real. I'm told there were rumors and legends, stories about the place even back then, but my uncle thought it was all a load of bullshit. Whether it is or not, I don't know, but I know what happened with him lends credence to there being some kind of curse or bad luck or evil spirit, whatever you want to call it, attached to the place. My dad died a few years ago; Mom passed over the summer. I've inherited the place, and I'm not sure what I want to do with it."

"I'm sorry for your loss," Lauren said.

"Thanks," Paul said. "When I saw what happened with you guys in the old dorm house over the holidays, it occurred to me that I could possibly hire you guys to go in and see what you can find out about the place. I want to know the whole history of the place, beyond what I know happened with my uncle. I want to know if there really is evil there or if it is just a string of bad luck and coincidences that just randomly happened there."

"If you don't mind my asking," Aiden said, "just what did happen to your uncle?"

Paul ran a hand through his short hair in a nervous gesture. He hated having to retell this part of his family's history. But then, who would enjoy talking about being connected to a murderer? "My uncle, it is assumed, went crazy. He killed his wife and his two kids on that property. He then killed himself. There was no note, no obvious reason; it was just something that happened one day. My dad was attending college in Boston at the time, so he wasn't here. He never liked talking about it, so I know only the bare bones of the story."

Paul paused and opened his attaché case, pulling out a plain manila file from it. "This is the info I have on the house. It isn't much, but it should be enough to spur on super research man here," Paul said with a thumb gesture to Derrick, who was sitting to his left. "It's sad to admit, but I've always been hesitant to do the research myself. I am a bit afraid of what I might find since my family is connected to the place."

"That's understandable," Lauren said. "Have you ever been to the property before?"

"No," Paul said with a shake of his head. "I guess I'm more superstitious than either my dad or uncle were. I don't want to invite trouble if it is there to invite."

"That's a smart decision, to be honest," Aiden said as Derrick pulled the file over to him. "You have no idea how many people decide to go looking for stories and legends only to find out that they are true in the worst ways."

"And most of them aren't prepared to deal with it," Derrick added as he opened the file.

"We'll take the case, but we won't be able to get out there for a couple of nights. Last night was a little rough, and I'd like to give Derrick time to work his magic," Lauren said. "Do you want to be with us when we investigate the property?"

"Is it necessary?" Paul's apprehensiveness showed as he asked the question.

"No." Lauren smiled. "But we will need the keys to the house if you aren't going to be there."

"Sure." Paul nodded, pulling his key ring out of his pocket. He detached a second key ring from it that had a simple blue plastic tag on it, as opposed to the Harley Quinn comic book character on his main key ring. "The key to the house is the big one. The smaller key is for the padlock on the shed. At least that's what I've been told."

Lauren took the keys with a smile and a nod. "Derrick has a way to contact you, right? We'll let you know before we plan to go in, and then a day or two later, we'll let you know what we come up with. Sound good?"

"Sounds good," Paul agreed, reaching over to shake the hands of the three of them in turn. "I appreciate it." The professor gathered his things and headed out,

Derrick walking him to the door to lock it behind him. The college senior then returned to the table his friends were at.

"So, what do you think?" Derrick asked.

"I think you forgot to order extra sauce on the meat in my pho," Aiden said as he ate.

"He seems genuine," Lauren said, giving Derrick a straight answer. "I like the fact that he's cautious. Can you tell anything from what he gave you?"

Derrick sat back down and began looking through the papers in the file. After a moment, he let out a low whistle. "Guys… this place is Scarecrow Farms."

Aiden nearly choked on his pho.

"Hey, just because the property has a history of stories doesn't mean those stories are all true," Lauren said. "We don't do ourselves any favors by buying into the hype. You both know that."

"Well, I'll get into the research," Derrick said. "I should be able to have a more solid grasp of the real stories versus the story stories by tomorrow."

"You do that." Lauren nodded. "And get some sleep. You look like hell. Aiden, you and I should swing by the hospital and check on Liam and Teeny."

"Yeah, that's a good idea," Aiden agreed.

Derrick slipped the file regarding Professor Phillips's property into his backpack and hoisted it onto his shoulder after he rose from his chair. "Give me a call later. Let me know what's up with them."

"Have fun storming the library," Aiden said, giving Derrick a wave. Derrick waved back to Aiden and Lauren and headed out.

CHAPTER 6

Notes, Part 1

"**W**ell, that was fruitless," Cadence said with a sigh as she sat back down at her desk.

Whitfield was at his desk, waiting for them. He offered them a sheepish smile and waved in greeting.

"Were you able to catch up with Sam?" Cadence asked the NHD agent.

"Yes, he filled me in. Again, I'm sorry about last night," Whitfield said.

"So long as it doesn't happen again," Snow said. "We need you here."

Whitfield nodded. "What is it that was fruitless? The interrogation?"

"Yeah," Cadence grumbled, annoyance plain in her voice. "He's not talking. No one else seems to know too much. This is so damn frustrating. I feel like I have a jigsaw puzzle with all the pieces in front of me, but no idea how to begin putting it together."

Snow walked to his desk and sat down. "Let's walk this through. I've a feeling we've been dealing with the same case all along, just different stages of it." Snow looked over to Cadence, his sharp blue eyes regarding her. He knew she would know what he meant when he said to walk it through.

Cadence nodded, tucking a stray honey-colored bit of hair behind an ear as she opened her desk drawer. She pulled out a box of silver thumbtacks, a square pad of paper, and a few different colored pens. She took a few moments to write down five things on five different squares of paper. Once done, she rose from her chair and walked, with a slight limp, over to the wall in front of the U-shape their three desks made.

The first square she pinned up on the left side said "WOLF" in capital letters. The second said "SHALDOXZ," and she pinned that a couple of feet to the right of Wolf's square. Then underneath Wolf's square, she pinned a square that read "Lexington Hills Chaos NH," with the NH standing for non-human. The fourth square read "Dorm Massacre," and she pinned that one several inches below Shaldoxz's name. The last note read "Marcus Overton." Cadence pinned it to the wall below and to the left of Shaldoxz's name and the dorm massacre.

Grabbing a pen, she drew an arrow down from Wolf to the Lexington Hills note in black ink. She then selected a red pen and drew a double-ended arrow from Shaldoxz to Overton and another double-ended arrow from Overton to the dorm massacre.

"Really, Cadence, you didn't need to draw on the wall," Snow admonished.

"You want me to walk it through. I'm walking it through." Cade didn't bother looking at her partner. Her eyes were fixed on the notes, and the gears in her mind were turning.

"Wolf is directly connected to Lexington Hills because we know he was ultimately responsible for the Chaos Entity that was unleashed there," Whitfield said. He had been quiet as Cadence had been pinning up her notes, but now he spoke.

"Right," Cadence nodded, scratching out another note. She moved to the wall again and pinned up a white paper square that read "Ritual." "But Whitfield, you told us that the ritual in question had been removed from circulation by our side a long time ago. So it stands to reason that someone on our side gave it to him." She quickly wrote another note and put it up on the wall attached to the ritual one. This one read "Who?"

"In the meantime," Snow began, "we had Marcus Overton possessing the body of Michael Caulfield. He possessed that body prior to the dorm massacre, and in fact, he was the one responsible for it."

"Right, and Overton was a disciple of this non-human entity, Shaldoxz," Cadence said. "He was trying to get enough blood and pain going on the prize wheel to release Shaldoxz from his prison. Do we know where Shaldoxz's prison is?"

"Non-humans don't go to the kind of prison we have downstairs for human spirits," Whitfield said. "Each non-human is different, with different strengths and weaknesses. They're generally somehow chained to a thing or place that is their weakness."

"Like chaining Superman to a rock of Kryptonite." Cadence nodded slowly.

"Yeah," Whitfield agreed as he watched Cadence write another note and pin it to the wall. This one read "What's its kryptonite?" and she pinned it right by Shaldoxz's name.

"We do know that what is believed to strengthen him is, as you said, blood and pain." Snow steepled his fingers beneath his chin as he spoke.

"So, his weakness would be warm fuzzy feelings? I'm not so sure it's that easy." Cade shook her head.

"If that were the case," Whitfield said, "he could be tied to a church. I mean, there's a lot of love there, right? Weddings, baptisms, love of God."

"I'm sorry. I just don't think it's that easy," Cadence repeated with a shake of her head.

"Given the multitude of churches in the world, it's not entirely easy," Snow said. "But I am curious as to your line of thinking. Why do you think a place of love and happiness would not be a prison for it?"

"Anytime, anyplace, there is blood and pain all over. A guest at a wedding could be in serious emotional pain because they are there alone or in physical pain if they are sick. It could be a shotgun wedding with no love involved. The baby being baptized could be unwanted or a representation of the parent's life ending. And love of God doesn't always equal happiness. Just ask the Catholics and Jews. They are masters of guilt in worship."

"What about an amusement park?" Whitfield offered another possible place.

"Tummy aches from too much sugar, headaches from screaming kids, sore feet from walking and waiting in line, skinned knees, bloody noses." Cadence ticked the reasons off on her fingers.

"I can see I've never taken enough time to properly admire your ability to be pessimistic about the most innocuous of places." Snow gave a wry grin to his partner.

Cade chuckled and shrugged. "I'm looking for holes to poke, is all."

"But you are forgetting," Snow said, "that a symbol has to be carved or placed on the offering or on the one doing the offering for it to work."

"True," Cadence acknowledged. "Let's move on to what we learned last night."

A few more notes were written out, and she approached the wall with a thoughtful look on her face. The first one she pinned up read "Barrington Prison." This she put in between Wolf and Shaldoxz with no arrows yet. The second note she put up read "Emma." She drew a double-ended arrow between Emma and Wolf.

"We know that Wolf is responsible for summoning Emma," Cadence said, backing away from the wall, even though she had a couple more notes in her hand. "He promised her she could possess the little girl in order to live again, like Overton did, but he double-crossed her. From what Sam said, he seemed to have no interest in following through with that promise. God only knows what he wanted Ava for."

"Your brother said Wolf was at the house in order to cut the power, which means he was orchestrating

Emma's taking the girl out of the house," Snow added. "There was some kind of plan."

"Right, we just don't know what yet," Whitfield said.

Cadence moved back to the wall and pinned up the last two notes she was holding. They both went under Barrington Prison, one to the left, the other to the right. The first one read "Roy Pruitt" and the second one read "Portal." Cadence then took a green pen and drew double-ended arrows between all three of those notes, making a triangle.

"Roy Pruitt was helping prisoners escape through a portal at the prison. I would say twenty at least have escaped," Cadence said.

"It wouldn't surprise me at all if it were more," Snow said.

"Me either," Cadence said. "It had obviously been going on for a while."

"But does the prison even tie in with Wolf and Shaldoxz?" Whitfield rose from his seat and walked over to get a closer look at the wall of notes. "I mean, it kind of looks like we have three separate cases here, not one. We have no idea what Wolf was doing at that house or what his intentions were with Ava. It might have nothing at all to do with Shaldoxz. And it looks like the prison was separate. Dangerous and troubling, yes, but separate from what seems to be going on with Wolf and the whole Shaldoxz thing."

"Let's not forget that Wolf was directly involved with Overton," Snow noted, and Cadence quickly moved to make more notes.

"Right," Cadence agreed. "Overton called Wolf to help him clean up, so to speak, when he had Andy in the basement of the dorm."

"I'd forgotten," Whitfield admitted with a nod. "Wolf told Overton to take care of his own mess; it looked like Wolf had higher ranking, or whatever you want to call it. It was like Overton was reporting to him."

"We also know that Wolf was the leader of the cult. Dan Kurtz said as much when he died," Cade added. "So, we can assume this cult is for Shaldoxz since we know the non-human thrives on pain and blood, and chaos is a close cousin to both of those things." She moved to the wall and between Wolf's paper and Overton's paper, she pinned a note that read "Shaldoxz Cult," another below that read "Wolf leads," and then another below it that read "Overton was part."

"You were wrong, Cadence," Snow said with a sigh. "While this is like a jigsaw puzzle, we don't have near enough to all of the pieces, let alone a guide to putting it together."

"No kidding," Cadence said. She frowned as she looked over the notes and the arrows, then turned and wrote a few more notes. She got up and moved back to the wall, pinning them up. The note that read "Where does it go?" was pinned to the note that read "Portal." The note that read "How much more to release?" was pinned to Shaldoxz's note. Beside Barrington Prison's note, she pinned a note that read "Is this connected to Shaldoxz?" She then sat back down in her chair as her feet were beginning to sting.

"You make a good point," Whitfield said, "in asking how much more is needed to release him. I think it might be a good idea to find this prison in order to see if there is a way we can reinforce it or keep this thing from getting out."

Cadence shook her head. "Sorry, man, I'm still not convinced that's the best way to go. That's like trying to find one special strand of hair in the entire universe. We'd have to search both the corporeal world and the incorporeal one."

"Well, we have a starting point now," Snow said, gesturing to the wall with his uninjured arm. "We now know what questions we need to be looking for answers for, and we can add more as we go. Though I hope we can add more answers than questions as we go along. It's been an arduous couple of days. I suggest we retire for the evening and get some rest."

"Do you need to check in with Ramon for your arm?" Concern was plain on Cadence's face as she asked the question. She had noticed which arm he had used when he pointed to the wall.

"No, I just need to get some rest," Snow said with a reassuring smile.

"See you guys in the morning," Whitfield said as he rose and left the room.

"Are you sure you're okay?" Cadence pressed the issue as she and Snow both rose.

"I assure you I'll be right as rain in the morning," Snow said. He hated lying to her, but he knew Ramon wouldn't be able to help him, and he didn't want to reveal to her what the root cause of the issue with his arm was. Sure, the punch to the force field had been foolhardy and useless, but he had used the same arm to punch with as he had to force the lock open to rescue

Cadence from Overton and the flames he was cooking her over. He had known the use of that power came at a cost. He hadn't quite realized how much of a price. So, he just gave Cadence a smile, and they left their office together, each heading home.

CHAPTER 7

The Producer

When Teeny woke to the beeping sound in the room, she realized that some nurse or CNA had covered her with a blanket. She was curled up in the chair beside Liam's hospital bed, and the golden light outside was dimming, letting her know without looking that the sun was setting. Looking over, she saw that Liam was still sleeping. The beeping was coming from the machine where two IV bags were hanging, one of which looked about empty.

Teeny winced as she unfolded herself from the chair. Her neck was killing her, and the rest of her body didn't seem too happy about her choice of sleeping position. Sore and stiff, she got to her feet, stretched, and moved the couple of steps to Liam's bedside.

His head was bandaged, as was his left hand. The rest of his injuries were shrouded by his blankets. He was pale, but he appeared to be resting without pain. Teeny picked up the call button to push for the nurse about the beeping when the door to the room opened and a nurse came in with a new IV bag. She wore green scrubs with a geometric design of triangles in blue and pink, and she had a long-sleeved blue shirt beneath her short-sleeved scrubs. Her long brown hair was pulled back into a ponytail and a stethoscope encircled her neck. Her white sneakers were soundless as she moved across the floor.

"I figured it was about time," she said, pointing to the machine. "I was hoping to get here before it started being vocal about it. You looked like you needed the rest. I'm Nancy, by the way. I'll be his nurse for a few more hours. Shift change is at 7, and I'll bring the night nurse by so you can meet her." Nancy spoke as she hooked the new IV bag up and took down the old one.

"Thanks," Teeny said, moving back to the chair to stay out of the nurse's way. "And thanks for the blanket."

"Oh, no problem," Nancy said, her voice cheery. "It gets cold around here, so I figured you could use one. You two obviously had a rough night last night."

"Yeah, him more so than me," Teeny said.

"True. Well, the doctor should be by in a couple of hours. I understand he spoke to you after the surgery?" Nancy had turned her full attention to Teeny now.

"Yeah, he did," Teeny said with a nod. Her mind was foggy and slow, and she was trying to recall what he had said.

"Don't worry," Nancy said. "Doctor Michaels is one of the best. If it means anything, he is who I would choose to be my orthopedic surgeon. Due to his condition, there won't be a dinner tray for Mr. McIntire later. The cafeteria is downstairs on the first floor if you want to go, or you can step out if you want food that might be a bit less bland."

"Thanks." Teeny nodded. She wasn't sure how hungry she was, even though she knew she should probably eat at some point. The thought of leaving the hospital while Liam was still unconscious was unacceptable.

Nancy gave her a warm smile and left the room. Teeny let out a sigh and looked over to Liam. She wished he would wake up; she would feel a lot better if she could talk to him. She wrapped the blanket around her shoulders. Nancy hadn't been lying; it was freezing. Teeny bowed her head, resting her forehead in her hands, willing her mind to stop being so fuzzy and sluggish.

A tapping sounded on the wide wooden door, and then it opened. A man with short, curly, sandy-colored hair poked his head around the edge of the door, and Teeny smiled.

"Russell." She smiled. "Jeez, you got here fast."

"One of my stars is in the hospital? Of course I'm going to get here as fast as possible," the middle-aged man said as he returned her smile. He was in a grey suit with a grey and black striped tie underneath his winter coat. He crossed the room to Teeny and hugged her.

"I'm glad. It's good to have a familiar face around." Teeny sighed.

"I can imagine," Russell made a face as he spoke. "God, Teeny, you look like hell."

"Gee, thanks," Teeny replied, her tone sarcastic. She knew she looked bad. She was still in the clothes from last night, and her hair was probably a knotted mess at this point from sleeping in a chair and on the sofa in the surgery center waiting room earlier. At this point, her makeup had to be half gone, too. Add to all that the dark circles she was sure were lingering under her eyes, and she had no doubt that she looked the worst he had ever seen her.

"Any news?" Russell looked over at the unconscious form of Liam as he asked the question.

"I haven't talked to the doctor since right after the surgery. The nurse just said he would be in later, though," Teeny answered. "I think I told you everything on the phone earlier. The leg is bad. He has a concussion. We won't know for a little bit when he'll be able to get on his feet again."

Russell frowned. "Why was he alone out in that area?"

"It's my fault." Teeny sighed and looked to the floor. "I got spooked when we were doing vigils in the solitary confinement cells. I didn't want to be alone. Also, the box worked. We got a spirit in there, and neither of us wanted to leave the thing alone unattended. So, Liam had Aiden stay with me, and he went to investigate the noises in the gallows room himself."

"So, Aiden stayed with you. I thought there were two other people on that team that were guesting on this episode. A woman and some college kid?"

"They had an emergency case come up." Teeny shook her head as she answered. "Lauren wasn't keen on being at the prison, anyway. She said she had bad vibes from it. Derrick is their researcher. We got him on video for the history of the place, but then he went with Lauren to do the other case."

"How on earth does some other case take precedence over their guest starring on your show?" Russell was incredulous at such a thought.

"I think a kid was in danger." Teeny shrugged. "At least, that was what I gleaned from it. So, Aiden came with us for the actual investigation. Everything was going fine until then. Thank God the cop you hired for security came in. I guess he heard something. He knew Liam was in trouble."

"I'll have to find him and thank him," Russell said absently as his mind worked. "I'm assuming you don't have any of the footage from last night with you?"

"No." Teeny shook her head. "I left everything at the prison. My first concern was Liam. The cop and Aiden locked up for us."

"Okay, well, we've got to get the keys from whichever one of them has them so that I can go pack up and see what we can salvage from last night. I'll tell the network to put us on a brief hiatus. I'll put out a press release about Liam's injury, and this episode can be what we come back with. Everyone will want to see what happened that put Liam in the hospital."

"I'm not sure yet what exactly happened," Teeny said. "But it was bad in there. The floor was covered in glass from a two-story tall window that had shattered. From what I could tell, he had been standing on the gallows trap door, and it gave out under him. He took a straight drop to a concrete floor covered in broken glass."

A knock sounded on the door, drawing the attention of both Russell and Teeny. Teeny smiled as she recognized Aiden and Lauren. "Hi, you guys," she greeted.

"Hi," Lauren said quietly. She entered the room and put the vase full of flowers she was carrying on the hospital bed tray table.

"We come bearing gifts." Aiden held up some bags from a grocery store in each hand.

"Thank you. You didn't have to," Teeny demurred, but she was glad to see them.

"It was no trouble," Lauren said with a soft smile to the younger, smaller girl.

"Oh, Russell, this is the group, or two-thirds of it, anyway. This is Aiden and that's Lauren," Teeny said, making the introductions. "Guys, this is our producer, Russell."

"Nice to meet you," Lauren said.

"Nice to meet you, too," Russell responded automatically, though Teeny could tell he didn't really mean it. "Aiden, Teeny here mentioned that you might still have the keys to the prison. I need to get them from you so I can go get their equipment and footage."

"Andy has the keys to the prison; he's the security you hired. I'll go grab them from him and then go with you." Aiden smiled. "Some of that equipment is going to take two people to carry, especially her box thing, which was heavy as hell. And if you need help, I'm the tech guy on our team. I can go through the footage for you to look for evidence." Aiden was trying to angle his way into viewing the footage so that he could discretely erase some of the most damning evidence. "I'm sure Liam's accident is going to set your production schedule back. It's the least I can do."

Russell eyed Aiden for a moment, sizing him up. "Let me think about it. We can go together to get the gear and the van. But let me think about the footage."

"Sure thing." Aiden nodded.

"Where's Derrick?" Teeny asked.

"He's doing some research." Aiden shrugged. "Or at class. The kid can't keep his nose out of books for long."

"Not that there's anything wrong with that," Lauren admonished Aiden.

"Never said there was," Aiden protested. "But I'm not wrong. He's constantly researching something."

"We brought you some food," Lauren said, directing the conversation away from Derrick and back to Teeny. "Snack stuff mainly, things that wouldn't need a refrigerator or cooking. Some drinks, too. We also grabbed a fuzzy blanket, some basic toiletries, and some clothes. I kind of figured you wouldn't want to leave his side too much."

Teeny hugged Lauren tightly, tears threatening to fall. "Thank you so much. That is so awesome of you. I don't want to leave him, not until I know he is out of the woods."

"We also picked up some stuff for you to do while you're sitting here," Aiden added. "Word puzzle books, adult coloring books with colored pencils, a deck of cards, a few books and magazines."

"Thank you," Teeny said again. "I couldn't have asked for more. This is so cool of you guys." She looked over at Lauren. "How did your other thing go last night? I thought

I saw you guys here at the hospital, but I could have just been imagining it. I wasn't in the best frame of mind."

"We were here." Lauren nodded. "The little girl got hurt, stepped on a nail. But otherwise, I think we took care of the problem. Only time will tell if it is for good or not."

Teeny nodded and opened her mouth to say something, but Russell interrupted. "What else do you guys have going on now?"

"We just picked up a case today, actually," Aiden answered.

"Anything interesting?" Russell asked as Teeny looked over at him, not liking where this was going.

"Possibly. There's an old property around here that has a bad reputation. Someone just inherited it and wants us to look into whether the stories are just stories or if there is something to them." Aiden shrugged. "Derrick really hasn't had much of a chance to research yet. Between everything last night and his classes and homework, I'm not sure where the kid finds time."

"When do you guys think you will go out there?" Russell asked.

"Russell, don't," Teeny warned.

Lauren frowned, looking between Teeny and Russell. "We aren't sure yet. Why?" Lauren answered before Aiden could.

"Well, if Liam is out of the woods and Teeny feels up to it, perhaps she could join you on your little investigation," Russell said. "After all, we did agree to all of you guesting on the show, and from what I hear, two of you broke that agreement. And Teeny tells me the reason Liam went haring off on his own was because he wanted Aiden to stay with her. Had you two been there, he wouldn't have been alone, and perhaps the entire accident could have been avoided."

Teeny sighed and looked at the ground. She had known that's what Russell was heading for when he opened his mouth. He was going to try to back them into a corner so that he could get another damned episode filmed while Liam was down for the count.

Movement from the bed derailed the conversation. Liam's right arm shifted, and he placed his right hand on his forehead. His fingers moved as he felt the gauze bandages on his head. His eyes were open, and he opened his mouth and tried to lick his lips, but it felt like his mouth was full of cotton. He tried to say something, but all that came out was a croak. Teeny was beside him in an instant.

Teeny grabbed the large, capped water mug with its plastic straw and lowered the straw to his lips. "Just sip slowly," she said.

Liam lifted his head a bit and took a couple of small sips. He wanted more, but he was going to do as Teeny said for now, given he couldn't remember why he was in the hospital. He leaned his head back on his pillow, and Teeny moved the cup away. "What happened?" Liam looked at Teeny but was aware of the others in the room. His voice was still croaky, and despite feeling like his mouth was a desert, he felt like his throat was full of phlegm.

"Do you remember going to the gallows room at the prison by yourself?" Teeny asked.

Liam nodded and the movement was slow and deliberate. Part of his slow response was because he was trying to think through the fog of his medications and head trauma. The other part of it was because he didn't want to hurt his head any more than it already hurt.

"Okay. I haven't looked at the footage yet," Teeny said, "but from what we can figure out, you were standing on the trap door for the gallows, and it gave out, dropping you. You shattered your left leg, got a concussion, and possible spinal issues. Jesus, Liam, this is why we don't go on our own to places." Part of her wanted to hug him tight, since she was just so relieved that he was awake. Part of her wanted to smack him for being so stupid, for going off alone.

"Sorry, Teeny," Liam said and cleared his throat, which led to a cough. He winced as the movements caused pain to ripple out into his body from a thousand different places.

"We'll let you guys talk. We just wanted to bring by those things for you," Aiden said.

"Teeny, you have our numbers. If you need anything, don't hesitate to call," Lauren said, giving the younger woman another hug. She then looked at Liam and offered him a compassionate smile. "I hope you heal up fast. We'll check in on you."

Liam gave the duo a weak wave as they made their way to the door. Just as they left, a CNA entered the room, pushing a cart to take Liam's vitals.

CHAPTER 8

Ruminations with the detective

A knock on his door brought Andy to his feet from where he had been sitting on his couch with Darwin, the cat. He ran a hand through his light brown hair as he wondered who could be at his door at this hour. Looking through the peephole, he saw the familiar visage of Aiden through the bleary, curved glass. Andy unlocked his door and opened it.

"You look like I feel," Aiden said as the door swung open and he saw Andy. Dark circles hung beneath the detective's eyes, which were bloodshot.

"It was a rough night," Andy replied, opening the door wider so that Aiden could enter. "You know that just as well as I do. Come on in. Want a beer or something?"

"Nah, I'm good." Aiden shook his head. "Thanks, though."

Andy gestured to the living room. "Take a seat. I have no doubt there are things to discuss." Both men made their way to the living room, Aiden folding himself into an armchair while Andy retook his place on the brown leather couch. Darwin lifted his head from where he was curled up, gave Andy a disapproving glare for disturbing him, then put his head back down.

"Yeah, a few things," Aiden admitted with a nod. "The trickiest is likely going to be the fact that the show's producer is in town. He wants the key to the prison to get the equipment out."

"That's not tricky. I can go with him tomorrow after my shift." Andy shrugged.

"That's not the tricky part." Aiden sighed.

"What is?" Andy lifted an inquiring eyebrow as he asked.

"Oh, a laundry list of things at this point," Aiden said with a sigh. "First off, he made thinly veiled accusations that Liam's accident was somehow our fault."

"You're joking," Andy scoffed, unable to believe that.

"I wish I were." Aiden grimaced. "He also threatened breach of contract. He stated that all three of us were, by contract, supposed to guest star in this show. All three of us did the interviews, so I would think that covers us. But he said if Lauren and Derrick had been there, then Liam wouldn't have gone off on his own to the gallows room, and the accident wouldn't have happened."

"Have you had any word from our mutual friend on what actually did happen?" Andy was, of course, referring to Cadence.

"Nope, not a damned thing." Aiden frowned. "To be fair it, was probably a hell of a night for them, too. But I wish I had heard something. I would love some answers."

"You aren't the only one," Andy said. "So, this guy is trying to hang you out to dry for breach of contract and for negligence in causing Liam's accident?"

"Not only that, but it gets better," Aiden said with a bitter smile. "We wound up with another case this morning. One of Derrick's professors inherited a mildly famous haunted house, and he wants us to go in and investigate. See how much of the legend around the house is true and how much is just a story. This Russell guy wants us to take Teeny with us so she can film it since Liam is apparently going to be down for the count for quite some time. He's using that as a quote-unquote favor that we would be doing for him that would make him forget about the breach of contract and supposedly causing Liam's accident."

"Jesus," Andy whispered in disbelief as he shook his head.

"Oh, and there's a cherry on top of this mess, too," Aiden said.

"There's more?" Andy couldn't believe there could be more manipulation going on than he had already heard.

"Oh yeah. I haven't seen the footage from last night, but I know for a fact Snow is on it. Teeny got him trapped in that box thing of hers that she made. I tried to get Russell to let me work on the footage, or at least review it to pinpoint areas of interest for them to save time in the editing room."

"You want to try to make sure that any concrete footage finds itself missing, right?" Andy could plainly see where this was going.

"Yep. But the guy is reluctant to let me. I mean, to be honest, if I were him, I would be hesitant as well," Aiden said. "But if they find that footage of Snow, or if there is more than just that, there is no way I am going to be able to get a television show to sit on it."

"True," Andy said. "But I think the producer is probably more interested in seeing what caused Liam's accident. How agreeable do you think the new owner of the haunted house would be to letting a TV show come in and film?"

"I don't know." Aiden sighed, rubbing a hand over his face. "I can get Derrick to ask him."

"You might want to," Andy said. "You can use it as a bargaining chip to maybe have a hand in reviewing the footage or getting them to sit on something critical."

"Good idea. I'll ask Derrick to ask his professor." Aiden nodded.

"Nothing else came to light about what happened, huh? How's Liam doing?" Andy asked.

Aiden sighed, leaning back in the chair. "He's not great. He looks like a reject from a mummy movie he's so covered with bandages. Not to mention all the tubes they have him hooked up to. We stopped by earlier with a care package for Teeny since I'm sure she is going to be spending a lot of time there."

"That was nice of you guys," Andy said. "I know I saw Lauren and Derrick at the ER when we came in, but I never got the chance to ask: what were they there for?"

"The case they were working on got a little hairy, too, but not nearly as bad as the prison," Aiden explained. "A little girl ended up in a strange place and stepped on a construction nail. It went through her foot, but the doctor patched her up. She's home with her folks."

"What did the docs say about you?" Andy looked at Aiden as he asked the question, his gaze sharp.

"Me? I wasn't seen by a doc." Aiden shrugged.

"Why not? Just because I was preoccupied doesn't mean I didn't notice that you looked hurt, too," Andy said.

"I'm fine." Aiden waved a hand dismissively.

"Don't bullshit a bullshitter," Andy replied, his voice flat. "What happened?"

"I was attacked by a ghost." Aiden sighed. "As crazy as it sounds, I know. It felt like someone reached into my chest and had a grip around my heart and lungs."

"And you didn't think that it might have been a good idea to get checked out?" Andy couldn't hide the disbelief in his voice. "Do Lauren and Derrick know?"

"Yeah, they do." Aiden nodded. "And they wanted me to see someone, too. I just felt it was better not to have to explain the handprint bruise on my chest."

"You're serious," Andy said after a minute of scrutinizing Aiden's face.

Aiden nodded and, predicting Andy's next question, lifted his shirt to reveal his chest. Beneath the brown chest hair was an angry purple and black bruise. There was no denying that it was in the shape of a large hand. Aiden let Andy see it for a moment, then put his shirt back down.

"Holy shit," Andy murmured.

"There don't seem to be any lasting effects aside from the bruise," Aiden said.

"Well, that's good, at least," Andy said, then shook his head with a bitter chuckle. "You know, three months ago, I wouldn't have imagined sitting here having a conversation like this."

Aiden grinned. "Talking with a ghost hunter?"

"Not so much with a ghost hunter, but talking with any seriousness about ghosts," Andy said. "Never believed in them until you guys showed up at my door. That set off a hell of a chain of events."

Aiden chuckled and nodded. "That time, you were the one to end up in the hospital."

"Only overnight. Nothing like what Liam has to go through," Andy pointed out.

"True." Aiden nodded. "Hey, if we do end up having to do this next investigation with cameras rolling, would you be willing to be security again? It's nice having someone there as backup who believes in what is going on."

"Have to see what's going on with work before I can say yes or no," Andy warned. "But if I'm available, sure."

Aiden nodded once more. "Well, if you are anything like me today, you have pretty much been biding your time until you can go back to bed and sleep. I think it is probably time we do that." Aiden rose from his chair and Andy followed suit, rising from the couch. This earned him another accusatory glare from Darwin, who got up, arched his back in a stretch, yawned, then hopped off the couch and headed for his food bowl in the kitchen.

"Yeah, I'm beat, too." Andy yawned as if his statement prompted his body to realize it. He walked Aiden to the door. "Be careful driving home."

"Thanks," Aiden said. "I'll be in touch."

Andy closed the door behind Aiden and locked up for the night. He rubbed his face with one hand as he debated if he had enough energy for a shower before bed. Deciding that a shower in the morning might be the better option, he looked over at Darwin, who had once been Cadence's cat before her death.

"Come on, fuzz bucket," Andy said. "Bedtime." Andy turned and went down the hall to his bedroom. Darwin followed him, hopping up onto the bed and curling up on the pillow beside Andy's head.

CHAPTER 9

Research Reveals

"**D**o you think he got lost in the library?" Aiden was half joking when he asked this and was rewarded with a light chuckle from Lauren. They were talking quietly behind the front counter as there were still customers in the store. One woman was in the back area looking at candles, a teenage girl was nearby looking at Tarot card sets, and Lauren had just finished ringing up a gentleman buying some herbs.

"I don't think it's possible for Derrick to get lost in any library." Lauren chuckled. "But it is odd for him to be radio silent for two days. Every time I call, I get his voicemail."

"Same," Aiden nodded with a frown. "You don't think he would have gone there on his own, do you?"

Lauren thought about it for a moment and then shook her head. "No. He's too much of a thinker, too cautious to just run over there without calling us."

The door chimed as it opened, and Derrick walked in, backpack slung over his shoulder, looking like he hadn't slept much. He gave a wan smile to Lauren and Aiden as he made his way over to them.

"Well, look what the cat dragged in," Aiden said with a teasing smile.

"You look a little rough." Lauren elbowed Aiden and looked at Derrick with concern in her brown eyes. "Are you okay?"

"Yeah, I'm just tired," Derrick said. "Classes, home-work, getting a head start on projects, on top of the research for Professor Phillips."

"School comes first, Derrick," Lauren intoned. "If we need to table this until you have time, we can."

"Oh no, I'm good," Derrick said, giving a dismissive wave of his hand. "Just takes me a couple of weeks to get into the rhythm of the classes. Sorry for being off the grid, but if I haven't been asleep or in class, I've been working the Professor Phillips case."

"Still working it, or did you finish?" Aiden asked.

"Got as far as I think I can on it. I figured we could go over it tonight, figure out a game plan, then I can go talk to Phillips tomorrow about it," Derrick said. "Oh, Lauren, mind if I make some coffee?"

"Go right ahead," Lauren said as she slid closer to the register to ring up the teenager and the Tarot cards she had finally selected. As the girl left, the woman from the back came up with an armful of candles and a book about harnessing your inner energies. Aiden went into the back to help Derrick with the coffee before he let some smartassed remark slip about the woman's purchases as Lauren rang her up as well.

Sam, who was always around, pulled his phone from his pocket and hit speed dial. His call was answered after one ring, and he smiled. "Hey, sis," he said.

"Sam! What's up?" Cadence asked on the other end of the line.

"They are getting ready to have a meeting here about the next case they're taking on. Thought if you and Snow were free, you might want to come and listen in," Sam said. "Whitfield, too, if he can find the time," he added, his voice sour. He still hadn't forgiven the NHD agent for bailing on him a few nights ago when they were supposed to have been working together.

"I think Snow and I have time. We'll be there soon," Cadence said. Sam recognized the tone in his sister's voice. Something was up on her end, but he knew better than to ask over the phone about it.

"Cool, see you soon," Sam said. He then hung up.

Derrick had his coffee. Aiden had grabbed a cup too, the smell of the freshly brewed drink wafting through the store. Lauren was counting out her register and preparing her bank deposit bag as she closed the till. Sam moved over to her, touched her arm, and spoke to her.

"Cadence and Snow are coming, too," he said, using the link he shared with Lauren to communicate with her.

Lauren nodded, acknowledging his communication without uttering a word. She zipped and locked her bank deposit bag and put it in the back room next to her purse. As she came out of the back room, she heard the crystals by the front door start tinkling together as

Snow and Cadence entered. The two men at the back table glanced to the door, then to Lauren as she left the back room.

"I take it we're not alone," Aiden said.

"No, Cadence and Snow are here as well, as is Sam," Lauren said, though she knew they were already aware of Sam's continuous presence with her.

Derrick's computer had booted up and he had the manila file folder out on the table beside the laptop. Lauren grabbed her tumbler of water from behind the counter and made her way to the table, sitting down between the two men.

Sam and Cadence hugged briefly, and Snow shook the young man's hand in greeting.

"How has it been here the last few days?" Cadence looked from her brother to the three gathered around the table and back again.

"We've meant to come by, but there has been much taking our attention elsewhere," Snow said.

"It's okay, but depending on where this goes, we may have a lot more to talk about," Sam said.

"Oh?" It was Cadence who asked this as the trio of ghosts made their way over to the breathers at the table.

"Yeah, the TV show producer is in town and trying to strong-arm them into making this next case into an episode."

"You can't be serious," Snow said, astonished.

Sam, who looked very serious, nodded. "Yeah, but we need to know what their plans with this are first," he said, gesturing to the breathers.

"Are we all good?" Derrick asked, looking at Lauren.

Lauren nodded to Derrick. "So, what have we got?"

"In short? A mess." Derrick sighed, taking a sip of coffee.

"That good, huh?" Aiden asked.

"Yeah." Derrick nodded. "Phillips told us about what happened with his uncle, but his story was lacking in detail, so I looked that up first. His uncle was the normal family guy by all accounts, but one day he just snapped. He grabbed a shotgun; he killed his wife as she was coming out of the downstairs bathroom. Apparently, the two kids, aged 6 and 8, heard the shot and ran out to the shed to hide. He found them there and gunned them down. Then he went inside, up to the master bedroom, and killed himself. Here, I have a floor plan of the house that I printed up. I marked the shooting locations on it." Derrick paused to hand out two papers. One was the floorplans with the murder locations marked in red. The other was a general layout of the property.

"This is the entire property?" Lauren was a little awed at the prospective size of the land.

"Yeah," Derrick answered. "Five acres. Two were apparently used for the house, the shed, and the family's personal farming needs, including a barn that burned down ages ago. The other three, on the other side of this tree line here, were the fields used for crops to sell."

"Did Paul's uncle burn down the barn?" Aiden took a sip of his coffee after asking the question.

"No. It burned down over a century ago. Scarecrow Farms was built after the civil war. The legend is that prior to being built, the land was used as a kind of dumping ground or unmarked graveyard. Back then, if you needed to dump a dead slave, that's where you went. Kill your wife's lover? Dump the corpse there. No one has tried to legitimize these stories, but that has more to do with the fact that the property was in the Phillips family by the time the equipment had been developed to look for bodies underground without having to just pick a spot in the ground at random and dig.

"There is also a story about a demon inhabiting a well on the property and another story about a summoning circle there. I figure if the circle is there, we will find it, and if there is a demon, Sam can probably verify that.

"The original house was built in 1870 by Jacob Chalmers, a freed slave who bought the land from his former master. I doubt Chalmers knew about the history of the land when he bought it. It was originally a one-story house with a cellar. The second story was added in the 1930s. The shed is original, too. There was a barn, but as I said, it burned down in 1926. At the time, according to the papers, there were several theories as to why it burned. Some used the old Chicago fire story of an animal kicking over a lantern. Others said Jacob's kids were in the bootlegging business since this was during Prohibition, and something went wrong with their equipment. This was largely discounted as no actual moonshine equipment turned up, just ash and animal bones. Still, others said it was other former slave owners, pissed that Jacob and his family were doing so well. Often though, people simply said that the land was cursed because Chalmers had built his place over a graveyard, even if he hadn't known it."

"Jesus," Aiden said, his voice low.

"No kidding," Lauren agreed.

Derrick nodded, agreeing with them, and picked up his tale. "The land stayed with the Chalmers family until the 1950s. There were a lot of mishaps, accidents, wives miscarrying children, livestock turning up dead for no reason, crops failing. I guess the last of the family, who was 27 when he sold the property, decided to protect himself and his family from the curse of Scarecrow Farms as the place had come to be known. He sold it in 1952. In the following fifteen years, the property changed hands that many times."

Aiden gave a low whistle. "Damn."

"Yeah," Derrick agreed. "And in that time, the legends only grew. More accidents, more strange occurrences, kids on the property talking about having a friend who lived in the well, and all of the kids, when they were asked, gave roughly the same description. What basically boiled down to a creature that resembled a goat walking upright.

"In 1967, Professor Phillips's uncle bought the property. He was vocal about thinking that the stories were all bullshit. He was a man of science, no such thing as ghosts; you know the type. Two years later, in 1969, was when he snapped and killed his family. You know the rest. Phillips's dad inherited the place but wouldn't set foot on the property. There have been squatters there, high school partiers, people like that, but just about every time, someone ends up in the hospital or in the ground."

"Did your research ever uncover why it was named Scarecrow Farms?" It was Lauren who finally broke the silence as they digested the information Derrick had just given them.

Derrick chuckled and nodded. "Jacob Chalmers named it that. He was generous in his use of scarecrows on his farming land, wanting to keep as many crops viable as he could. It's said on those 3 acres of land he farmed commercially, he had at least 20 scarecrows. That doesn't count the ones in his family garden."

"With everything you've read and everything you've uncovered, do you think the graveyard theory is legitimate, or is the demon theory more legitimate?" Aiden posed this question as he finished his coffee.

"I'll be honest. I'm not sure. It could be a bit of both; it could be neither," Derrick said. "We won't really know until we get out there."

"And that brings us to the possibly literal million-dollar question..." Aiden sighed. "Do we approach Paul about allowing *The Dead Show* to film our investigation there, or do we tell Russell to go fuck himself?"

Lauren pursed her lips as she thought, frowning. "This place has a sinister history. As sinister as the prison, it seems. If something happens to Teeny while we're there, I have a feeling nothing will stop Russell from raining down holy hell on us."

"I kind of get the feeling he's intent on doing that no matter what we do," Aiden grumbled in annoyance.

"Well, the first thing we need is to plan when we're going to go out there," Lauren said. "Derrick, can you ask Paul if he is okay with us going on Sunday? I would like to walk the property as a whole in daylight first."

"I'll talk to him," Derrick said with a nod. "I'll also talk to him about the possibility of bringing Teeny and the show with us. I'm not sure he'll be jumping for joy about it, he's kind of private, but I'll broach the subject with him, and maybe we can negotiate from there."

"If he wants to negotiate, maybe we should set up a meeting between us, him, and Russell," Aiden said as he thought. "That way, the two of them can hammer out whatever details they want without us having to constantly be go-betweens and middlemen."

"Good idea," Derrick said with a nod. He then turned to Lauren. "Sam or the others have anything to say about all of this?"

The three ghosts had been standing by, listening to all of the information that Derrick had come up with. Sam looked at Cadence and Snow.

"As this is the first we've heard about this place, we'll have to see if we have any information on it in our files," Snow said. "We will check with Whitfield about the possibility of a non-Human on the property."

Sam nodded. "They will check it out and get back to us about what they can find out," Sam said to Lauren.

"Cadence and Snow are going to see if they can find anything out," Lauren said.

"Okay," Derrick said. "Gives me time to talk to the professor about what he may or may not want to do, and we can all reconvene tomorrow or whenever is convenient."

"Sounds good." Aiden nodded.

"Hey." Derrick looked over at Lauren. "I never got the chance to ask you. Have you had a chance to check in with Robin and Doug about Ava?"

"I did," Lauren said with a nod. "I talked with Robin this morning. She said Ava hadn't seen any spirits since that night. She will call if that changes, however."

"And Ava's foot?" Derrick asked.

"Robin has been keeping her off it as much as she can and keeping it bandaged. The doctors expect her to heal just fine though she will likely have a scar on her foot for the rest of her life," Lauren replied.

"I'm just glad the kid is okay," Derrick said.

Lauren nodded in agreement and looked over at Aiden. "What about you?"

"What about me?" Aiden asked, surprised at the abrupt turn of the subject.

"Your chest." Lauren's tone was annoyed at his feigning ignorance.

"It's fine, Lauren. I'm fine," Aiden said.

"Did you ever get checked out?" Lauren persisted.

"No, I didn't. There was no need." Aiden sighed. "I'm fine. Other than a bruise on my chest, everything is good. No lingering effects, I promise."

"It could have done damage to your heart," Lauren said, her voice rising as her temper flared. "I don't know why you are being so stubborn about getting it checked out by a doctor."

"Because I don't want to explain to a doctor why I think my heart may have been affected when it's just a big old handprint bruise on my chest. I'm pretty sure the real explanation will get me committed to a nut house damned quick," Aiden said, frustration showing in his voice.

Cadence moved over to Sam. "This has less to do with Aiden being hurt and more with the fact that Dan, her ex-husband, died of a ghost-induced heart attack. She's afraid of losing Aiden, too."

Sam's eyes widened a little as he realized his sister was right. He hadn't been involved in the Lexington Hills case, but he had heard plenty about it from Snow. Having not known Lauren back then, though, it hadn't clicked for him, at least not as quickly as it had for Cadence. He moved to Lauren and put a hand on her arm, trying to calm her a little.

"Good thinking." Snow nodded to Cadence.

"I don't know why you are being so difficult about this." Lauren stood and put her hands on the table, looming over Aiden. She was fighting back against Sam's touch in her mind, trying to stay agitated and angry.

Aiden slammed a hand on the table and rose as well. He opened his mouth to say something, then stopped as the look in his eyes changed from aggravation to understanding. He sat back down. "I'm not Dan, Lauren. I'm not going to have a heart attack."

At those words, it seemed like the wind went out of her sails. She slumped back down into her chair and covered her face with her hands. Aiden leaned over and put a hand on her shoulder. She was shaking, and it took a moment for them all to realize she was quietly crying. Derrick, who had stayed silent as the two argued, jumped up and grabbed a box of tissues from behind the counter. He put it down on the table by her and retook his seat. He then reached over and put a hand on her other shoulder.

"We're here, Lauren," Derrick said. "We're not going anywhere."

"We ain't afraid of no ghost," Aiden said, quoting the famous song to try to lighten the mood a little for her. He was rewarded with a half sob, half chuckle from Lauren. She dropped her hands and grabbed a tissue from the box.

"I'm sorry," she said after she blew her nose. "It just scares me. You two are my family, and I can't lose any more family."

"You won't," Derrick said.

"I wouldn't do that to you," Aiden said. "If there was even a hint that something was wrong, I would go to a doctor. But other than the bruise, there hasn't been any pain, any shortness of breath, nothing. I swear."

"He got very lucky that Pruitt wasn't able to do more damage to him," Snow said, looking at Cadence.

"I know," she replied, her tone somber. "It's something that I'm grateful for."

"I don't think there's going to be any more information tonight," Sam said, finally taking his hand away from his charge now that she had calmed down.

"We'll see what we can find out and let you know," Cadence said, walking over to Sam and giving him a hug goodbye.

"Talk to you later," Sam said, giving his big sister a hug and offering a parting wave to Snow which the Englishman returned.

Cadence and Snow then left the shop, leaving the ghost hunters to tend to their friend's grief.

CHAPTER 10

The Game Changer

"**I** can't believe those assholes are trying to strong-arm Lauren and Aiden into making their next case into a TV show just because Liam got hurt and now they are stuck there," Cadence fumed as she and Snow re-entered their office after the meeting at the New Age Shop.

"Calm down, Cadence," Snow said as he closed the door to their office. "I'm sure they will find a way to negotiate the issue." He stopped when he saw Whitfield.

Cadence saw the NHD agent as well, looking a little less harried than he usually did. Something caught her attention as she made her way to her desk, a niggling distraction that something was off. "Hey, Whitfield. What's up?"

"I was just about to ask the same of you," Whitfield said. "You're all riled up about something."

"The idiot producer of that TV show our paranormal team helped out is trying to blackmail them into letting the girl from the show film their next investigation since Liam got so badly hurt and is going to be laid up for a while," Cadence said, falling into her chair with a huff.

"That's a little over the top, isn't it?" Whitfield looked between Snow and Cadence as he asked this.

"A bit," Snow said with a nod as he took his seat behind his desk. "They did fulfill their obligations by doing the interviews, from what I understand. Participating in the actual investigation was something that Liam and Teeny sprung on them at the last minute. Then again, I have no idea what their actual contract states."

"What is their next case?" Whitfield continued looking between the two as they talked.

"Some old estate," Cadence said with a shrug. "Scarecrow Farms, I think was the name."

"Scarecrow Farms?" Whitfield almost seemed to pale. "Isn't there a non-human on that property?"

"They mentioned that there might be, yes," Snow said. "Which puts it right in your wheelhouse, doesn't it?"

"Yeah," Whitfield said, giving a nervous laugh.

"Oh, come on, you can't still be nervous about going out in the field with us, can you?" Cadence was still trying to figure out what was bothering her about the room as she asked this.

"Only a little," Whitfield confessed. "It's easier when it's just spirits. Non-humans, going out after them, that still makes me nervous. You never know how nasty they are going to be."

"Son of a bitch!" Cadence stood up suddenly, her gaze fixed on the wall she had pinned her notes on.

Snow blinked at her outburst, then saw what she was looking at and, more importantly, what she was seeing. The wall was just a wall. There were no notes, no markings, and no pins. It was all gone. Whitfield turned and widened his eyes in shock.

"What on earth happened?" It was Snow who broke the silence as they all stared at the blank wall.

Cade walked over to the wall and ran her hand over the smooth surface. "The pin holes are gone," she said, her voice quiet. "The pen marks, all of it. So, what happened to the notes?"

"You were here before us," Snow said, looking to Whitfield. "Were the notes up when you came in?"

"I think they were," Whitfield said with a frown. "I think I would have noticed if they were gone."

"But you're not sure," Cadence scoffed.

"I can't be sure. Sorry," Whitfield said.

"Other than us, did anyone come in that you are aware of?" Snow was wondering if there had been some visitor who may have managed to remove the notes despite Whitfield's presence.

"No, it was quiet." Whitfield shook his head.

Cadence turned and flung herself back into her chair, letting it roll back a little with her effort. "This is ridiculous," she growled. The fury was plain on her face, even though she had no one to direct it at.

"I am going to head upstairs and see what I can find out about Scarecrow Farms and its non-human, if it has one," Whitfield said. "If I can think of what might have happened to the notes, I'll let you know."

"Thank you, Whitfield. Yes, it is best to start preparing for this next case," Snow instructed.

Whitfield nodded and left the room.

Cadence got up once more and walked over to Whitfield's desk. She opened two of the drawers there, beginning to rifle through them.

"Cadence, what are you doing?" Snow's voice sounded weary as he asked this.

"You're a detective, figure it out," Cade snapped back. She slammed one drawer shut and began sifting through another.

"You think he had something to do with your notes going missing," Snow said.

"Snow, he was the only one in here. Or at least that's his story. That means he did it, or he let it be done," Cadence said.

"Or it happened in between the time we left and he arrived, and he just didn't notice the notes were missing," Snow said. "It did take you some time to notice they were gone, too."

"No." Cade shook her head vehemently. "Something has been off about him since I came back. Not being available, not showing up for an investigation, now the notes disappearing."

"So, you think he is somehow a traitor because of strange behavior?" Snow seemed suspicious of her reasoning but not dismissive of it.

"Look, I know what you're thinking, Snow." Cadence sighed. "It's all just circumstantial at best. But my gut is telling me something is off. I don't mean he's a bad guy per se, but something is off about him right now."

A knock sounded on their open door, and Cadence quickly shut Whitfield's drawers. The partners looked over to see the dark, impressive form of Croft in their doorway. Normally, he would greet them with a smile. Now he just stood there, looking almost somber.

"Alistair," Snow greeted with his usual smile.

Cadence was immediately on alert. Something was wrong. She wasn't sure how she knew it, but she did. Not that something was wrong with Croft, but with whatever news he was bringing with him. His tone, his body posture, it was all too stiff, too serious. Croft was usually at least affable with Snow. The man looked troubled and made no effort to return Snow's smile. This wasn't going to be something they were going to like.

"We need to talk," Croft said, looking at them both. "In my office. Now."

Derrick's headlights swung around as he turned the corner into the parking lot. He knew it was a long shot that Professor Phillips would still be here at almost nine at night, but he knew that sometimes the man would teach an odd night class or two. His eyes strained as he slowed his car to a crawl, looking back and forth for the professor's car. The lot wasn't full by any stretch of the imagination, so it didn't take Derrick long to spot the professor's black Nissan sedan.

Derrick pulled up and parked in the empty space to the right of the professor's car and waited. He had no idea what his class schedule was like this semester, so he had no idea how long to expect to be here. He waited roughly half an hour and had completed several levels of the match-3 game on his phone before Professor Phillips came around the corner of the building.

Derrick turned off his car and got out, the movement of which caught the professor's attention. The older man tensed for a moment, then relaxed when he recognized who it was.

"Isn't it a little late for you, Professor?" Derrick said as a greeting.

"Derrick, what brings you to a dark parking lot this late at night?" Phillips asked with a slight grin. "Oh, and to answer your question, I have a night class I am teaching this semester." He finished walking to his car, pressed a button on the fob that made the car beep twice, then opened the back door and put his briefcase in the backseat.

"I wanted to talk to you about a few things regarding your case," Derrick said.

"Have you heard of this little invention called a phone?" the professor asked with a grin.

"This is kind of an in-person conversation." Derrick shrugged.

"That bad of a place, huh?" Phillips said, as the smile evaporated from his lips.

"No. Well, yes, but … okay maybe. This isn't about the history of the house or the stories that have come out of the estate," Derrick said, walking around the car to properly face his old teacher. "Do you remember when we met at Pho-Q, and I told you were just coming off of a case that had run really late the night before?"

"Yeah," the older man said with a nod.

"Well, for Aiden, who was helping the *Dead Show* people, it ended with Liam from *The Dead Show* in the hospital. He's going to be there for a long time as he had emergency surgery that morning for a break in his leg, among other things," Derrick said.

"Ouch," Paul said with a wince. "Someone should have told him that the 'break a leg' phrase is just a phrase, not an order."

"No kidding," Derrick said with a nod, not quite jiving with the levity of his teacher. Then again, he had seen the results of what had happened to Liam firsthand, having visited him in the hospital with Lauren and Aiden the previous day. Professor Phillips had not. "Well, since they are in town with Liam laid up, the producer is sniffing around, trying to find ways to get another episode filmed. He wants Teeny to go with us when we investigate Scarecrow Farms, and he wants the investigation filmed."

"I don't know how comfortable I am with that," the professor said with a shake of his head.

"I understand," Derrick said. "We can try to arrange a dinner with you, the producer, Teeny, and us if you want to talk to them about it. If it's a hard no, don't worry about it. We'll tell them you passed."

Paul leaned against his car for a moment, one hand idly scratching at the goatee on his chin as he thought. At length, he looked back over at Derrick.

"Set up the meeting." Paul sighed and cracked his neck, a sound that always made Derrick cringe a little. "I'll think about it, and this will give me time to do so. I'll have questions I'll want answered before I agree to this. Let them know that."

Derrick nodded. "I'll let them know. I'll give you a call when we settle on a date and time. What nights are you free?"

"I have this class on Tuesday and Thursday nights, so any night other than those," Professor Phillips said.

"Sounds good," Derrick said with a nod. "I'll call you." Derrick then walked back around to his car.

Snow and Cadence had followed Croft back to his office in complete silence. Neither one was sure what had brought on the man's dark mood, and neither one had the temerity to speculate about it in his earshot. The tension grew with each step. Bonnie was not at her desk as they passed it, and Croft held the door open for them. After both had entered, he shut it firmly behind them.

"Have a seat," he said, his voice commanding.

He gestured to the two chairs in front of his desk, not to the more comfortable, less formal conversational arrangement of sofas in the corner of the room. Snow and Cadence exchanged glances and then made their way to the two chairs. Croft walked around them to take his seat behind the desk.

As Cadence sat, she looked at the desk for any indication of what may have upset him. Antique scales, check. Quill pens with bottled ink, check. Paperwork, no check. No indication at all. The only thing new that she could see was a small paper heart on one side of the scale and one of the feathers on the other. The scales were equally balanced.

Croft sat there, his eyes moving from Snow to Cadence and back again. It was obvious he was looking for one of them to start talking first. Cadence had never been intimidated by Croft until this moment. He could be harsh and judgmental, yes, but this was the first time he had ever come across as scary.

"Alistair," Snow said, finally breaking the heavy silence. "What in the blazes is going on?"

Croft folded his hands in front of him on his desk. "Several things, as a matter of fact," he said, his deep voice almost a rumble of thunder in the atmosphere in the room.

"Are you planning on telling us?" Cadence asked, unable to keep her snark in check. "Or are you going to just keep us in suspense forever?" Snow cast a quick look of warning to Cadence, but Croft cracked a smile.

"You never back down, do you?" Alistair said, amused by Cadence's words.

"Not even when she should for her own good." Snow sighed.

Croft nodded. "I will admit, it is going to be a bit of a road to get to the point. There is a lot to discuss. But first, Osmund, would you take off your jacket, please?"

Snow blinked at the odd request. "I'm sorry, I think I misheard you. What?"

"Take off your jacket and then roll up your shirt sleeve, please," Croft said a little slower. "You know which sleeve."

"Alistair, I hardly see why—" Snow began but was interrupted by Croft.

"Osmund, I don't care if you do or do not see why I have asked that of you. Do it. She needs to see," Croft added the last part in a gentler tone, but there was still no doubt that this was an order.

Snow sighed and rose. He took off the blazer he had been wearing and then unbuttoned the cuff of his sleeve, rolling it up. He had used the mental image trick to make his hand look normal, but he let that drop now. Cadence gasped as she saw it. His hand was black and withered. Thick ropes of that shadowy ink crept up his arm, under his skin. The areas of blackness weren't swollen; in fact, they seemed to be caving in on themselves.

"Jesus," Cadence swore, her voice just above a whisper.

"I'll heal," Snow said, glaring a little at Croft for bringing this up with Cadence. "It's just taking longer than I expected."

"Does Ramon know about this?" Cadence couldn't believe Ramon would let Snow out of his care if it was this bad.

"The good doctor is aware that there is nothing he can do for it," Croft answered, sparing Snow whatever lie he was about to tell.

"Nothing he can do?" Cadence was flabbergasted. "I didn't think that was possible."

"What caused this affliction," Croft said, "was a perfect storm of instances."

"Instances? I thought this was all from him trying to punch his way out of the force field at Barrington," Cadence said. "'Instances' makes it sound like more than one thing happened."

"More than one thing did," Croft said with a nod. "Osmund, please tell Detective Riley exactly how she was rescued from that fiery cage several weeks ago."

"I thought we had agreed to not talk about that." Snow glowered.

"Oh, we did back then." Croft nodded, then shrugged. "That was before Barrington, however."

Snow closed his eyes in irritation and sighed. "I'm sure you'll recall that the area that Overton had you in was a null. An area where our day-to-day spirit powers don't work."

Cadence nodded. "I tried to teleport and couldn't, tried to make a weapon and couldn't."

"Exactly," Osmund said, nodding. "I'm not sure how aware you were at the time, outside of your pain. Overton and I were fighting. I got the best of him, but I wasn't about to waste precious seconds asking him for a key to your cage. So, I used an ability I was taught long ago. I used a little bit of my soul to blast the lock open. Sam got you out; I shoved him in and then used a little bit more of my soul to fuse the lock shut. That last part was childish, I'll admit, but it felt good at the time."

Cadence blinked, taking a few moments to digest this new information. She had known Snow was there. She had even been aware that Snow and Overton were fighting as her brother managed to rip her limbs free from the metal chair. But the pain of Sam freeing her had overwhelmed her, and she hadn't been aware of what had happened after that until she woke up in the new hospital. It hadn't occurred to her to ask how they had managed to set her free. She had just been so grateful that they had.

"You spent part of your *soul.*" She emphasized the last word. "How can you say this like it's no big thing? That's your life force, Snow. You can't just go slinging that stuff around because finding a set of keys is a little inconvenient. Don't get me wrong, I am amazed and grateful you would do that for me, but am I going to lose you now because of it?"

"If I hadn't, we wouldn't have been able to get you out in time. The breathers were working on the incantation to reseal the prison," Snow explained.

"Leave me behind then." Cade frowned.

"Leave you behind? Would you do the same, then? Leave me behind in that hell if I had been the one he had taken?" Snow had turned to fully face Cadence now.

"No," Cadence answered, not even needing a moment to think. "I wouldn't. You're right."

"I did what I had to in order to free you and get you, your brother, and myself out of there before the door closed for good," Snow said. "I don't regret it for a moment. I do regret letting my anger get the better of me in that damned box, however."

"When you use some of your soul," Croft said, "it takes part of you. Like a wound, it can heal with time and rest. It takes more rest and more care to heal it, however. Time and care that Osmund didn't see fit to spend."

"I was busy," Snow protested.

"And now you will be busier, though in a different way," Croft said with a nod. "But we're not at that point yet. We still have a part of this tapestry yet to weave. While I am not that familiar with the kind of box the young woman employed at Barrington, there is no doubt she did something right on her end, as it did hold you. When you tried to punch your way out of it, were you using soul to power your hit?"

Snow looked down at his lap.

"That's a yes." Cadence sighed in resignation.

"Somehow, the field of energy created by the box took what you offered it and fed back something else. It's something that is slowly spreading. Something that Ramon recognized right away as something he wouldn't be able to heal." Croft eyed the two of them carefully as his deep voice carried across the room.

"What is it?" Snow asked, lifting his eyes from his lap to look at his mentor.

"It is slowly disintegrating your soul," Croft said.

"No!" Cadence yelled the word as she stood. "There must be a way to fix this. I will not let this happen."

"You have no say in the matter, Riley," Snow replied, but his voice was rough, even though he tried to control his emotions. In trying to save her and save knowledge of the afterlife, he had unwittingly given up his own.

"It's true. She does not," Croft said. "But I do." Both looked at their boss in shock.

"What say do you have over this?" Snow asked, raising his blackened and withered hand.

"Think, Osmund," Croft said patiently, as a teacher would to a child. "Who taught you that power?"

"You did," Snow said with a shake of his head, failing to see why it mattered who taught him.

"How many other spirits have you seen wield that kind of power?" Croft was prompting him, hoping to get him to figure things out a bit before dropping his mask.

Snow frowned as he pondered, and his brow creased. Cadence thought, too, even though she hadn't encountered as many spirits as he had. But none she had met or had heard of had the ability to wield their soul as a weapon.

"I haven't heard of anyone else being able to do what you taught me to do, not a spirit or ghost anyway," Snow said.

Croft nodded, prompting Snow with a simple gesture of a finger to follow that train of thought.

Snow's face changed as little things clicked into place. "The only ones I've heard of having anywhere near that kind of power are gods, demi-gods, or non-humans," Snow said at length, his eyes never leaving Croft's face as he said it.

With that, a smile spread across Croft's face. "And there you have it."

"Wait, so, you're one of those three?" Cadence was suddenly apprehensive. *Could it be that he took the notes down in our office?* Had they somehow been stumbling too close to the fact that he was a non-human and was involved in the whole non-human revolution thing Shaldoxz seemed to want to bring about?

"Your expression does little to hide your thoughts, young Riley," Croft said with a laugh. "I am not a non-human."

"Are you seriously telling us you're a god?" Cadence couldn't hide the skepticism in her voice.

Croft nodded. "I am."

Snow's eyes narrowed and he frowned as he thought. "It does make a kind of sense." He nodded. "You're right; I've not seen anyone else wield that power. But why would you be here? Why would you be taking on officers to train?"

"Osmund, you know about the council of gods and that all of the gods take their turns and such," Croft explained. "What you don't know is that when a god is not serving on the council, they are allowed to do as they please. They can work on this side. They can go to the corporeal plane. While there are limits depending on how high you were in your religion, freedom is allowed."

"So, you thought it would be fun to slum it with cops?" Cadence couldn't believe how shattered her image of the gods was right now.

"Fun, useful, a change of pace, mainly." Croft shrugged. "I chose Osmund to be my protégé in this line of work. Given his service at the Yard and his background of the family and religion, he was a perfect choice."

"Why was I a perfect choice?" Snow had no idea why Croft had chosen him, of all souls, to be his student.

"You are what I would want in one of my priests," Croft said with a shrug. "Back when I had them, at least. You are just, you are well educated, you keep excellent notes, and you do your best to not only uphold the law but to be fair. You know how to take the measure of a man in an instant and judge his motivations."

Silence hung in the room for a moment as Snow digested this, only to be broken by Cadence, who was looking at Croft with her jade-colored eyes wide. "Who are you?" she asked.

"I will tell you before we are done, but there is still more ground to cover here," Croft said.

"There's more?" It was Snow who asked this, stunned by the fact that there could be more to this discussion.

"Yes." Croft nodded. "I mentioned the council. Apparently, one of the gods didn't show up for their turn."

"Since you are bringing it up, I can assume it means one of two things. One being you want us to find them, or two, that you are taking their place," Snow said.

"The latter," Croft confirmed with a nod. "Another of their pantheon had been filling in for the last few years, but they've decided to go looking for their missing patriarch."

"Who's missing?" Cadence couldn't keep the curiosity out of her tone. How does a god even go missing?

"Zeus," Croft replied. "Hermes was filling in for him, but now he has gone to the corporeal plane to find him. Hermes asked me to fill in, since he and I were often regarded as the same kind of deity, just from different geographic areas and time frames."

That made Snow sit up straight, and Cadence could almost see the lightbulb go off over his head. "I know who you are," the Englishman said.

Croft nodded, as he was pleased with his student. "I thought you might reach that conclusion before we were done."

"So, you are leaving to go take a seat on the council and be all god-like," Cadence said. "Where does that leave us? Who is going to be our new you?" She had a feeling she knew, but she didn't want to be right. She didn't want to give up her partner.

"With Osmund's current affliction, he won't be able to remain in the field much longer," Croft said, and Cadence felt her heart and her stomach sinking. "I can stop the progression of the sickness eating at him, but to do so will turn him into a demi-god. So, I would like it if he were the one to take over my position. You would take over his and have another partner assigned to you."

"I have a question." Cadence measured her words, trying to not be as reactive as she knew she usually was. "And maybe this is just my brain playing catch up with everything you have been dumping in our laps with this conversation, but you said you chose Osmund. Was I just randomly assigned? Or was I chosen, too?"

"I chose you to be his partner," Croft said in answer. "I wanted to see him challenged a bit, and you did provide that. But you proved yourself worthy, Cadence Riley. You are quite the asset to us all, now more than ever."

"If I'm such an asset, I won't need a new partner then," Cade said with a shrug, the knee-jerk reaction kicking back in. She had managed to hold it off for a few seconds, at any rate. "I'll just work with Whitfield or something."

"Don't worry," Croft said with a smile. "I have someone in mind who I think will be a perfect match for you."

"Besides, it's not like we'd never see each other," Snow said. "I still live across the hall from you, and you would come to talk to me about your cases, I hope."

"So, you've already decided?" Cadence said, her emotions torn between sadness and anger. "Take the promotion and screw the old partner." The bitterness in her voice was almost tangible.

"You would rather the sickness eat him into nothingness?" Croft's voice was pointed as he spoke.

"No," Cade replied, looking at her lap in guilt. "I don't want that at all. I want him well; I just don't want to give him up. He's my partner."

"Cadence, one way or another, he has to go back to where he belongs," Snow said. He knew this was going to be hard for her. She hated change, and she had been through so much of it in the past year. He also knew she tended to react with emotion, but he was still going to try to reason with her because that's how they were with each other. "He was always going to have to go back at some point. He has set us on a path to where we need to be for him to be comfortable turning the reins over to us."

"The reins of what? Last I heard, this was a whole department. Worldwide and all that, to keep the ghosts from talking too much, keep the living from finding out too much," Cadence said.

"The reins of a new department," Croft said as he rose from his chair. "A specialized task force, if you will, that works with the living and the dead to contain threats to both. Your cases will inform how the NHD handles things. And at some point, I have a feeling Snow will call on you to do more, to find trustworthy breathers to work with. But that will likely come when you have more people under you."

"More people?" Cadence's eyebrows lifted in surprise.

"The NHD has instructions to begin grooming their best to work with you." Croft smiled.

"I don't believe this." Cadence shook her head.

"There is a little more." Croft shrugged.

"I'm not sure how well we'll be able to handle many more of these surprises," Snow said.

"This one will be brief. Whitfield will not be returning to work with you," Croft said.

"Son of a bitch, I knew it." Cadence sprang to her feet to begin pacing. "He's been distant, not showing up when he should, and then this thing with the notes. He's taking our research and running it back to the NHD or something. He's trying to sink our little task force experiment before it's even had a chance to really get on its feet."

"I think you may be overreacting just a tad bit, Cadence." Snow chuckled a little.

"She is and she isn't," Croft said.

"What?" Both Snow and Riley asked the question in unison.

"I have people trying to confirm things, but what I can tell you is that Whitfield isn't Whitfield," Croft said. "The spirit that was Bradley Whitfield was lost for good about a century ago. This one has apparently been fooling some of the newer supervisors in the NHD. I'm not sure what he's playing at, but he is not Whitfield."

"Good to know." Snow frowned, unsettled by this news.

"I'll let Sam know in case he turns up over there," Cadence added.

Croft nodded and tapped the scales on the corner of the desk. "This makes sense now, doesn't it?" He posed the question to Snow.

"Yes." Snow nodded. "It does. As does the Ibis painting behind you. The heart in the scale is a new addition, though."

"That was placed there by a very clever doctor who alerted me to the danger you were in, my friend." Croft smiled at them both.

"Wait, Ramon put the heart there?" Cadence couldn't believe it.

"He did." Croft nodded.

"So, he's figured out who you are, too? I feel like I'm the last person to know now," Cadence said with a frown.

Croft chuckled and then a golden light filled the room. It became so bright both Cadence and Snow had to shield their eyes. When the light dimmed, Croft was still standing there, but his visage had undergone a wild transformation. He wore a large Ibis head on his own head, his dark-skinned face visible beneath the beak. A wide, beaded gold and blue necklace covered the base of his throat all the way to his shoulders. His dark chest was bare except for a cream-colored sash that went diagonally across him to affix itself to a tied wrap-style skirt in cream and gold. The skirt went to his knees, revealing his calves and feet, which were clad only in sandals with straps that crisscrossed up his legs.

"I am Thoth," the man Cadence had formerly known as Croft said. "Egyptian god of arbitration, magic, writing, science, and judgment of the dead."

CHAPTER 11

Planning and Confrontation

Teeny was curled up in a chair near Liam's bedside as Lauren walked quietly into the room. The younger woman looked up from her phone, and it was clear to Lauren that despite the hospital staff bringing in a recliner for her, Teeny hadn't slept much. Teeny set her phone down and stood up as Lauren crossed the room, embracing the middle-aged woman in a hug.

"I'm sorry for stopping by so late," Lauren said.

"It's fine, but you got lucky. They kicked Russell out twenty minutes ago," Teeny said with a chuckle. "He was not happy."

"How is Liam doing?" Lauren asked, gesturing to the sleeping man in the hospital bed.

"He's in and out of consciousness because of the pain meds," Teeny said. "I try to be here for him when he wakes up."

"I'm sure he is appreciative of that," Lauren said. "Look, I must be honest; I'm glad Russell's not here. But I have information on that next case he wants you to take part in."

"I am so sorry he acted that way with you guys," Teeny said. "Most of the time, he's a good guy, but he can be an asshole when he wants to be."

"Don't worry about it," Lauren said. "Yes, he was being an asshole, but I do understand his being protective of you two and of the show."

"Okay?" came a croaky male voice from the bed. Both women turned to see Liam had woken up.

Teeny smiled and returned to her place by his side. "Yeah, we were just commiserating about Russell being an asshole."

Liam tried to laugh at that but winced and ended up coughing, which made him hurt more.

"Shhh, just lie back and rest," Lauren said to him. "Everything is fine."

Liam nodded, and his head fell back to the pillow as his eyes slipped closed.

"I didn't mean to wake him," Lauren said, whispering. "I just wanted to tell you that we're going to put together a dinner. We'll talk to Russell tomorrow and see if we can arrange it for tomorrow night. The owner of the property has several questions he would like answered before he agrees to let the show film there."

"Understandable," Teeny said, sinking back into her recliner. "It's not some derelict building that no one owns. It's someone's property."

"I'll call you if Russell agrees and let you know the time," Lauren said. "In the meantime, you need to get rest yourself. You'll be no good to anyone if you keep exhausting yourself."

Teeny nodded. "You're right. I'll try to get some sleep. Hit the light on your way out?"

"Sure thing," Lauren said with a nod. She left the room, turning off the light and closing the door for Teeny. A nurse caught sight of her leaving the room and frowned. Visiting hours were long over, but since the woman was leaving, she left it alone. She had to get meds to another patient and try to find thirty seconds to go to the bathroom before her bladder exploded. The late guest was just not that important.

"You knew and you didn't tell me?" Cadence let the door to her apartment close behind her after she and Snow entered. Her remarks, however, were directed toward Ramon, who sat on the couch.

"I knew what?" Ramon looked quite confused as to what was going on as he looked between Cadence and Snow.

"About Croft," Cadence said, feeling fire at what she felt was his betrayal. "And about Snow."

"Ah," Ramon said and looked at the floor for a moment as he thought about how best to answer her.

"I should leave you two to talk," Snow said.

"Oh, don't think you're getting out of this either, Mister," Cadence said and pointed to the armchair beside the couch. "Take a seat." She moved to stand in between the coffee table and the television set so she could talk to both easily. She leveled her eyes at Ramon and crossed her arms in front of her chest.

Ramon could feel the laser-like glare boring into him, and he looked up, meeting her gaze. "For the first thing you are mad about, Croft, I didn't know. Not with any certainty. But I will admit I suspected."

"For how long?" Cadence's voice made it clear she was not the least bit mollified by his answer.

"Since they brought you back burned to a crisp, and Snow explained how he had gotten you out of that place," Ramon said. He was still a picture of calm reasonableness as he answered her.

"And when did you realize you wouldn't be able to heal him?" Cadence pointed to Snow as she asked this.

"The morning you brought him in," Ramon explained. "I knew what I was looking at and that I could do nothing about it. I went to Croft, given I had my suspicions about what he truly was. I encouraged him to help Snow if he could, or give me a way to help him. And before you accuse me of not telling you about Snow's condition, that was not my place. It was his decision whether he wanted you to know or not."

Cadence turned her fiery glare to Snow. "Fine. Then why didn't you tell me how bad it was? And if you give me some shit about not wanting to worry me, so help me God, Osmund Snow, I will never talk to you again."

Snow thought about his answer for a moment, focusing on the coffee table as he did so. He then looked back at Cadence as he answered. "At first, I didn't think it was as bad as it was. Then, as it began to sink in that it was serious..." He trailed off for a moment. "If I'm to be honest with you, I believe I was masking it from myself as much as from you. If everything looked normal, then I could go on pretending that it was. As much as I lectured you about not needing to put facades or walls here, I was the one who ended up doing it in order to hide the truth from both of us. You have my most sincere and deepest apologies, Cadence."

His answer took the fire out of Cade's anger, and her arms dropped to her sides. She was silent for a moment before nodding to Snow. "Apology accepted." She frowned and walked over to the couch, dropping down beside Ramon and leaning into him a little. "And I'm sorry for jumping down your throat the minute I walked in."

"I can understand why," Ramon said, slipping an arm around her. "I take it you guys have had an eventful day?"

"That would be a hell of an understatement," Cadence said, and Snow nodded, echoing her sentiments.

"What's happened?" Ramon looked between the woman in his arms and Snow.

"In the course of this day, we found out that the breathers we associate with have another case," Snow said. "The case is on an estate that could have a non-human entity on it, in addition to a summoning circle of some kind and a very nasty history of bloodshed. We then had a meeting with Croft, wherein he made me reveal how bad the disintegration had gotten. He had me reveal to Cadence exactly how I got her out of Overton's cage, which caused the initial weakness. He then revealed that the feedback from my punching the force field of the box injured me further, to a degree that it will just keep doing damage. He disclosed his godhood and told us that there will now have to be changes since he has been summoned to take a place on the council."

"Take a place on the council?" Ramon couldn't keep the surprise from his voice. "We're not due for a change-over on the council for almost eighty more years."

"Well, from what he said, Zeus is missing, and the guy who was bench warming for Zeus asked Croft, or I guess Thoth, to take over so he could try to find Zeus," Cadence said. "But wait, there's more! So, Croft is going to the council, Snow is taking his spot, I'm taking Snow's spot, I'm going to get some new partner, and Whitfield isn't Whitfield."

"What?" Ramon had no other words than that for the last bit of news Cadence delivered.

"Yeah, we're not totally sure what's going on with that either, but apparently, the real Whitfield met his end a century ago, and this guy, whoever he is, has been pretending to be him," Cadence said.

"That is just…incredible," Ramon said after a moment of searching for the right word.

"Indeed," Snow said.

"Snow, since you've shown Cadence how your arm is, would you mind showing me? I've not seen it since the morning you came in," Ramon said.

Snow nodded and rose, taking off his blazer and rolling up the sleeve before dropping the mental image of a normal hand that he had gone back to using since leaving Croft's office.

Ramon rose and walked over to Snow. He examined the hand and arm closely before shaking his head. "This must be hurting like hell," Ramon said.

"A little," Snow conceded. "To be honest, with all we've dealt with today, my mind hasn't been on it."

"I wish there was something I could do for you, Snow," Ramon said, moving to sit back down beside Cadence. "I hate that this one is beyond me."

"I'm only glad Cadence's wounds weren't beyond you," Snow said.

"Oh, so it's okay for me to lose you as a partner, but not you lose me?" Cadence tried to keep the bitterness from her voice but failed.

"That's not fair, Cadence," Snow said, chiding her. "I am getting a promotion. I will still be here for you to talk to. Were I not to accept Croft's proposal, I would eventually cease to be as this poison spread through my soul. This promotion is not kicking you to the curb. It is saving my life. As for what happened with you, we were all afraid that we were going to lose you for good with the wounds you had after Overton burned you."

"That's true," Ramon said, hugging her closer with the arm that he had around her. "Even I wasn't sure you were going to pull through those first few hours."

"I don't want a new partner," Cadence said with a pouty frown.

"Cadence, you're not going to be able to do all of this by yourself, impressive as your skills are," Snow said. "You'll need a partner you can trust to have your back."

Cadence gave Snow a look that screamed sarcasm but said nothing.

"Let's just leave the workday at the door and enjoy the evening, shall we?" Ramon suggested. The other two both nodded and their talk turned to more cheerful things.

# CHAPTER 12

Meeting of the Minds

The bells over the door at Pho-Q jingled as Lauren, Derrick, and Aiden walked in, the smell of barbeque filling their noses and making their mouths water. They spotted a free table that was large enough for the party of six that they were going to be. It had a small sign on it that said "Reserved."

"Cool of Tom to reserve the table for us," Derrick said.

"Was it Tom, or was it Chris you spoke to?" Lauren looked at Aiden as she asked this.

"It was Tom," Aiden said with a nod. "But I think he said Chris was going to be the closing manager tonight."

As if on cue, a skinny man of Vietnamese descent sporting a very close buzz cut stepped out of the kitchen.

He walked over to the three of them with a smile. "Hey guys, how's it going?" he asked.

"Hi, Chris," Lauren said with a smile. "Going okay, thanks. You?"

"Oh, you know, work, kids, life," Chris said with a shrug.

"How are the wife and kids?" Aiden sat down as he spoke.

"The baby is going to turn two in a week," Chris said. "I can't believe she is getting so big. The boys are doing well in school. So, I hear you have some kind of big thing going on here tonight."

"Yeah," Aiden said with a nod. "So, bring out your best samplers and such. And make sure the bill goes to Russell," he added with a wink.

Chris laughed. "Sure, no problem. Which one will he be?"

"The one who has a stick up his ass," Derrick replied with a wry grin. "Can't miss him; he looks like your stereotypical Hollywood slimeball."

"Does he leave a slime trail where he walks? I'm pretty sure that would be a health code violation," Chris joked back. "Don't worry. I'll run up the bill for you guys." He turned and went back to the kitchen.

The cheerful bells above the door jingled as a pair of customers left and Professor Paul Phillips entered. He spotted Derrick and his friends easily and made his way, weaving through tables and chairs to them.

"Evening," Paul said in greeting.

"Hey, Professor," Derrick said, and both Lauren and Aiden echoed their hellos as well.

Everyone took their seats, and a waitress brought out water for the four of them. "Y'all are waitin' on more, right?" the waitress said as she set the last of the red bubbled plastic cups and paper-wrapped straws on the table.

"Two more, yeah," Aiden said.

"I'll bring out two more waters, then get y'all's drink orders when they get here, okay?" Her southern accent was charming, and Lauren had to try to not laugh as she saw how all three men at the table looked at the waitress with googly eyes. It was easy to guess that the young woman got great tips from most of her male customers, and maybe some female ones, too.

"Who exactly will I be meeting tonight?" Paul took a sip of his water to try to ease his nerves. "I know you said the show producer and one of the talents, but do we have names?"

"Yes," Lauren said with a nod. "Russell is the producer. Teeny DeLucca is the talent that will be here. She and Liam are the stars of the show, but of course, Liam is in the hospital now."

Sam had been hovering nearby, as was his practice. He smiled at Cade as she entered the restaurant. "Hey, sis," he said, waving her over. "You're just in time."

"Glad I'm not late," Cade said, giving her brother a brief hug. "I was helping Snow move into his new office."

"How is all of that going? I know how much you love change," Sam said, the sarcasm in his voice hard to miss. Cade had called him and let him know what was going on with Snow and Whitfield, so he wouldn't be as surprised when she showed up alone or with someone new in tow.

"Croft is fixing the damage to Snow's arm," Cadence said with a shrug. "He's been spending time with Snow to show him what he does and how he does it."

"Leaving you all alone?" Sam was surprised at that, given how protective Snow was of Cadence.

"Yeah, well, you know me." Cade shrugged. "I do love change. I haven't exactly been doing cartwheels over the idea of a new partner. I think they are focusing on their changeover before they worry about the battles I'm probably going to give them."

"Go easy on them, tiger," Sam said with a grin. "Snow doesn't need you to be difficult for him."

"When am I ever difficult?" Cade said, as she gave her brother an impeccable, practiced, innocent smile.

He snorted a laugh in reply as the bells above the front door of the restaurant jingled and Russell entered, followed by Teeny. Teeny looked annoyed, and Russell had a smug look on his face. Whatever argument they had been having in the car, Russell had apparently won. His smug look melted from his face as he took in the restaurant and the fact that it was not a high-class establishment. Teeny, however, couldn't help but grin as she watched Russell's smugness fade.

Teeny walked over to the table that the four others were already at and hugged each of the three she knew in turn. "And who is this?" she asked as she looked at the professor.

"Teeny, this is Professor Paul Phillips," Derrick said.

"Tina DeLucca," the tiny woman said, extending her hand to the professor. "It's a pleasure to meet you. Feel free to call me Teeny; everyone does."

"Nice to meet you, Teeny," the professor said, shaking her hand. "Call me Paul."

"And I'm Russell," the blonde man interjected, offering his hand to Paul. "I take it you are the owner of the property in question?"

"I am," Paul said with a nod. He now understood why Derrick referred to Russell as the stereotypical Hollywood slimeball. The man had a toned physique and wore clothes that were fitted to him to show it off. Blonde hair, tanned skin, a blinding smile, and a general attitude of being better than anyone or anything he was around. Paul was already beginning to have doubts about this venture, not that he wasn't before.

The waitress, whose name tag proclaimed her to be "Pam," came back to the table with two more waters. "Oh good, y'all are here," she said. She pulled her pad of paper and pencil from a pocket on her apron. "What drinks would y'all like?"

Cola was the order of the day by everyone until it got to Russell. "Highball," he said.

"Sorry, what?" Pam looked a little confused.

"A highball," Russell said again, rolling his eyes at the waitress's incompetence.

"Dude," Aiden said. "I'm going to make this easy on you. Soda, beer, or stick with just water. They don't have a bar here, just a few taps."

Russell made a face and shook his head. "Fine, I'll have what they're having," he said with a sigh. He picked up a paper-wrapped straw and tore it open, letting the plastic cylinder slide into his water.

"Thanks, Pam," Lauren said with an apologetic smile to the waitress.

Pam nodded and walked back to the kitchen.

"What crawled up that guy's ass and died?" Cadence asked her brother.

"He's the producer of *The Dead Show*. I think it's his job to be a douche," Sam said, and Cadence chuckled.

"So," Russell said as he began, "have you given the offer much thought?" He looked at Paul as he asked this.

"Well, that's part of the problem," the professor said. "You haven't made an offer. There has been no negotiation between us at all. You heard I had approached them, and you asked them to let Miss DeLucca tag along and film everything. To boil it down even further, you want to put land I own on TV with barely a thought to compensation or privacy."

Russell had the decency to look embarrassed. "I was angry when I did that. I had just gotten in from LA, I had just seen how bad Liam looked, and to be honest, I was worried about the fate of the show and its stars."

"So, are you no longer interested?" It was Aiden who asked the question, even though it was running through more than one mind. The conversation paused as Pam brought out their drinks, setting the sodas and a fresh batch of wrapped straws in front of them. "Appetizers'll be up in a little bit."

Russell looked apprehensive as Pam walked away. "Appetizers?"

"Yeah, you know, those things they sell at the beginning of a meal," Derrick said, being his usual smart-aleck self.

"Is the food here safe?" It was obvious Russell was skeptical about this, but his question elicited a sharp elbow in the side from Teeny.

"It is actually much better than you think it will be," Lauren said. "Trust me; don't judge this place on appearances."

Russell nodded. "To answer your previous question, no, it does not mean I've lost interest. It just means that I have come to realize my strong-arming you into it was wrong. I apologize."

The three ghost hunters nodded in response before Russell turned to Paul. "I would like to see if we can negotiate a way to do this. To be explicit, what I want is to have Teeny join their group," Russell said, gesturing to Aiden and the other two. "I want them to agree to film their investigation. No dramatics, no theatrics, just the investigation. You guys have the lead. Teeny is guest-starring with you, although it will fall under *The Dead Show* title with her as the star. We would do a special introduction explaining that since Liam is injured that she is accompanying a local paranormal team and has been given permission to film."

The conversation paused again as Pam set down a large tray of appetizers. "Okay, so here we have traditional pot stickers, and here we have pot stickers with the Pho-Q twist. Then on this side, you have Pho-Q spring rolls, and then there is the Pho-Q twist on Vietnamese Chicken Curry Puffs. Barbecue sauces, hoisin sauce, and soy sauce are all in the center of the table for y'all. Can I get anything else for you right this minute?" After they all shook their heads no, Pam nodded. "Alright then, ya'll just call me if you need anything!"

As Pam sashayed away, Paul looked across the table at Russell. "Look, this property has been in my family for some time, and I have yet to see anything good come of it. Derrick tells me that the research he turned up isn't any better. So, first of all, I don't want my family's name dragged through the mud more than it was when the tragedy happened. Secondly, I do not want to be held responsible for whatever may happen out there if someone gets hurt. The property hasn't been lived on for a long time."

"The indemnity clause is a usual thing. It's why I'm not talking to an attorney about suing the state for what happened to Liam on their property," Russell said. "Your family's history is part of the story of the estate. We will have to delve into it as it's a matter of public record, from what I know. However, we can have you as an anonymous speaker. Do lighting so you are a shadow and use voice-changing tech so you can't be recognized."

"If this does happen and Teeny comes with us," Aiden said, "it is going to have to go differently than Barrington did. No cool bleeding edge, high-tech experiments. Just the usual trappings of the job."

"We'll also do it in at least two parts," Lauren said. "We want to walk the grounds in the daylight so that we can learn our way around. A daylight walkthrough of the house itself will be necessary because I don't love the idea of going in there with no prior knowledge of any structural weaknesses in the dark. Then we will do a nighttime investigation of the home and any other parts of the property we think might have activity."

Russell nodded. "Fair enough, but would you let Teeny tape a special beginning?"

"What kind of special beginning?" Paul and Aiden both asked the question in stereo.

"Something outside or inside your headquarters, just saying that Liam was badly injured on the Barrington Prison episode and that you have agreed to partner with her while Liam is recovering," Russell said.

"Our headquarters is my shop at the other end of the complex," Lauren said with a shrug.

"Oh!" Russell did nothing to hide his shock at this. "I thought you would have an office somewhere, or at least someone's home."

"No, my shop has served us well," Lauren said with a shrug.

"It must make it nerve-wracking to have all of that equipment in such a public place," Russell said.

"I keep the equipment at my apartment," Aiden said.

"Perhaps we could pretend that your apartment is the group's headquarters? No offense meant to your shop," Russell said.

"None taken," Lauren said. "But that would be up to Aiden."

"I think we're getting ahead of ourselves," Teeny said, piping up. "Paul has yet to say yes or no. It seems to me that all other plans hinge on that."

"True enough," Russell said, turning on his Hollywood smile. "So, what do you say, Paul?"

Paul thought for a moment, considering his words. "I understand that what happened with my uncle is public record, but I don't want you to deviate from what is known as fact. No crazy theories or stories that will get people worked up and wanting to investigate it all again or trespass on my property."

"We can do that." Russell nodded. "Stick to the facts, got it."

"And will there be compensation for using my land as the backdrop for your show?" Paul wasn't overly concerned about money, but an extra cushion would be nice to have.

Russell nodded and took a pen from the inside pocket of his blazer. He folded the paper napkin by his plate in half and wrote on part of it. He folded it closed and passed it to Paul. "I hope this will suffice."

It must have been enough because Paul's eyes boggled behind his glasses. "Yep, I'm good with that," Paul said.

Pam came back to the table with a pitcher to refill the drinks. Chris was right behind her with a large tray with several large bowls and a stack of smaller ones. Pam put the pitcher down on the empty table next to them after refilling the glasses and was swift in clearing off the tray of appetizers. Chris set down the large tray, and Pam took the stack of smaller bowls off it.

"Here you have a sampling of all the Pho we offer," Chris said. Each bowl had a ladle and a small handwritten card stating what was in the bowl in front of it. Meanwhile, Pam was setting one of the smaller bowls in front of each person. "You've got everything from vegetables only to beef, chicken, pork, seafood, and a spicy one. Enjoy!" He and Pam then disappeared back into the kitchen.

"So that's settled then," Russell said as everyone began serving themselves some of the soup. "I'll draw up the contract tonight and have it sent to you tomorrow."

Paul nodded his agreement as he pocketed the napkin with the number on it.

"Good! Now we just need to hammer out the details with the three of you," Russell said.

CHAPTER 13

New Kid on the Block

"Hey, Bonnie." Cadence greeted the secretary who sat outside of Croft's office.

"Detective Riley," Bonnie said with a cheerful smile. Her horn-rimmed glasses were currently hanging from a pearl accented gold chain around her neck. Her silver hair was done up in a modest beehive hairdo, and her voice was sweet and breathy. "It's good to see you. How are you?"

"Eh." Cadence shrugged her shoulders noncommittally. "Waiting to see how all of this is going to play out."

"I know," Bonnie said, her voice dropping to a conspiratorial whisper. "I had no idea that Alistair was really … well, you know."

"No kidding," Cadence whispered back. "So, are you staying here to work for Snow?"

"Yes," Bonnie assured Cadence with a nod and a smile that lit up her eyes like a giddy schoolgirl. With that look in her eyes, Cadence could almost see the young woman Bonnie had been before age took its toll on her hair and skin. She would have been one hell of a beauty in her day.

"Glad to be working with Ozzy, huh?" Cadence said with a grin, ribbing the woman about her obvious crush.

Bonnie's cheeks turned a nice pink, as did her ears beneath her silver hair. "Inspector Snow is a good man," was all she said. "They are waiting for you; I shouldn't keep you out here chit-chatting. Go on in."

Cadence smiled at Bonnie and let the teasing go. "Thanks, Bonnie. See you later." Cade then entered the office, closing the door behind her.

Croft and Snow were both on the couches to the right of the door in the conversational area of the office. Cadence hadn't seen much of Snow over the last couple of days, as he had been spending time with Croft. Croft had been healing Snow, and they had been going over the particulars of the transfer of power and position.

"Have a seat, Detective Riley." Croft's deep, warm voice welcomed her into the office as did his smile. Gone were his halo and clothes of godhood, and he was back in his normal "Croft" suit.

Cade moved to the couch Snow was on and sat down on the opposite end of him. They smiled at each other in greeting. Cade turned a little on the couch and tucked one leg up underneath the other so she could better see both without having to crane her neck to the side.

"You look better," Cade remarked to Snow.

"Thank you." Snow nodded. "Alistair has done a wonderful job of helping me." He flexed his hand as if showing it off. "No façade. The damage is repaired."

"Good, I'm glad." Relief was obvious in Cadence's voice and face. "Have you guys worked out how all of this is going to go now?"

"Among other things," Croft said with a nod. "This will be my last day down here, and this will be Snow's office from now on. Bonnie will stay on as his secretary. I've been familiarizing him with the current concerns and goings-on with the non-human issues we've been facing, not just with the Shaldoxz issue, but with others as well. You will continue, with your new partner, working with the breathers you have made inroads with."

"You don't have to trouble yourself about a new partner," Cadence deflected. "I'm good on my own. Plus, if I'm working with our group of ghost hunters, Sam will be there anyway."

"As good as you may be, Cadence," Snow said, "you do need to have a partner. You know that even from your own mortal life, for safety, if nothing else. What if you had been alone at Barrington, and Pruitt had shoved you into that infernal contraption the girl made? You would have had no way to escape and no one to help you."

"Why do you have to make good points?" Cadence's voice was sour but not venomous.

"Why are you so resistant to change?" Snow countered. "You would think I, as the older one, would be the one more resistant to it."

"I guess we've rubbed off on each other." Cadence feigned an innocent smile as she shrugged. "And you have to admit that I've had a whole lot of change in the last year."

"Granted," Snow said with a nod. "I forget how short a time it has been for you on this side."

"And yet you have flourished," Croft said, trying to steer the conversation back on topic. "So, I have no doubt that you will be just as resilient with this change as you have been with all the others."

"Okay, but how do we know that this new person isn't going to be some kook or someone like Whitfield who isn't who they say they are?" Cadence was frowning as she presented two of the things that had been troubling her about getting a new partner. "Besides, do you really want someone who is less than a year dead training someone? I barely have the answers to my own questions."

"You aren't partnering with someone newly dead," Croft explained.

"Okay," Cadence said, drawing out the word slowly as she thought. "So, an older cop, like Snow?"

"No, he wasn't involved in law enforcement at all." Croft held up a hand to stop her as she opened her mouth to protest. "You do your best work when you think outside of the box, so to speak. Your new partner has the same penchant for that as you do."

"Her new partner is as unpredictable as she is?" Snow couldn't keep the surprise from his voice as he had been sure that Cadence would be partnered with someone reasonable to balance her out. "You're trying to give me as many headaches as possible."

"No, my friend," Croft said with a laugh. "I think these two will make an excellent team, and you will still be here to help keep them in check if they get too wild."

"Well, if it's going to annoy Ozzy, I might be more apt to not hate this new guy too much." Cadence grinned at Snow.

"We will send him to your office soon," Croft assured her. "In the meantime, tell us, how did the meeting with the breathers go?"

"They all ended up coming to an agreement," Cadence recounted. "The producer offered the professor enough money to make the guy's eyes bug out of his head, so the professor, of course, agreed. Then they hammered out a deal so that Teeny will join our ghost hunters and get to film the investigation for an episode of that damned show."

"When do they go?" It was Snow who asked.

"Tomorrow," Cadence said. "They are going to do a daytime walk around to get a feel for the property and see how bad the house is since it has been, for all intents and purposes, abandoned for the last few decades."

"The video from the Barrington Prison incident," Croft said. "I've not heard you mention it. Have they even reviewed the footage?"

"No, that was part of the agreement they made. Aiden gets to help go through the footage. That, they will be starting on in a few hours." Cadence was just hoping that Aiden would be able to get the damning footage away from the show by hook or by crook.

"Good. You and your new partner will have plenty of time to meet and then go to the video review session," Croft said. "The priority on that remains the same.

No conclusive evidence can make it onto that television show."

"I'll do what I can," Cadence nodded. "I'm sure Aiden will, too."

"I'll check in on you later," Snow said.

Getting the impression that she was now dismissed, Cadence rose and left the office. She gave Bonnie a smile and a wave as she passed her desk, then made her way back to the office. Whitfield's desk was now gone, and Snow's was barren. She frowned at the sparse state of her office and resolved to try to personalize it a little more. She sat down and began recreating the notes that she had pinned to the wall that had gone missing. Within thirty minutes, she had recreated the majority of what she had originally put up on the wall.

"What's all of that?" a male voice asked from the doorway as she pinned a note to the wall.

Cadence turned and looked at the figure in the door with trepidation, figuring it was going to be her new partner. Her expression changed from wariness to confusion as she saw the young man in the doorway.

He was in the vicinity of six feet tall, and his brown eyes looked like he was ready to crack a grin any second. He had short, light brown hair on his head, and he wore a pair of jeans and a Ghostbusters T-shirt. The belt on his jeans looked almost like a utility belt that a comic book character would wear, as it had pouches and pockets all over it. Cadence's confusion wasn't over the belt or the old-looking sneakers, but over the fact that he looked about sixteen years old.

"Who are you?" Cadence was proud of herself for not swearing.

"Name's Will McKinney," the kid introduced himself. "You're Cadence Riley, right?"

"Yeah," Cade said with a nod as her stomach began to sink. They wouldn't have partnered her with a teenager, would they?

"I'm your new partner." Will smiled as he walked across the office with his hand outstretched to shake hers. For a moment, she was so stunned she shook his hand without giving it a thought, but then she came to her senses and took her hand back, just shy of yanking it out of his grip.

"You can't be my new partner." She shook her head. "You're a kid."

"The term is teenager if you want to get into technicalities," Will said. "And, so what? You're a girl."

"What does being a *woman*," Cadence said, stressing the word, "have to do with anything?"

"What does my age have to do with anything?" Will asked as he crossed his arms over his chest. He still looked like he was about to laugh, despite posturing like he was angry.

"You don't have any experience for one," Cade said.

"Wrong. I've been holed up in Design & Invention for the last thirty years," Will said with a bit of a grin. "Next argument?"

"That actually is my argument," Cadence said. "You seem like a decent kid, but you have no law enforcement experience."

"Not true," Will said. "I've watched *Miami Vice, Hunter, The Equalizer, T.J. Hooker*. I know how all of this is supposed to go down."

"It's not like it is on TV, kid, trust me," Cadence said.

"How about this, then? You stop calling me kid, and we talk about what you expect of me in this job as your partner," Will said. "I've been transferred. It's a done deal, and we're stuck with each other. So, let's try to figure this out. From what I've heard, you're cool. Inspector Snow said he thinks we'll get along. Can we try?"

Cadence sighed in defeat. Snow was going to hear it from her about sending her a kid, but that would come later. "Okay, fine." Cade gestured to the desk that would be his. "Make yourself at home."

She went back to her desk as he made his way to his. He sat down and kicked his feet up on his desk.

"You never did tell me what all that was about," Will prompted as he gestured to the notes on the wall.

"The cases that Snow and I have been working on seem to all be interconnected with a breather trying to free a non-human entity at the center of them all." Cade explained. "We were just trying to work out how it all fits together. We know someone on our side is working with the breather to try to bring back this Shaldoxz, and it's been going on for a while."

"Wicked," Will said. "Do you have a file on all of this that I can go over? Kind of get up to speed. I hear you have a group of breathers that you work with."

"Yeah," Cade said with a nod. "It all started out by accident, but the partnership has worked out well. It's a three-person group. Lauren is the psychic, Aiden is the tech guy, and Derrick is their researcher. My brother Sam is Lauren's spirit guide."

"Your brother is on this side?" Will couldn't keep the surprise out of his voice or off his face. "That kind of sucks. Sorry to hear it."

"I'll be honest. It sucked more when I was still alive. He was killed ten years before I died, and after he died, both our parents did, too," Cadence said.

"Damn," Will said, shaking his head. "I mean, it sucks being here alone, but I know I would hate it if my sister was here. She was younger than me. Of course, I guess she could die in a couple more decades since she's mid-forties now."

"I know I'm not supposed to ask," Cadence said. "But how…" She trailed off, trying to find a decent way to put it without being offensive.

"How did I die as a teenager?" Will wasn't a stranger to that question, and it didn't bother him as it did most spirits.

"Yeah," Cade said with a nod. "I'm sorry. I know it's rude."

"You aren't the first to ask," he said, giving an easy smile. "Cancer. Acute Lymphoblastic Leukemia."

"I'm sorry," Cadence said with a wince.

"It is what it is," Will said with a shrug.

Cadence tilted her head a little as she looked at Will. "You know, I think you and Sam will get along great. He really isn't that much older than you, or he wasn't when he passed. He was 19 when he was killed."

"Killed, not died," Will said, noting the difference.

"Yeah," Cadence said with a sigh. "He was a college freshman; a killer took out a bunch of people in his dorm."

"And how long did you have to live with that before you ended up here?" Will opened a drawer of the desk and took out a red rubber ball. He began tossing it up in the air and catching it as they chatted.

"Ten years," Cade said as she watched him. "I was a junior at the same college when he was murdered. I went on to become a cop, made it to detective, but then was killed in the line of duty."

"So, the Riley siblings have a penchant for getting murdered. Good to note. I'll try to make sure we never visit any lakeside campgrounds," Will said with a grin as he tossed his ball in the air and caught it again without even looking.

"Was that a *Friday the 13th* joke?" Cadence couldn't keep the surprise from her voice or face.

"Yeah." Will stopped tossing the ball up in the air and looked across the desks at her. "Why?"

"No, nothing. I'm just used to being the one that makes those kinds of jokes and then having Snow not get it at all," she said, shaking her head.

"See? Now you have a cool partner, one who gets the jokes." Will grinned. "Believe me, you have no idea how grateful I am for this transfer."

"Why's that?" Cade leaned back a bit in her chair.

"Design and Innovation is cool and all, but no one got me there." Will shrugged. "You have no idea how many things I tried to get passed into circulation that could have made life here, or even your work with bad spirits and non-humans, a little easier. It felt like I was the only one at the party, you know? No one could loosen their sphincters enough to have a little imagination."

"Now you have my attention. What is it you wanted to design that would have made our work easier?" Cadence had to admit that maybe Croft and Snow had gotten the pairing right.

"Well, you know how it works, right? Someone puts the energy into something to make it permanent and make it work against whatever they are designing it to work against, even if the person using it doesn't know," Will said, explaining. "So, I could make a little glass ball with liquid in that would work as a kind of knock-out gas for specific kinds of spirits. Anyone could pick it without knowing what it does and use it. Now, of course, if they don't use it against the kind of spirit it is designed for, then it might not be as potent, but it's still going to have a slight effect."

"Really?" Cadence was intrigued. "Why on earth wouldn't they put that through?"

"According to my manager at the time," Will said, "no one wanted to try to figure out which marble would work against what and that there were other more tried-and-true methods that were better."

"Well, their tried-and-true methods are backfiring in their faces," Cade said sourly. She opened her top desk drawer and pulled a file from it. She then got to her feet and walked a few steps to let the file fall to Will's desktop. "Take a look."

"What is this?" Will moved his feet to the floor and sat up, putting the ball on top of his desk for the moment. He opened the file and began looking at what it contained.

"It's a report from the hospital," Cadence said.

"We have a hospital? You have got to be kidding me." Will shook his head as he chuckled. "A hospital for ghosts?"

"We get hurt," Cadence said with a shrug. "Some of us more than others. Especially when we're going up against non-humans and their human devotees." Cadence paused for a moment as she thought. She then opened the top drawer of Will's desk and pulled out another file. "This is the caseload Snow and I worked that you'll want to read up on. We have a few hours before we go out," she said, checking the time on her watch.

"We're going out?" Will made a joke of it and waggled his eyebrows at her. "I didn't think you moved that fast."

Cadence chuckled and shook her head. "No, not like that. I'm still working on a case. We have to review video evidence gathered from a ghost hunt at a prison. We'll be there with my brother, Sam, and with Aiden, one of the breathers we work with."

"Who's Aiden? Oh! Never mind, tech guy," Will said. "Gotta get used to the names," he added with a smile.

"Hey, who's this?" Both Will and Cadence turned to see the speaker in the doorway, and Cadence was shocked to see Whitfield standing there.

"Whitfield, hey." Cade smiled, trying to not act as surprised and suspicious as she felt.

"Hey." He smiled back, but looked curiously around the office. "What's going on? Where's my desk? Where's Snow?"

Will sat back in his chair, thinking it was the better part of valor to stay quiet and let his new partner handle this person. He had noticed the perceptible change in Cadence's body language and tone.

"Snow is in Croft's office. I think you're off the team, something about the NHD deciding they needed you more. Might want to check in with them." Cade shrugged with a bit of a smile. "You know how they like to keep me out of the loop sometimes."

"Are you serious? The NHD asked for me back full time?" Whitfield looked hurt at the notion of not being there with them anymore. "Oh, come on! I loved being a part of this team." Whitfield frowned and looked at where his desk used to be. "Is it because I screwed up the other night?"

"I couldn't say," she answered with a shrug. "I've been a little busy since the prison case isn't entirely closed yet."

"Not closed? I thought it was," Whitfield said with a frown. "You have the old monitor incarcerated; the TV show won't be filming there any time soon, right?"

Will leaned forward and grabbed his red rubber ball from the top of his desk and started tossing it and catching it, but not like he had been earlier. The ball only went a few inches up before descending back into his waiting hand.

"It's a little more complicated because of what happened to the guy from the TV show," Cadence answered. "But I've got it in hand," she said, trying to reassure Whitfield that all was normal in their little slice of the afterlife. "Maybe you should go talk to your bosses at the NHD and see what's going on."

"Yeah." Whitfield sighed as he ran a hand through his unruly ginger locks. "I guess I'll have to."

"Cheer up, man," Will said to him. "Everything happens for a reason, right?"

"I'm not sure I believe that," Whitfield grumbled. "Who are you?"

"Oh!" Will got up from his chair and crossed over to Whitfield. He offered out his hand and they shook. "I'm Will. Nice to meet you."

"Agent Whitfield, likewise." Whitfield winced for a moment and took his hand back. He looked at it for a second as if he had been bitten, but there was nothing visible.

"Are you okay?" Cadence asked the question as Will made his way back to his chair with a smirk on his face that had melted by the time he turned back around to face Whitfield again.

"Yeah, yeah, I'm fine." Whitfield said, almost muttering the words. "I'll see you later, Cade."

"See you soon," Cadence said, not wanting to sound like she didn't want to see him again.

As soon as he was gone, Will looked up at Cadence from his seat. "You know he's non-human, right?"

"Wait, what?" Cadence's eyes widened as she looked down at Will.

"I told you I came up with stuff," Will said with a shake of his head. "Ye of little faith." He picked up his red rubber ball from the desk where he had set it down when he went to shake Whitfield's hand. He turned it and showed Cadence that there was a small hole in it. "See there? There's a little thing of liquid in there that I can squeeze out onto my hand. That liquid is a litmus test of sorts. You know those papers that can tell you how acidic—"

"I know what a litmus test is," Cadence cut him off. She wasn't trying to be rude. She was concerned with what he had just said about Whitfield.

"Right, anyway, the liquid is nothing to us," Will said. He squeezed the ball, and a drop began to appear and grow larger in the hole. "Touch it."

Cadence lifted a skeptical eyebrow but was willing to play along. If he was right, this answered a lot of questions. Her finger ran along the ball, smearing the drop of liquid. It just felt wet to her. "Is this supposed to do something?"

"Not to you or me," Will said, putting the ball down again. "To us, it's like hair gel or a kind of thick water. To a god, it won't hurt them, but wherever I had that liquid on my hand would be glowing golden." He then raised his right hand, opening his palm to show Cadence. The center of his palm, where Whitfield's fingers had touched, was a dull gray, as if it had been covered by ash. "To a non-human or a spirit with evil intentions, it will feel like an ant bite or a bee sting. It doesn't hurt me. It just makes the gel look like this. If it is an evil non-human, it actually hurts them, like a stabbing pain, and the mark it leaves on my hand would be dark red."

Cadence looked from the dry, crumbling gray flakes on his palm to the inoffensive red rubber ball. "That's genius." Cadence was dumbfounded by the invention her new partner had just used to out Whitfield.

"Thank you," Will preened. "It's nice to hear someone finally appreciates my work."

"Come on, we've got to talk to Snow," Cade said, tugging on the sleeve of Will's T-shirt. "Bring your ball."

Will decided he didn't know Cadence well enough, just yet, to make the obvious smart-assed reply. Instead, he grinned and just rose from the chair, following her.

Of Tests and Theories

"It makes no sense." Snow seemed inordinately aggravated by what Cadence and her new partner were proposing.

"It makes a startling amount of sense if you would stop to look at the evidence," Cadence said.

"Fine, show me this test you conducted," Snow said as he stopped pacing and turned to face them. Cadence looked at Will and nodded.

"Okay," Will said. "But first, I want to just thank you again, sir, for the opportunity to work at this level." Will reached out with his left hand and shook Snow's hand. "You were right; she was argumentative at first, but once we got talking, she warmed up."

"Hey!" Cadence protested.

Snow closed his eyes for a moment and counted to five. He didn't have the time to count to ten. "I am glad the two of you found common ground so fast. However, I would like to see the test you say you ran." He opened his eyes and saw Cadence grinning. "Now what?" Snow's voice reflected his annoyance as his accent became more clipped.

"You just saw the test," Cade said, still smiling.

"I don't think I have ever been this close to getting punched by a demi-god before," Will said. He opened his hand to reveal his palm. Unlike the black ash that had been there after Whitfield's handshake, there was a silvery sparkle as if someone had drawn a smudge mark on Will's palm with a silver metallic marker.

Snow blinked, then shook his head. "I'd heard you were one for practical jokes, Mr. McKinney," Snow said. "But to fake something like this is irresponsible."

"It's not a joke," Cadence said. "I saw him do it. I saw Whitfield's reaction. And think about it. His convenient absence a few nights ago when he was supposed to be our eyes and ears on the family case was more than just him being tired or losing track of time. He deliberately was out to make one or the other case fail."

"Why, Cadence?" Snow asked, exasperated. Croft telling them that Whitfield wasn't who he said he was had been more than bothersome to Snow. He had put faith and trust in the NHD agent, or whoever he really was, and now that was gone. "Just because he managed to fool every single one of us into believing he was who he said he was doesn't make him non-human."

"But the positive non-human test does," Will said.

"Forgive me, Mr. McKinney, but our acquaintance has been far too short for me to believe in your toys as legitimate tests," Snow grumbled.

"Why can't they be both?" Will looked offended and hurt.

"Just hold up, both of you." Cadence cut into the conversation before their argument over testing methods took them too far off track. "Snow, you and Croft told me that you had the perfect new partner for me, right? That he was creative, imaginative, liked to think outside the box just like I did, right?"

Snow looked at Cadence and nodded. "Yes, you are right."

"This is part of his thinking outside the box. Creating a test like this out of something as innocuous as a toy," Cadence said. "Creative, innovative, and outside the box. As much as you know this hurts me to say it, you were right. He's a great choice."

"Setting that aside," Snow said after a moment, acknowledging her comments with a grudging nod, "what else makes you think Whitfield is a non-human?"

"I don't just think he's a non-human," Cadence said with a shake of her head. "I think he is working for Shaldoxz."

Snow tempered his initial reaction of incredulousness and instead tried the more rational approach. "Explain to me why you think that," he said, gesturing for them to have a seat on the couches that still inhabited the corner of the office.

The three of them moved to the couches and had a seat, Snow at the end of one couch while Cadence sat on the opposite couch at the end nearest him, Will sitting next to Cadence.

"Okay, so you know I've been trying to piece all of this together, hence the notes all over the wall," Cadence said.

"Yes, go on," Snow said.

"If we take it back to, what is it now, six? Seven months? Anyway, take it back to when we started at the beginning at Lexington Hills. The spell that Dan and the others used to conjure up that chaos entity. Whitfield told us that it was a spell that had been removed from breather circulation by the rulers and authorities on our side a couple of centuries ago." Snow nodded in response, silently encouraging her on. "Well, I've been doing a lot of research into those runes, into that particular spell. The runes are legit, we saw the proof of that, and they do work together and do conjure a chaotic spirit that has never been human. The spell he talked about is bogus. It never existed. I've been running all kinds of research at home—you can ask Ramon or Sam. I have yet to be able to find a spell like that in any religion or cult or occult theology. Unless it is something superclassified, some knowledge only the gods have, and they keep it guarded, it does not exist.

"Veronica Banks wasn't who she said she was either, remember?" Cadence said, continuing her explanation. "She grabbed our request off the pile and thought she could run it on her own, being newly dead. At least, that was the story we got from Whitfield. Who's to say that she wasn't given the file by Whitfield? That her answers weren't fed to her by him? That he gave her those weapons that barely did squat to the monster. And ultimately, when she was destroyed, he stepped in himself to keep close tabs on us, to see how we would or could handle what he had been responsible for?

"Shaldoxz, we have been told, is a non-human that thrives on chaos, pain, and blood," Cadence said as she continued barreling down her path of explanation. "That those are the things it would take to release him from whatever prison he is in. Well, this was a chaos entity. It took blood to summon it, and the damn thing caused plenty of fear and pain while it was free, to humans and spirits alike."

"We knew nothing of Shaldoxz during the Lexington Hills case," Snow said. "While you are correct in pointing out that the entity summoned would have been a good vehicle to bring about the reclamation of him from prison, what makes you think that case is linked to the others where we know a Shaldoxz follower was involved?"

"Wolf," Cadence said with a shrug.

"Wolf?" Snow repeated.

"Dan said that was the name of the cult leader. We know that when Lambert attacked Andy during the dorm case, Lambert called Overton for help, and Overton called Wolf, who threw Overton under the bus and told him to clean up his own mess."

"We only know what Overton was told by Wolf because Whitfield was out there," Snow said. "Why would he help us if he was in on their plot? For that matter, why would he have helped us with Lexington Hills if he was part of the scheme in trying to help with Shaldoxz's release? Why help us destroy the creature that you are saying he caused to be summoned?"

"You said yourself that the people who had our area before were pretty lax when it came to doing their actual job," Cadence said. "We saw how they let Barrington

Prison go and what happened with that. In giving Wolf the runes and creating the spell, it's not out of the realm of possibility that he thought Lexington Hills was just as untended. When Banks was put out of the picture, it's possible that he responded to us to see just how well we did or did not do our job. It's possible that he was taking our measure while trying to clean up something that had become a bigger mess than he had intended. After that, he was a victim of his own success. Croft appointed him to help us out, and then the new team was created, and it rolled from there.

"We know Wolf can see spirits. He saw that girl at the family house, and he saw Sam. It's very possible that Whitfield going out to check on Overton was more of a way to help himself and Wolf. We were preoccupied with getting Andy help. It's possible he gave Wolf some kind of sign to dump Overton, which could be why Wolf left Overton to fend for himself. Whitfield knew enough about us by then to know there was no way in hell I was going to leave Andy or the other breathers to get hurt, and that you wouldn't let that happen since it was important to me."

"Why break our confidence in him now, then?" Snow said after a moment of thinking.

"Desperation, pure and simple," Cadence said. "From what Sam said, Wolf spoke like the girl, the living girl, was important to him somehow. That's why he was using the ghost child to lure her away. With Lauren's group involved in that, we were going to be there. With the prison being as dangerous as it was, he knew we would have our hands full there. All he had to do was give a little push to make both things happen on the same night so that our resources were stretched thin and then disappear. Sam was on his own, and Whitfield would know that Sam would call me if there was trouble, which there was. I was still injured, and I think that box contraption just was a stroke of luck on his side. It made it so that neither of us could leave the prison to help Sam, which in turn left Sam on his own dealing with Wolf—not to mention the very sloppy attempt to undo our little wall of notes. Maybe he knew the jig was up? Maybe he was tired of playing along with us? But he had to have been the one who took the notes down. Even you looked like you were suspicious of him."

"Granted, at that time, it did look like he was the one who had taken down the notes," Snow said. "And you make a lot of good points, but they all hinge on maybes and what ifs. Conjecture isn't something you can use to put a criminal behind bars, Cadence. You know that."

"I do," Cadence said with a nod. "But he doesn't know we're on to him. I told him that you and Croft had talked, that I wasn't there for the conversation, but that his old boss at the NHD wanted him back focusing on that line of work. I made it seem like that was something I had vaguely heard and that I was waiting to talk to you again to get more details. We ended it with a see you later, not goodbye forever. I figure that might give us a little wiggle room to keep the connection and see if he slips up any more. Keep it social, no case details anymore, but just see what happens."

Snow looked at Cadence and then over at Will. The younger man had been listening quietly the whole time, and he just shrugged at Snow.

"I don't know the particulars of these cases yet, but the logic she's presenting is sound," Will said.

"And all of this was brought on by your hand gel test," Snow said, musing over everything Cadence had said.

"When he said that Whitfield was a non-human, it just kind of clicked into place. I know it is a lot of maybe this and possibly that, but it makes sense, Snow. It makes a scary amount of sense," Cadence said. "So don't hold back. Tell me what you think."

"I just want to interject one thing," Will said before Snow could answer Cadence. "Like I told Detective Riley, Whitfield's test was gray. That means he is a neutral non-human. A straight-up evil non-human would have left a dark red mark, like you left a glittery silver one."

Snow nodded slowly as he listened to Will, then thought over everything the two of them had presented. "I think that putting the two of you together as partners was a stroke of genius on Croft's part," Snow said.

CHAPTER 15

Video Review

Cadence led Will down the hallway of doors that led to locations she and Snow had jurisdiction over or that they frequented. Aiden's apartment had its own door now, and that was where Cade stopped. She opened the door, and they stepped through into the living room of Aiden's apartment.

The tall audio/visual expert was waiting on his couch, a tablet in his palm, reading an E-book. On his coffee table, he had his two usual props when he thought Cadence and Snow might show up—a green felt shamrock for Riley and a white felt snowflake for Snow. Aiden would look up from time to time to check the clock.

"This is something he usually does, so we can let him know we're here," Cadence said as she moved to the coffee table and used a bit of energy to knock the four-leaf clover shape off the coffee table. Aiden didn't notice it until he looked up to check the clock again.

"Oh! Hi Cadence," he said. "No Snow tonight, huh?" He looked at the table for verification to see if the snowflake moved. When it didn't, he nodded. "Okay. Russell should be here soon. We'll be reviewing the footage in the back room."

"I still think it's weird you guys interact so casually with these guys," Will said. "I thought the whole point was to not talk to the breathers."

"Yeah, well, sometimes circumstances can spiral to a point where they are the only solution," Cade said. "You read the reports. With the Lexington Hills case, we had no way of fixing the situation without their help. And they've kept our secret. They're good people."

"He seems like he is fine with the idea of you hanging out here and watching what he and the producer do." Will was amused by the situation. "If I'd known there were ghosts around when I was alive and kicking, I'd have been freaking out! It would have been hella cool, but freaky, you know?"

Cadence laughed and shrugged. "Yeah, but they go looking for ghosts, so they're more used to the idea of ghosts being around."

"Point," Will agreed with a nod.

A knock sounded on Aiden's door sounded, and he rose from his couch, setting down his tablet on top of the felt pieces. He checked through the peephole and opened the door, letting both Russell and Teeny in.

"Come on in," he said in greeting. "I'm surprised you came, Teeny. I figured you would be at the hospital with Liam."

"They keep him well medicated. He's asleep most of the time," Teeny said with a shrug. "He's stable, so now it's just a waiting game until he recovers enough for them to start tapering him off the meds. And we did get good news. The swelling around his spine is going down, so there may not be much permanent damage there."

"That is good news and a relief. I'm glad he's stable," Aiden said, closing the door. "Can I get you guys anything?"

"No thanks," Russell said. The producer was carrying a small plastic storage box under one arm. "Where's your setup?"

"Back here," Aiden said and led them down a short hall to the bedroom that Aiden had set up as his computer and equipment cave. His pc was already humming, and he had set a chair near the desk. "Let me just get another chair from the dining room."

"Aiden, was that fresh coffee I smelled when we walked in?" Teeny asked, hope in her voice.

"Yep," Aiden said with a smile. "Want some?"

"*Please*," Teeny said with emphasis on the word.

Aiden chuckled as Russell rolled his eyes in impatience. Teeny followed Aiden out of the room, and Russell set the storage box on the desk. He began looking at the items on Aiden's desk, but whether it was out of genuine curiosity or a desire to try to get dirt on Aiden, Cadence wasn't sure.

"So, this is all we do?" Will asked as he, too, began looking at things in the room. "Just hang around and watch the videos?"

"Right now, yes," Cadence said. "Snow and I already did the actual investigation part, so this is part two.

"And if they have something on video they shouldn't have?" Will looked at Cadence as he asked this, curious as to how they were supposed to be able to do anything about it.

"Given how this case played out, I would wager they do. I'm sure they have footage of Snow from when they had him trapped in that damned box, at the very least," Cadence said. "Aiden knows we can't have that out there in circulation, though. I have no doubt he will do what he can to keep us safe." She knew he would try, but Cadence really wasn't sure how Aiden would be able to persuade a TV exec to sit on footage that would make his ratings go sky-high.

Aiden and Teeny came back into the room. Aiden was carrying an extra dining room chair, and Teeny was carrying a cup of coffee. Soon enough, they were all settled around the desk and Russell handed Aiden the box.

"These are the memory cards from all of the cameras you guys used in the prison," Russell said as he handed the box over to Aiden. "I tried to keep them as organized as I could, but you guys didn't leave a ton of notes to go by."

"We didn't exactly have time, Russell," Teeny admonished.

"When did you go there to get them?" Aiden hadn't had the chance to ask about that earlier. "I said I would help you with the equipment."

"I hired some movers," Russell said with a shake of his head. "I had to pay the superstitious idiots extra when I told them where the pick-up was."

"Did you go there yourself?" Teeny was surprised by this news.

"With the officer you guys hired as security," Russell said. "It gave me a chance to talk to him about what happened that night."

"And?" It was Aiden who asked, trying to prompt the conversation to see how things had gone between Andy and Russell.

"He took me in, showed me where he found Liam," Russell said, then paused. "I can see why people would get spooked there," he admitted. "But I have no idea what Liam was thinking, going off on his own into that gallows area."

"Why don't we watch his camera first?" Teeny said. She was anxious to be able to see what had happened to him at last. "I remember him putting a new battery and a new memory card in the camera before he went out there. We were still trying to get that one ghost we caught in the box to talk when we heard that noise coming from the gallows."

"I'm interested in seeing that, too," Russell said, flipping through the memory cards. "If that box you designed worked as well as you said, and it caught on film, then that is going to be one hell of an asset to the show." Russell found the card he wanted and handed it to Aiden, who proceeded to put it in the memory card reader he had hooked up to his computer. In a couple of mouse clicks, the wallpaper of his desktop was replaced by a video window and the footage from Liam's handheld camera.

Liam was walking through the hall of the prison that led out to the backyard area where the gallows building was. To his left and right were doors that had once been marked, but time's erosion had taken the identifications away. His footsteps echoed on the concrete floor in the audio, and until he spoke, that was all they heard.

"Okay," Liam said, "while we were back in the center atrium, we all heard this really weird noise. Of course, it happened while I was changing out the batteries and memory card on this thing, so I'm hoping the equipment the others have on picked it up. Teeny doesn't want to be left alone after what happened in the solitary cell, which is understandable. I left Aiden with her, so I'm going out on my own to investigate the noise. In the horror films, this is where everything goes to hell, right?" Liam could be heard chuckling. "Good thing this isn't a movie."

Liam stopped in front of the doors for a moment, pushing against them to get them to open. With a creak, they budged at last, and the cold air from outside hit him in the face. "The good thing about doing nighttime investigations when it's cold like this," Liam said, leaving the main prison building behind him now, "is that stepping outside in the middle of the night is just the slap in the face you need to wake up and keep going."

The crunching of Liam's feet on the half-frozen, half-dead grass stopped short as a noise could be heard on the tape. It was a strange noise, like someone was bellowing, screaming, and crying all at once, but it was far enough away that the camera only picked up a quarter of the volume.

After a quick and nervous comment to the camera, he began walking, although this time, he was picking up the pace. He got to the door and found it chained. The camera jostled as he tucked it under his arm and fished out the keys. It took a few tries, the frame of the camera jiggling as he moved. Finally, he got the right key because you could hear the padlock move and then the chains moving as Liam pulled them out of the door handles and tossed them on the ground.

For as creaky as every door in the prison had been, the doors to the gallows building opened with no issue and no sound. There was no squeaking of rusty hinges, no scraping of the metal door on the concrete floor, just a slight whoosh of air as Liam opened a building that hadn't been opened in a few decades.

The camera, which Liam had well in hand now, panned from right to left and back again. Right in front of him was a plain wall, though the paint had aged more in some areas than others, giving the indication that there had been plaques or pictures on the wall that had been removed before the prison was decommissioned. To the right was a staircase that went up to a door, and to the left was a double doorway. Liam turned to the left and made his way through the double doors. He followed a small corridor around and it let out into the viewing room, where people, usually family and authorities, would sit to view the death of the criminal. Liam proceeded to say as much to the camera.

Liam let the camera linger on the dark, imposing carcass of the gallows in the next room, separated only by glass from him. He then turned back the way he came and went to the stairs, narrating as he went for dramatic effect. His narration ceased as he opened the door and stepped onto the gallows platform, moving the camera in a slow sweep from left to right.

Teeny leaned in closer to the computer monitor. Aiden knew off the bat what she was studying; he had seen it, too.

"Are the shadows in that corner moving?" she asked.

"What corner?" Russell asked, looking up from his phone's text messages to look at the screen.

"There," Teeny said, pointing to the screen which Aiden had paused for her.

"It could be," Aiden said, treading carefully. "But it also could be artifacts or digitalization. It's hard to tell."

Aiden hit play on the video once more, and they watched as Liam explored the gallows area. Liam began speaking again, talking about how oppressive the atmosphere in the gallows room was. He was silenced as a deafening scream rose in the room. Even though this was recorded, you couldn't miss the tones of agony and fury in that sound, which seemed as if it was made up of many different voices. Aiden and Teeny both paled, and even Russell looked up from his phone.

"What the hell?" Russell looked amazed.

"That was something," Aiden murmured.

"He should have left right then," Teeny said, annoyed. "He knew better. He should have come and gotten me."

On the screen, the camera was shaking a little as Liam's hands trembled. He made his way to the edge of the gallows, panning down. "Hell of a first step," he muttered. As the camera traveled back up the glass window, looking out over the viewing room, a brief arc of blue light, almost like a tiny lightning bolt, flashed in the glass, and it shattered.

"Wait! Back up," Teeny said.

Aiden backed the video up. He had seen the same thing, but he had been hoping they would miss it. In the glass, as the electric-like light appeared, there was a faint reflection that could be seen. The face of a man with a long, bushy mustache was there in profile, as if he was turned to the side and talking with someone else.

"Who is that?" Teeny asked, leaning in closer to the computer monitor to try to see better.

"It could simply be shadows, or a reflection of something else in the glass from underneath the gallows. We didn't get the greatest of looks at what was underneath there," Aiden said, trying to think of ways to debunk the footage. He rubbed gently at the bruise on his chest without thinking.

Russell looked up from his phone to the video screen and frowned. "A shadow? You must be kidding. That is clearly a person."

"Skeptics will pick that apart as being something else," Aiden said.

"Skeptics don't watch our show. They figure it's all bullshit anyway," Russell said with a dismissive shrug. "Our audience believes in ghosts, or at least is open to the idea of them."

"Just saying," Aiden said with a shrug. "I know Teeny wants to be as scientific as possible. It could be pareidolia. When your brain makes something like a face or logical image out of random shapes and glares. Like seeing things in clouds."

Russell's cell phone rang, and he left the office to go to the living room to take the call. Aiden looked over at Teeny with one eyebrow raised. Teeny just shrugged and shook her head.

"I do want to be scientific," Teeny said. "And in the beginning, we had a producer who was behind that. When Kath, our old producer, left, we got Russell. He does far more to promote Liam's party-boy mentality than I like. And loves to downplay the science. As long as it gets ratings, he is happy. So no, he doesn't care how well people can debunk things."

"It has to be a pain, working with someone like that," Aiden said.

"Yeah, it is. This is my last year on my contract, though, so I can leave the show if I want to," Teeny said.

"But will you?" Aiden was curious if the change of tone in the show would sway her away from the celebrity and money.

"I'm not sure," she said with a sigh. "Part of me likes the money, I'll be honest. But I hate the bullshit that Russell and Liam try to pull."

Aiden nodded, filing that away. Maybe she could be reasoned with, although he was really hoping they wouldn't find anything too awful in these videos. The flash of a face could be explained away since it was faint—the crashing glass was odd but not incontrovertible evidence of the afterlife, just evidence that maybe the glass had finally run its course.

"Let's keep going," Teeny said after a minute. "He was bored to tears anyway, and his phone calls can go on for a while."

"Yes, Ma'am," Aiden said. He was glad to be going on without Russell, though he was pretty sure Cadence would be having an invisible conniption fit behind him.

The glass falling onto the concrete was almost musical, but it was also thunderous in the close confines and stillness of the room. It was joined by the sound of Liam shrieking in surprise and fear.

Liam's lens zoomed in on where the glass had fallen as he stepped closer to the ledge of the gallows. "What the hell was that?" Liam asked in a hushed voice. "This is insane." He panned down, showing millions of pieces of shattered glass covering the floor beneath him. The glass had to have been twenty feet high and twenty feet wide, so the bits and pieces of broken glass were innumerable.

"Okay, no bullshit, this place is freaking me out," Liam confessed. Liam's hands were full-on shaking now, and it showed in the video. The disembodied noise was not screaming, but it was audible again after the crashing of the glass. Liam began to back up, away from the edge of the gallows. His camera focused on where the glass had been in case something else happened. "I think I caught a light anomaly down there right before the window exploded, maybe an orb or two. We'll have to go back through the footage to be sure." Liam took a deep breath and blew it out to try to calm himself. "This place is insane!"

Liam was still slowly backing up. There was a loud voice suddenly, this one clear and quite recognizable to Aiden.

"No!" Cadence could be heard on the tape. A split-second later, Liam screamed as he fell through the trapdoor of the gallows. The camera that he had been holding crashed to the ground and broke.

"Shit," Cadence said as she stood behind Aiden.

"This is bad, isn't it?" Will asked.

Cadence nodded her head. "And we haven't even seen the footage of the Faraday cage that Pruitt threw Snow into. This is catastrophic if it gets out."

"Who was that?" Teeny asked the question to Aiden as the playback stopped itself due to the end of the recording. "It sounded like a woman yelled 'no.' It didn't sound like Lauren, and she wasn't with us, anyway. We both know it wasn't me. So, who was that?"

They could hear Russell on his phone in the hallway, and from the tone of his loud voice, he was annoyed about something.

Aiden made a snap decision and turned to face Teeny, taking her hand in his. "This isn't going to make any sense to you, but please don't tell Russell what we just saw on the tape. Tell him the glass breaking was the last of it until the trapdoor fell and so did Liam."

"Aiden—" Teeny started, pulling her hand out of his and shaking her head, but Aiden cut off whatever she was going to say next.

"I'm serious. This is serious," he said. He glanced at the doorway as it began to sound like Russell was finishing up his conversation.

"Why?" Teeny asked, disliking the position Aiden was putting her in.

"Because it's important," Aiden implored, another frantic glance given to the doorway. "You have no reason to trust me. I am aware of this. I promise I'll explain what I can. But please, Russell can't know." Aiden stressed those last three words as much as he could.

Teeny frowned, her brow furrowing as she considered the matter.

"Please," Cadence whispered. "Just agree with him."

"And if she doesn't?" Will was watching the two breathers as he asked the question, tension lying thick in the room.

"Then I have a feeling we are screwed," Cadence replied.

"I find myself not loving your cheery outlook," Will said.

Russell hung up the phone as he came back into the room. "Sorry about that. Did you see what happened?"

"It's what I thought," Teeny said, her eyes never leaving Aiden's. "He backed up onto the trapdoor, and it gave way."

"Damn," Russell said, "I was hoping after that light and the face in the glass that we might have had more. Mr. Perkins, I'm afraid I am going to have to take you up on your offer of going over the footage. With news of the show's hiatus, some of our people have jumped ship for other work."

"Sorry to hear that," Aiden said as he was inwardly doing jumps of joy at the news. "Don't worry. Your footage is in good hands, I promise."

"Yeah, yeah," Russell said, waving Aiden's assurances aside. "Can you give Teeny a lift back to the hospital? I have to catch a flight back to LA."

"Right now?" Teeny was surprised and didn't keep it from her voice. "With Liam still in the hospital?"

"Look, babe, I can't stay here and hold your hand while your show falls apart," Russell said. "I need to save your jobs. Liam would want me to go back and save the show."

"Fine," Teeny said, though it was apparent even to Aiden that it was anything but fine.

Russell was oblivious to this as he smiled and nodded. "Great. Text me, keep me up to date on Liam and any good footage you got."

"Sure," came the monosyllabic response from Teeny.

"Oooo," Will said, shaking his head. "She's pissed. Fine and sure were two of the words you never wanted to hear my mom use. They meant someone's ass was grass, and my mom was in charge of the lawn mower."

"You aren't wrong," Cadence said.

Russell left and they heard him let himself out, the front door slamming behind him in the quiet apartment.

Teeny brought her sharp gaze back to Aiden. "Now, please tell me why I did that."

CHAPTER 16

Daytime at Scarecrow Farms

The van, driven by Aiden, pulled onto the overgrown grass to the side of the house. The phantoms of wheel ruts were still visible, no matter how hard the grass on either side tried to obscure them. Lauren, Derrick, and Teeny bounced in the van with Aiden as he ran over a dip in the ground.

The house itself was obvious in its abandonment. The white paint had yellowed in the sun and weathered to the point that it was falling off in flakes from the wood. The concrete that made the foundation of the house had been covered with spray paint tags. The steps to the front porch were gone—not just broken or dangerous, but flat out not there anymore. As they went behind the house, they could see part of the roof on the second floor had opened up in a jagged hole, and parts of the roof had collapsed, no doubt due to water damage or heavy snows. The steps to the back porch remained, but their safety was in question. Whatever railing had been on the porch was gone. One lone beam of it was left, attached to the pole holding the roof up over the porch, while the other end had fallen through the rotting wood that made up the floor of the porch.

The house was on their left as they parked in the grass at the back. To their right and in front of them, the rest of the property stretched out. A line of trees was directly in front of them, about 50 yards away, and divided the home and its private field from the fields used for produce grown for sale. About 30 yards from the back porch of the house, almost by the row of trees, stood the tool shed. Once upon a time, there had been a barn off to their right somewhere. One lonely scarecrow, old and bereft of most of its straw, was hung on a pole in that field.

"Well, this is a cheery place," Teeny said, trying to break the silence that had hung heavily over them all as soon as they drove onto the property.

"No kidding," Lauren said in a soft murmur, grateful to know that she wasn't here alone. As much as she had been iffy about the idea of Sam tagging along in her life, she was finding that, often, she was happy to know he was there, protecting her from spirits that might not want to respect boundaries.

Aiden and Derrick went to the back of the van and got out their hand-held camcorders. Aiden went into another bag and tossed Lauren an audio recorder, then handed Teeny a still camera.

"We have plenty of daylight to explore this place. Let's take our time and see what we can find," Aiden instructed. "Also, be careful. This place probably needs to be condemned."

"Also, if I may," Teeny said, "don't go off alone."

"Yeah," Derrick said. "We just need to get an idea of what we might be up against here when it gets dark."

"Let's get to it then," Lauren said. "Start with the house?"

"Might as well," Aiden said with a nod. He made sure that he had a pocket full of fresh batteries as he and Derrick opened the camcorders and began recording.

"I wasn't sure you were going to make it," Sam said as Cadence and her new partner materialized in front of him.

"I'm Will. You must be Sam." Will extended his hand to Sam, not waiting for Cadence to introduce them.

"Nice to meet you, Will," Sam said with a nod.

"Seen anything here yet?" Cade asked. "Sorry we're late."

"No, nothing," Sam said with a shrug. "We're just getting here, too."

The ghosts followed along behind the breathers as they made their way through the tall grass to the steps of the back porch. The steps up to the porch landing were almost all intact, though it was obvious that it was only a matter of time before rot caught up with them. As it was, the third step up was broken in the center, the two sides landing at angles on the second step.

"Be careful," Aiden said as he stepped up, his long legs making easy work of the space with the missing step. He turned and reached out his hand, helping Lauren and

Teeny up. Derrick waved Aiden's hand away, determined to do it himself.

The wood of the porch was curling up in some areas and felt spongy beneath their feet as they made their way to the back door. Aiden pulled the keys out of his pocket and unlocked the back door. Swinging the door in, they stepped inside and found themselves in the kitchen. The walls had once been blue, but time had taken its toll in here as well. The curtains, which had once been blue and white gingham, had faded to the point that you could barely see the squares. There was a stove, turned over on its side, on the left side of the kitchen between two doors. Otherwise, the room was empty. There was no refrigerator, no sink, not even any cabinets.

"Talk about sparsely furnished," Derrick said, trying to make light of it. A somber atmosphere had settled around the group as they disturbed the silence of the house, and it was unsettling Derrick's nerves.

"No kidding," Teeny said, her own voice hushed.

"This place is too silent," Cadence said.

"What do you mean?" Will asked as the breathers began to make their way to the farther of the two doors that led into the house.

"Do you hear any birds?" Cadence looked around the room as they followed the living, trying to stay out of the way of Teeny and her still camera.

"Gotcha," Will said after a moment of listening, which was his way of acknowledging that there were no bird sounds.

With Aiden leading the way, the group investigated a small alcove that also served as a short hall. The floor in the center of the small room had caved in under the worn and faded orange carpet. To the left was a bathroom. To the right was a small sitting area large enough for an armchair and bookcase, not that there was anything there. They were able to skirt around or jump over the foot-wide spot of non-existent floor.

As Lauren started edging around the hole in the floor, bringing up the rear of the group, she looked up and her eyes widened. The bathroom had been a dirty, dusty, dimly lit gray a moment ago. But now she saw the bathroom as it had been. A cheery white and yellow with a couple of rubber ducks sitting on the edge of the tub.

The cheery scene was shattered with a noise that startled Lauren, a loud boom, and the bright yellow and white was now blood-spattered. The flowers on the wallpaper were obscured by the viscous liquid running down the walls. A pool of blood was quickly forming under the door of the bathroom and edging its way out from under the door. The rubber duckies dripped blood from their bills like vampires after a messy meal.

Sam jumped in front of Lauren, waving his hands to catch her attention. Hands caught at Lauren's arms, and she screamed as a shadow exited the bathroom behind Sam.

"Lauren!" It was Aiden's voice and hands catching at her. She was wobbling on the edge of the hole in the floor and would have fallen if not for Aiden pulling her backward.

Sam touched Lauren's arm. "It was a memory from the house," he said to her. "Nothing more. You're safe."

Lauren tried to relax as she heard Sam, but the vision of the bathroom, of what had happened, was disturbing. She knew she was trembling and didn't care for the moment. Derrick and Aiden helped her across, and they went into the living room. There was a fireplace in there, missing half of its stones, and the front door, which was still intact.

The three spirits followed the breathers into the living room. They could see the bathroom as it used to be as well, and none of them particularly wanted to be around it either. It may have been a simple traumatic memory that the house had, but that didn't make it any less unsettling.

"Is that going to happen a lot?" Will asked.

"I don't know," Cadence said. "From what they said about what happened here, it might. There have been enough traumatic things that have occurred here to probably make Stephen King shudder if he saw them all."

"Houses remember," Sam said. "Especially with things like murder."

"What happened?" Teeny asked.

"Are you okay?" Aiden was concerned as he looked at Lauren's pale face and held her still trembling hand.

"I'll be fine," Lauren said. "That was just a little sudden."

"What happened?" Teeny repeated. "It looked like you saw something before you lost your balance."

Lauren took a deep breath and then recounted to them exactly what she had seen. "I know it's a shadow, a memory, but it was still vivid as hell," she said.

"Here's hoping you don't see anything else like that," Derrick said.

Lauren nodded, agreeing with her young friend, but she had her doubts.

Teeny had stepped back over to the alcove and was taking still pictures of the alcove, the short hall, and the bathroom doorway. Will followed her to watch what she was doing. This was still so new to him that he was fascinated by it all.

Cadence walked over to Will, leaving Sam standing guard by Lauren. "How are you holding up so far?"

"This is a little intense, I have to admit," Will said. "Is it always like this?"

"Not *always*," Cadence said, stressing the last word. "But it does have a habit of being like this more often than not."

"How do we keep evidence from them when crazy stuff like this happens?" Will was beginning to feel more out of his depth than he had expected to.

Cadence chuckled. "I used to ask Snow that all the time. There's a distinction. We need to make sure no absolute concrete evidence of the afterlife gets into breather hands. Orbs, shadows, voice fragments, those are all fine."

"Good to know," Will said with a nod.

"Are you okay to go on?" Aiden voiced the question, though they had all been giving Lauren a few minutes to recover from what she had seen.

"Think so," Lauren responded with a thin smile.

They crossed the living room, noting where the floor was weak but hadn't caved yet, so they could be careful later. They passed the solid wood front door and opened a set of double doors perpendicular to the front door.

The room housed yet another fireplace. Stones were also missing from this one, but it looked like they had all been tossed in the middle of the grate. An old, stained twin mattress was on the floor in one corner of the room, along with several empty beer bottles and cans. A doll in a blue dress with red trim, dirty and faded, was abandoned in another corner of the room, its blonde hair greyed by dirt and dust, beyond the hope of any brush or comb. Other debris and trash littered the floor as well. One wall had a faded mural of a prince and princess having a tea party with stuffed animals under a tree in a garden. More recently, spray paint had been employed to add to the mural, making the children's eyes black, red blood on their clothes, and giving the stuffed animals fangs.

"Because this place wasn't creepy enough," Derrick said. "I'm beginning to think we need to just go back and tell the professor to sell this dump."

"No kidding," Teeny said as she snapped pictures. "This isn't a cool haunted house. This place is a horror show."

"Sam," Cadence said, getting her brother's attention as he hovered beside Lauren. "Are you getting anything from this place?"

Sam nodded, moving over to talk to Cade and Will. "Yeah, this place is bad. We haven't seen what's here yet, but there is something evil in this house. Evil and old."

As Sam moved away from his charge, Lauren saw something else. The shadow she had seen from the bathroom came into this room. It hefted up something that could only have been a gun, aiming toward the fireplace. Looking over, Lauren could see the translucent images of children, a boy and a girl. Shrill screams of terror echoed in Lauren's ear as she watched the children leap out of the window, running toward the back of the property.

Aiden saw Lauren stiffen and went over to her, putting a hand on her shoulder. "Are you going to be okay here?" His worry for his friend carried in his voice.

"Yeah." Lauren nodded, her breath coming a little faster than normal and her heartbeat racing. "Yeah, this place is just very strong. I'm getting a bird's eye view of some of the things that happened here."

Sam made his way back over and touched Lauren's arm. "Don't go upstairs," Sam said. "There's something strong up there, and I don't know how it will react to you."

"All of us or just me?" Lauren's voice was barely a whisper.

"What?" Teeny had heard Lauren whisper, but not what she had said.

"Oh, nothing," Lauren said. "I mumble to myself sometimes." She didn't feel like going into the explanation of Sam.

"You," Sam said to Lauren. "Whatever it is, I can feel it down here. It's strong, and given your gift, I'm not sure how it will react to you. The others should be fine."

Aiden still had his hand on Lauren's shoulder, and he guided her out of the room as the others followed. There was a small hallway that had a door along the wall. The paint on the long wood paneling was cracked and peeling. Just beyond the door was a stairway leading up to the second floor. Beyond the stairway was an open archway back into the kitchen.

"I wonder if these are still safe," Derrick said as they approached the steps.

Teeny had stopped at the door and was toying with the knob.

"Locked?" Aiden asked as he watched her move the knob back and forth but not open the door.

"No." Teeny dropped her hand from the brass handle, giving them a nervous smile. "I was just wondering if it was better to find out what's behind the door or just leave it alone."

Aiden chuckled a little, trying to lighten the mood of the group, which was tense, to say the least. "We are explorers at the heart of all this, right?" He put on a fearless façade and took hold of the doorknob as Teeny stepped back. For her part, Teeny looked as if she didn't believe a word he was saying. Aiden cleared his throat, and with his heart pounding so hard he was sure they could all hear it, he pulled the door open.

The door protested, hinges caked in rust screaming at the forced movement. Beyond the door was darkness. As their flashlights spilled in through the now open doorway, a stairway going down was revealed. The stairway was plain wood with no attempt at any kind of adornment. It was impossible to tell if the floor below was dirt or if it was just bathed in dust. Several boxes could be seen at the base of the stairs, but nothing was visible in the cloak of blackness beyond since their flashlights were unable to penetrate that far.

"If you want to split, I'll volunteer to go down there," Lauren said. When they all looked at her like she was a lunatic, she added, "I'm not going upstairs. It's dangerous for me up there. The basement will be just fine."

"Why is upstairs dangerous?" Teeny asked.

"You know how I said this house is strong?" Lauren cast a nervous glance at the stairs going up as she spoke.

"Yeah," Teeny said with a nod.

"Well, there is something upstairs. I can feel it from here. It's that strong," Lauren said as she looked between the three of them, feeling Sam at her back. "Whatever it is, it's not going to react well to me. Now I will admit that it is possible the strength of what is upstairs is masking anything coming from below. But I am not sensing anything from down there."

"If upstairs is that bad, maybe we should just skip it entirely," Teeny said.

"We promised the professor that we would check this entire place out," Derrick said. "Maybe we should split up. Two go upstairs, two downstairs."

"Derrick is right," Aiden said to Teeny. "We agreed to check the whole estate out. That includes the creepy upstairs. It's okay to be nervous about this. Especially after what happened at Barrington. No one is going anywhere alone; it will be okay."

Teeny looked down at her shoes for a moment and took a deep breath, the smell of must and dust invading her nose as she did. "Fine," she sighed. "You're right. So how do you want to break it up?"

"Why don't you and I go upstairs?" Aiden suggested. "Lauren, Derrick, you guys can take the basement. We meet back here. Sound good?" Everyone nodded and he nodded in response. "Okay then. Let's get going."

CHAPTER 17

Upstairs, Downstairs

Derrick went first, leading Lauren down the stairs. Sam preceded them, having teleported to the bottom of the stairs. The beams from the flashlights were relentless as they pushed back the dark gloom of the basement, revealing a large room packed to the brim with an assortment of items. The duo joined Sam at the bottom of the stairs, their lights playing this way and that around the room. There were boxes, crates, suitcases, and random items, both large and small. There were walkways extending out from the central landing, but otherwise, all room was taken up storing these remnants.

"Well, the professor could definitely have the garage sale of the century with all of this stuff," Derrick said as he moved his light and the camcorder he was holding around to take in and record the view of all of it.

"No kidding," Lauren said. She moved halfway down one narrow aisle drawn by a stack of old records, their covers faded with age and dust.

"Hey, don't wander off," Derrick said as he scurried down the aisle after her. He was careful not to knock over anything as he moved. "It would be all too easy to lose you in this maze of crap."

Something bounced off Derrick's right shoulder, having come from behind him, and hit the stack of records. The records slid sideways, some toppled over into the next aisle and landed on the floor there with a series of light thuds.

Derrick let out a startled "Hey!" and both he and Lauren jumped. Their flashlights followed the item that had hit Derrick as it landed on a suitcase. The wooden car that had been tossed was still now.

"Did you knock that over or off of something?" Lauren felt Sam leave her side as she asked Derrick the question. She knew her spirit guardian was searching the room for other spirits.

"I don't think so," Derrick said. His hands were shaking a little. "I was careful to not hit anything as I came over here."

"Maybe the ghosts just don't like you calling their stuff crap." Lauren chuckled, trying to make light of the situation.

Sam moved through the stacks and piles of old, unused things easily. A benefit of being a ghost that his sister still hadn't gotten used to, moving through objects. He had seen the car come at Derrick; he knew it had been thrown. It didn't take long for him to catch the toy-tosser.

"Hey, kiddo," Sam said to the little boy, who looked like he had been about eight when he had died. Brown hair crowned his head, and big brown eyes kept a baleful watch on the movements of the older ghost. "It's okay," Sam said. "I'm not going to hurt you. I just wanted to know why you threw your toy."

"It's not crap," the boy said, his tone defiant despite still watching Sam like he was a hare about to sprint off at a moment's notice.

Sam laughed and his smile seemed contagious as the boy smiled and seemed to relax. "I'm Sam. What's your name?"

"Ronnie," the boy said in answer. "Why are you here? Why are they here?"

"I'm here because I'm with them. I watch over the lady and try to keep her safe. They are checking this place out for the guy who owns it," Sam said.

Ronnie looked up at the ceiling with a frightened frown.

"Hey, are you okay, Ronnie?" Sam wasn't sure what had spooked the kid, but it was plain that something had.

"S-sure," Ronnie managed to say, looking back at Sam. "He's just angry. He never comes down here, though."

"Who?" Sam stepped closer to Ronnie as he asked the question and was pleased that the boy didn't run from him.

"He's always been here," Ronnie said with a shrug as if that explained everything. "Dunno his name, or if he's really a him. He's the one that made Daddy scary. I know that."

Sam nodded. He had figured Ronnie was one of the siblings killed by their dad years ago, he just hadn't wanted to ask. "I'm going to guess," Sam said at length, "that you're smart enough to stay away from him, right?"

Ronnie nodded, a very determined look on his young face.

"Good," Sam said as he reached out and ruffled the kid's hair, which elicited a smile from Ronnie. "Where's your sister?"

"She's in the shed," Ronnie said. "She doesn't come to the house anymore, so she stays in the shed or just out in the woods or fields."

"But you come here to play with your toys," Sam said.

Ronnie nodded.

"Besides you and your sister and him," Sam said as he pointed a finger upstairs, "are there any other spirits here?"

"It changes," Ronnie said with a shrug. "There's us and the old man from a long time ago. There's a lady who screams about a fire, but she never seems to do anything else. It's like she's a movie or something. She never talks to us. Old man Ed says to ignore her. Others come and go sometimes, but don't stay. Then there's the circle. We keep away from there. But I've seen spirits down there. Different ones always, but always men. And then there's a thing down here, but it don't come out much. It sleeps a lot. Which is good, cause that one's scary, too. But not as scary as the one upstairs. Old man Ed says to keep away when it's awake."

Sam's brow furrowed as he tried to puzzle that one out, then shook his head. "And is Ed the old man from a long time ago?"

Ronnie nodded. "He's nice. He looks out for me and Renee as much as he can."

"Renee is your sister?"

"Yep," Ronnie said with a smile.

A crash caught the attention of both Ronnie and Sam. The crash was quickly followed by the sound of Derrick cursing. Sam darted in the direction of the sound and Ronnie disappeared. Moving through stacks of boxes, Sam found Derrick on the floor with several boxes on him. Lauren was beside him, trying to help dig him out of the stuff that had spilled out of unsecured time-worn boxes.

Women's clothes and shoes were strewn all over Derrick, even as he scrambled to his feet. Lauren pulled a crinoline skirt liner off his arm then, laughed as she noticed that the spaghetti strap of a negligee had hooked itself around his neck. Derrick dropped the high heel in his hand and pulled the strap over his head, tossing the satin and lace garment to the dusty ground.

"It's not funny," Derrick said.

Lauren grabbed the camera from him before he could react and pointed it at him. "The intrepid paranormal investigator, felled by lady's lingerie." Lauren laughed again, moving the camera down to record the pile of clothing at Derrick's feet.

"Yeah, yeah, yuk it up," Derrick said with a frown.

"For the record, I saw that," Lauren said. "You didn't walk into anything. That all just randomly fell over on you."

"I feel so special," Derrick said, rolling his eyes.

"Come on," Lauren said, trying to rein in her laughter. "You go first. I'll record."

The wooden steps groaned beneath Aiden and Teeny's feet as they ascended to the second story of the house. Aiden was first with Teeny behind him. They could hear the steps of Derrick and Lauren as they descended into the basement. As they neared the landing, they both felt the change in the air.

"It's not as musty up here," Teeny said.

"No, it's not," Aiden said, agreeing with her. "Watch that step second from the top. I don't like the give it had." He reached out and offered a hand to help steady her as she took the last two steps carefully. She made a face on the step he had indicated.

"It feels spongey," she said.

"Yeah, well, given all of this, I can only assume it's water damage," Aiden said.

Cadence and Will were with the two breathers on the second floor and were likewise in amazement at the state of it. The second story was all one room. There was evidence of a bathroom at the far end, but the fixtures were gone, as were the better part of the walls that had once enclosed it. The roof had an enormous hole in it, as if a bomb had been set off beneath it. Some stray boards and shingles had fallen beneath the hole due to time and weather weakening their bond to the structure. Dead leaves and dead birds were scattered on the floor like discarded candy wrappers left by kids during trick-or-treating on Halloween.

"Jesus," Teeny said, her voice quiet. "It's like a room of the dead."

Teeny didn't know how right she was since she couldn't see what was in the far corner of the room. Cadence and Will could see it, however, and neither of them liked it.

The creature was bulbous and huge as it hunkered under the roof at the far end of the room. Its skin looked like a mixture of tar and an oil slick. It was froglike in look, though it had two extra sets of arms and three extra eyes. The extra arms had three thick finger-like tips with curved claws that had to be at least five inches long. Its eyes were yellow and cat-like, all of them blinking at different intervals. Three of those eyes turned to regard Will and Cadence while the other two kept watch on the breathers near the stairs. It was obvious that this thing had never been human.

"Who?" the deep, thunderous voice of the creature boomed in both Cadence's and Will's heads. They both clapped their hands over their ears as they staggered underneath the weight of the sound.

The two ghosts exchanged a look between themselves and then Cadence took one step, albeit small, toward the creature. "I'm Detective Cadence Riley. We're here to monitor the breathers while they are here investigating. Who are you?"

"Here. Mine," the creature said and puffed himself up to be even more enormous than he had been. "Go."

"Not the best communicator, is he?" Will asked, a grimace on his face as his hands were still clapped over his ears. He knew it had nothing to do with physical volume, but the creature's voice was so loud in his head that it felt like his skull was vibrating.

"The opposite," Cadence said. "He gets his message across in the fewest possible words." She turned her attention back to the creature. "Your name?"

The creature bristled at the fact that Cadence hadn't been cowed by his size. "X'Haldzos."

Aiden had moved farther into the room and was midway between the creature and the stairs with Teeny right beside him. When he kicked a beam of wood out of his way, all five of the creature's eyes refocused on the two breathers and narrowed. It let out a belch of mustard-colored gas.

"GO," it said in Cadence's mind even louder than before.

As the gas disseminated into the air, the atmosphere changed. It became darker, despite the sun pouring in from the massive hole in the roof. It felt thicker, like trying to move through water. And a repulsive smell arose in the room, forcing Teeny and Aiden to cover their mouths and noses and gag.

"What is that? What did you kick?" It was Teeny who spoke, regretting the action as she could even taste the foulness of the air.

"Wood," Aiden said, turning and ushering Teeny toward the stairs. "Let's go. Be careful on those steps."

The creature at the end of the room settled himself back down, somehow managing to look pleased with himself despite his monstrous face.

"Will, follow them," Cadence said. "I'll be right behind you."

"If something happens to you, you do know that Snow, Sam, and Ramon will have my head, right?" Will knew he was only half joking as he said this.

"I'll be fine," Cadence said, reassuring her young partner.

Will frowned, then handed her what looked like a ping-pong ball. "If Mr. Toad tries to get handsy with you, just hit him with this," Will said.

Cadence took the ball without question and nodded. Will then followed the breathers down to the first floor. Cadence turned back to face the creature.

"X'Haldzos, are you the one making innocent people turn into murderers?" Cadence had her arms crossed loosely in front of her chest and was doing her best to look casual and unimpressed.

The creature shifted, focusing all five of its yellow eyes on her. "So? Land mine. Food. Toy. Play with. Eat. Better with more pain. Tasty," the creature said.

Cadence was sorry she had asked. Images flooded her mind, sent by the creature. She saw the farm over the years. The people that X'Haldzos had manipulated into doing something cruel, something evil. Then she saw him eating them, body and soul, and felt the pleasure he derived from their guilt and pain. She dropped to her knees in dry heaves, disgusted by the images and their accompanying feelings. The images left, and she got another feeling of self-satisfaction from the creature that he had brought her to her knees.

"Go," he said again, his voice deafening in her head.

Cadence teleported back to the first floor, bristling with anger that she had backed down despite knowing that right now, it was the best choice.

Aiden and Teeny were standing by the door to the basement and Will was with them. Will looked over as Cadence appeared at the foot of the stairs heading up.

"You look like hell," Will observed, moving over to her. "Are you okay?"

"Fine," Cadence said with a nod. "Just got subjected to some bad home movies." She looked around and noticed Lauren, Derrick, and Sam weren't there. "Are they still downstairs?"

"Yeah." Will nodded. "Aiden called down to them. They said they were fine and would be up in a minute. So, you think that thing is the cause of all the bad here?"

"Oh, hell yes," Cadence said with an emphatic nod. "It's tied with the land somehow, and it has been here for a very long time."

It was then that Lauren, Derrick, and Sam reappeared, climbing out of the dark depths of the basement. Derrick looked disgruntled and Sam looked amused, so Cadence knew something had happened. When Sam saw his sister, his amusement vanished, and he teleported over to her and Will.

"What happened?" Sam asked, but couldn't help himself and added, "You look like you saw a ghost."

"You had to go for the pun, didn't you?" Cadence said with a sigh.

Will laughed, and he and Sam shared a high-five.

"I wouldn't be me if I didn't," Sam said, bowing with a flourish. "But really, what spooked you?"

"That power you felt upstairs is a non-human," Cadence said. "A humungous, weird, bad-smelling non-human."

"According to Cadence, it's been here forever," Will said, piping up.

"What about you?" Cadence switched the subject. "What did you guys find in the basement?"

"Stuff. Lots and lots of old stuff," Sam said. "I'm guessing it's all from old owners and tenants of this place. Oh, and I did meet the ghost of the little boy that was killed by his dad in the 70s. He had some interesting information."

The breathers were beginning to move back to the door in the kitchen.

"You would think a room with a hole in the roof wouldn't stink," Derrick said.

"It didn't, at first," Teeny said.

"Sounds like you guys got a bit of activity in the basement," Aiden said to Lauren. "Did you have any visions down there like you were having up here?"

"No, none," Lauren said, shaking her head.

The group moved outside into the sunlight, and the breathers were careful to avoid the parts of the back porch where the wood had rotted through.

"Okay," Derrick said. "If we go that way," he pointed straight ahead, past where they had parked, "it's the area of the old barn that burned down. If we go that way," he said as he pointed to the left, "we get the tool shed, farmland, and then beyond that line of trees, even more farmland."

"Why don't we head down to the shed and the farmland?" It was Aiden who suggested it. "Then we can hit the barn area on the way back to the cars."

"Makes sense," Lauren said with a nod of agreement.

The group began walking and the grass got taller as they went. By the time they had gone twenty feet, the grass was taller than Teeny and was brushing Lauren's shoulders.

"Over there," Aiden said, pointing to the left. "I see the toolshed."

"Man, next time we're out here, we need to bring a bunch of lawnmowers," Derrick said.

"No kidding," Teeny laughed.

The mood had altered noticeably since leaving the rotting confines of the house. They were now bathed in sunlight, walking through a wild, unkempt field. It was still cold, but even the cold was more acceptable than the atmosphere in the house. Lauren looked back at the house as they turned to follow Aiden to the toolshed. The hole in the roof was visible and something there made her shiver despite her coat.

Aiden was the first through the wild grass to the door of the toolshed. The entire structure was about 12 feet wide, with the door smack dab in the middle of the length. The whole thing was made of wood that looked so old and dry it would take little but a spark to set the whole thing aflame. There were no windows that Aiden could see, but he could easily see the large padlock on the door.

"You have the key," Lauren said as she stopped beside Aiden.

"What's up?" Teeny asked. "Oh, never mind," she said once she spotted the padlock.

Aiden fished the keys out of his pocket once more and selected the key the professor had said was the one for the shed. He slipped the key into the hole and turned it. The padlock failed to open, however.

What the breathers could not see was the spirit of Ronnie standing there, resolute, his hand on the padlock. He was holding it together as tightly as he could. He didn't want to let them into the shed, the hiding place of his sister and himself.

Sam came forward as the breathers started wondering aloud what was up with the lock. He knelt beside Ronnie. "They aren't here to hurt you." Sam spoke in a gentle voice to the boy. "They aren't here to hurt your sister. You can let them in."

"No. I don't want to," Ronnie said defiantly. "I'm protecting her. She'll get scared."

Sam turned to Cadence and gave a helpless shrug before turning back to Ronnie. "They are trying to help clear this place of the evil, bud."

"There's nothing bad here. Just us," Ronnie answered. "Leave our place alone." The boy would not release his grip on the lock.

Sam sighed and stood up, making his way back to Lauren.

"Maybe it's rusted through enough or the wood is rotted enough we can just force this baby open," Aiden said, giving up on the lock. He grabbed the latch and tried to push and pull the door with force.

"If it won't open, we can just come back with a couple of big wrenches and get it open that way," Teeny said.

"Should we be worried that you know that?" Derrick grinned at Teeny as he posed the question.

"What? I work with tools and build things," Teeny said. "It's not entirely out of my wheelhouse to know that."

"Uh-huh," Derrick said, still smiling.

"Well, we may have to try Teeny's wrench trick," Aiden said with a sigh, wiping his hands on his jeans. "This thing isn't budging."

"Maybe the termites are holding hands to keep the place together." Derrick shrugged. He then turned, leading the way back to where they had been walking before turning off toward the shed.

"At least with us walking the property now, we're making small paths through the grass," Teeny said. "We might have a hope of remembering where things are when we come back and do this at night."

"If we come back," Aiden said. "I'm not so sure it's worth it."

"What do you mean?" It was Derrick who asked as Aiden passed him to take up the front of the line again as they walked toward the tree line.

"This place isn't good for your teacher, bro," Aiden said. "The house is a structural nightmare. I don't even know if it is worth it to try to fix it. It probably would have to be torn down. Then you have the problem with the land itself, the history here, the blood that's been spilled."

"You think he should sell it?" Teeny asked.

"I think the structures should be torn down and the earth salted and blessed from property line to property line," Lauren said.

"Isn't that a bit extreme?" It was Derrick asking this time.

"No, I don't think so," Lauren said. "Let me put it this way. Barrington Prison was dark and dangerous, but it was that way because of the people. Criminals, their traumas in prison, and the death sentences carried out there. This place..." She paused, shaking her head. "It's evil. I don't say that lightly. I know how cartoon-y it sounds. But there is something here that is old, and it hates with a power I've not felt before."

"If it's that strong, though, how can you be here?" Teeny asked as she climbed over a tree limb as they began to venture into the tree line that separated the farm plots. "I mean, no offense, but you had a hard time spending even thirty minutes inside the prison."

"I can't explain it," Lauren said. "I can guess that the pain, trauma, and bad intentions of multiple humans affects me more than the hate and bad intentions of a single non-human creature."

"So, you do think that whatever is here is non-human?" Aiden stopped moving and turned to face Lauren as he asked.

"Oh, I'm absolutely sure of it," Lauren said, nodding.

"Are we in serious danger if we stay?" Aiden asked, being careful to choose his words so that Lauren would know what he was inferring while Teeny wouldn't.

"I can't answer that," Lauren said with a shrug. "I wish I could."

Derrick and Teeny had forged a little farther ahead while Aiden and Lauren had been talking.

"Uh, guys," Derrick said. "You're gonna want to see this."

Neither Aiden nor Lauren liked the tone in Derrick's voice. Both made their way through the dead leaves and underbrush to where Derrick stood at the edge of the tree line. It didn't take long for either of them to see what he was talking about.

In the field beyond the trees, the grass was dead and had been flattened down. Stones had been laid in a circle, with a large flat rock in the middle. The quartet of breathers and trio of ghosts made their way down to the circle. Lauren knelt beside a rock on the outside of the circle, looking at the base of it, running a hand through some weeds that had managed to grow around it.

"These have been here for a while," Lauren said.

Aiden had moved to the center of the circle. The flat-topped rock there was more of a slab than anything. It went as high as his mid-thigh. He reached out a hand to touch the top of the rock, but then thought better of it.

"Is that blood?" Derrick broke the silence. He was looking at the slab of rock that Aiden had just pulled his hand away from. His statement got the attention of the ladies, who were still on the outside of the circle.

"I hope not," Aiden said.

"Lauren, look at this," Teeny said.

Lauren tore her attention from the central stone and followed Teeny to one of the outer ones, leaving the circle. Sam followed along with her.

"Oh shit," Sam muttered. "Cade, get over here."

"What?" Cadence asked as both she and Will joined him. As her attention was taken to what Lauren and Teeny were examining, Sam knew he didn't have to answer.

On the outer face of the circle, this stone had a symbol carved in it. She took out her phone and placed her hand over it. Using a trick Snow had taught her, she put what she saw into the phone, a way of taking a picture with the tools they had at their disposal. Cadence began walking the perimeter of the circle, using her mind to store pictures of the scene on her phone. Every third stone had a different rune etched on it.

"They're on the base of the center one, too," Will said as he did the same thing Cade was doing except focusing on the middle stone.

Cade finished her perimeter of the circle and looked around as she realized this place seemed familiar somehow. "No damn way," she said under her breath.

"Cade?" Will had heard her say something. He just hadn't heard what.

Cade ignored Will for a moment and walked to the center of the circle. She hated walking through things. It felt like a ticklish itch beneath the skin that she couldn't scratch. She avoided doing it if she at all could. Her brother knew that, which was why Sam was so astonished to watch Cadence willingly and without complaint walk through the slab and stand in the middle of it.

Cadence looked up, imagining the sky dark and full of stars. She turned a little bit so that she could face the tree line more. She frowned deeply and walked back out of the stone.

"What was that about?" Will asked.

"Sis, what's up?" Sam moved so that he was between her and Lauren, that way, he wasn't entirely ignoring his charge.

"Nothing I'm sure of yet," Cadence said. "I would need to talk to Snow. He saw it with me."

"Saw what?" It was Will who asked.

"The portal at Barrington," Cadence said. "This might be where it goes."

CHAPTER 18

Recovery and Discovery

Cadence closed the door of her apartment behind her, and she began to pace the length of the living room. She frowned as she wondered if she should go back to her office but quickly dismissed that idea. People would find her and interrupt her there. Here it was quiet. Sam was with Lauren, and Ramon was at work, so she had the place to herself.

The cases since Lexington Hills had all been somehow connected, if at times by the slimmest of threads. Even the case at her brother's dorm had been connected, although they had only discovered that toward the end of the case. The old woman in the house case had led to the ghost child case that Sam had been working. And he had been working alone because Whitfield hadn't bothered to show.

They knew Whitfield was somehow involved in things that had been going on, though what exact involvement he had, she wasn't sure yet. They knew he wasn't who he said he was. Was he working for Shaldoxz? Did he have his own plans?

Now there was possible proof that this case was connected to the Barrington Prison case—if that stone circle was indeed where the portal in the rec room of the prison let out at. She knew that Pruitt had been sending spirits from the prison through the portal and into waiting bodies on the other side to possess. The dried blood on the central stone of the circle gave indications that such a ritual was not without its cost. Even if it wasn't where the portal came out, something was definitely going on with that circle.

Were these all just coincidences? Was she giving more importance to them than they deserved? Or was she right? She had a hunch that this was indeed all connected, but why? How? These were all seemingly random incidents that, on the surface, had nothing to do with each other. So why was she trying to link them up?

She gave the blue velvet couch cushion a punch as she walked by it for the fifteenth time, letting out a grunt of frustration. She was linking them because she knew in her gut that they were all connected, and it all came back to Shaldoxz. Raising the chaos entity in Lexington had been Wolf's idea. Wolf was a known disciple of Shaldoxz. They knew that thanks to Bolton-in-a-Caulfield-suit calling on him for help when he had Andy tied up. The case at the old woman's house seemed unrelated until you figured in the fact that the breather's success at getting rid of the ghost led the wife of the home's new owner telling her friend about it. Her friend was having issues with a ghost talking to and scaring the bejesus out of her daughter. When Sam was on that case, he had come face to face with Wolf. Sam had been alone because Whitfield hadn't been there and because the group had split, due to the timing of both that case and the prison investigation. And now here they were, investigating an old property that could have ties to the prison. Was Derrick's old professor, Paul, in on it, too?

Cadence grabbed a pillow from the couch and vehemently threw it toward the front door, where it landed at Ramon's feet. Ramon, who had just walked in, looked at the pillow, then at Cadence, and lifted an eyebrow.

"What did the pillow do to warrant police brutality?" Ramon tried to stay serious as he asked the question, but Cadence could see the smile tugging at the corners of his mouth.

Cadence sighed and shrugged. "Existed around me. I think I'm going crazy. Know any good asylums?" She smiled as she walked over and picked up the pillow.

"None I would want to go back to," Ramon said. He then leaned down and kissed her slowly, trying to ease her tension. After a moment, Cadence tossed the pillow blindly behind her and wrapped her arms around him, giving herself into his lips.

"Now that," Ramon said, "is a much better greeting than a thrown pillow." That caused Cade to laugh, and she shook her head. She walked over to the pillow, which had landed halfway between them and the couch, picked it up, and tossed it onto the couch.

"Yeah, sorry about that. Didn't know you were there," Cade said.

"I could tell," Ramon said with a chuckle. "What's got you so riled up?"

"Just trying to figure this whole damned thing out," Cadence said with a sigh as she ran her fingers through her honey-colored hair.

"Your current case?" Ramon said. "Or the whole thing in general?"

"The whole thing, in general," Cadence said as she sat on the back of the couch.

"Have you talked to Snow about it?" Ramon asked this as he went around the couch to sit on it properly. He then reached around and grabbed Cade by the waist, dragging her backward off the back of the couch and onto his lap.

"Hey!" she said at the unexpected movement, then laughed. "Okay, I give you credit," she said, still laughing. "That was a smooth move."

"I'm so glad you approve," he said with a smile. "I'm being serious, though. Have you talked to him about this?"

"We were working on trying to tie this all together when he got promoted," Cadence said, letting her head fall back on his arm. "Today's investigation might have gained us another piece of the puzzle. Or another puzzle entirely. That's part of what I'm trying to figure out."

"What about Will?" Ramon stroked her hair gently as he asked the question. "You've brought him up to speed on your cases, right?"

"He got the *Cliff's Notes* version," Cadence said.

"I think your best bet is to have a meeting then," Ramon said. "You, Snow, Will, maybe even Sam. Talk it all through. That's what you guys do, right?"

"Yeah," Cadence said with a soft sigh. "I just don't want to bother him. I know he has his hands full adjusting to his new job, and I'm not the only person he oversees."

"I'm pretty sure he would make time for you, Cade," Ramon said, tweaking her nose. "Other personnel or not, you were his partner."

"I guess," Cade said, not arguing the point.

"Call him tomorrow," Ramon said. "See if he can meet with you."

"I could call tonight," she said but stopped speaking as Ramon put a finger to his lips.

"I have tonight free, and it is rare that we get time together," Ramon said.

"The whole night, huh?" Cadence asked as she gave him a teasing, wicked grin. Her jade eyes sparkled with mischief. "Whatever shall we do?" Before he could even answer, she leaned up and kissed him.

Derrick, Aiden, and Lauren tromped back into Lauren's store after saying goodbye to Teeny at the hospital. They all went back to the round table in the back of the store and sat down heavily. Aiden fished both the green felt clover and the white felt snowflake out of his pocket and set them on the table before leaning back in his chair. They sat in silence for a few minutes before Derrick broke it.

"Why are we all acting like someone died?" Derrick leaned forward, putting his elbows on the table as he spoke, trying to muster energy.

"There was a lot of paranormal there," Lauren said, making no effort to try to perk up. "It tends to drain us. You know this."

"Yeah, I know *that*," Derrick stressed the last word. "But I don't think I have ever seen us come back from a place like this."

"Once," Aiden said. "We did once, and it was when we tried to help at the college dorm."

"Well, someone did die that time if you want to be technical," Lauren said.

"True," Aiden said with a nod. He rotated his head and neck a little, trying to work some of the tension out. "I think it might just be the events of the last week catching up with us. The prison, the family case, now this."

Sam listened and watched, staying close to Lauren. He could see black streaks in their auras, dense and dark, like cracks in cement. They had all suffered a psychic attack from the evil presence attached to the farm. Aiden more than the other two, as he had been upstairs with the creature. He would need to talk to Lauren later to let her know that they had to protect themselves better before they went back.

"We should get something to eat," Aiden said.

"Yeah, food might help," Derrick said.

"Dinner, and then a well-deserved night off," Lauren said as she nodded in agreement.

"Ah, crap," Derrick said as they all rose from their chairs.

"What?" Lauren's tone was sharper than she meant it to be, but after the farm, she felt drained and on edge. Sam put a hand on her arm to try to calm her.

"Nothing important," Derrick said, waving away her concern. "I just remembered I have a test tomorrow morning. No rest for the wicked that are still in college, I guess."

"Will you be talking to Paul?" Lauren grabbed her purse as she asked.

"If I can catch him after my test, sure," Derrick said. "You want me to ask him to give you a call?"

"Or come by," Lauren said with a shrug. "I think we need to talk about what we found out there today."

"Man, if I were him, I would just cut my losses on that place and destroy it," Aiden said. "Dismantle that stone circle, bulldoze the house, then sell the land."

"And if whatever is there is attached to the land and not the structures?" Lauren looked over to Aiden as she asked the question. "That would be irresponsible and ultimately make him at fault for more pain and suffering. He knows something is wrong with the place, or at least suspects it. That's why he hasn't gone himself."

"Okay, time out," Derrick said, using both hands to make a "T" sign. "You know I hate it when Mom and Dad fight." He gave a bit of a grin, hoping to lighten the tension that had grown in the room.

Aiden gave a slight smile and nodded. "Right, food," he said.

They all shambled toward the door; their motions slowed by their tiredness. Lauren made sure all the lights were off and locked the door behind them as they left.

"Going after more ghosts tonight?" a voice asked. Andy turned in his chair to see who was being a smart-ass. He saw Detective Raynor perched on his partner's desk, smirking at him.

"Hmm, so you have nothing better to do than bust my balls, Raynor?" Andy was annoyed. He and Raynor had never gotten along well but kept it civil for the sake of work. The barbs and snide remarks had increased in the last few months, however.

"Not really," Raynor said with a shrug and a smirk.

"That tells me way more about your social life than I needed to know," Andy said in retort, turning in his chair once more to put his back between himself and Raynor.

"At least I have one and don't have to moonlight by doing security for some dumb TV show," Raynor said. "And then screw it up on top of that."

"I didn't screw anything up," Andy said with a sigh as he stood and turned to face Raynor. As Andy rose, so did Raynor. Andy was three inches taller than Raynor and was more muscular as well, but Raynor didn't look intimidated in the least.

"That's not what your last partner said," Raynor said, his smirk growing as he knew he was pushing Andy's buttons. That comment made a couple of other detectives in the room stop what they were doing and pay attention. Keller, who had been with Andy and Cadence on the case during which she had died, was one of them. He stood up, bristling with anger as well, but Raynor's attention was solely focused on Andy as he spoke. "Oh wait, she didn't say anything, did she?" He raised his hand to eye level, then pointed his finger down and lowered it again while whistling a single note.

Andy's temper broke, and he reached out and grabbed Raynor by the collar of his shirt with one hand. "You weren't even here when that happened, Raynor," Andy said, his voice a growl. "And don't ever let me catch you talking about Detective Riley like that again."

Keller moved, wanting to hit Raynor himself, but was more interested in keeping Andy out of trouble. He forced himself in between the two and began trying to push Andy away from Raynor. "He's not worth it, Halleran."

"Halleran!" The telltale squeak of the captain's office door sounded right before his voice bellowed the name across the room. "My office. Now." The smirk on Raynor's face grew. Andy narrowed his eyes at the other detective but released his collar. Without comment, Andy turned on his heel and stormed into Captain Rodriguez's office, slamming the door.

Rodriguez, still outside his office, looked over at Raynor and shook his head. "Go home, Detective."

Raynor nodded to the captain and smoothed out his shirt before gathering his things and heading out for the evening.

Rodriguez entered his office and shut the office door far more gently than Andy had. He then closed the blinds on the window in his office. Andy was already seated in the chair, one leg crossed over the other, his fists clenched in his lap. It was obvious that Andy was fuming. Rodriguez went around his desk and sat down in his chair. He regarded Andy for a few moments before finally breaking the silence.

"Shake it off. He'll be gone by the end of the week," Rodriguez said.

"He put in for a transfer?" Andy couldn't keep the surprise from his voice as he asked the question.

"No, I put in for him to transfer," the captain answered. "You aren't the only one he's been needling. Keller almost came to blows with him, too. Among others." Captain Rodriguez sighed and pinched the bridge of his nose, massaging there for a moment as if trying to ward off a headache.

"You okay, Captain?" Andy noticed the dark circles under the other man's eyes.

"For the most part," Rodriguez said. "I haven't had time to catch up with you about your little security job at the prison."

Andy sighed and closed his eyes for a moment. "What about it?" he finally asked.

"I saw your report," the captain said. "There's one thing I don't get, though. How did you know to go in?"

"I heard the glass shatter," Andy said, lying. As much as he knew it was the truth, he was not about to tell his superior officer that he went based on his dead partner's plea for help. "I was stretching my legs, walking around the car, and I heard the glass shatter."

"I see," the captain said. He looked like he was going to say something else, but he was interrupted by his coffee pot flying across the room. It came out of the machine, sailed over Andy's head, and smashed against the wall behind the captain. Hot coffee and broken glass rained down and stained the wall and floor as both men jumped to their feet.

"What the hell?" Andy was looking around for a culprit, knowing full well no one had come into the office because the door hadn't squeaked.

Captain Rodriguez, however, saw the culprit clearly. Her blonde curls, her white dress, and her blue eyes, which should look innocent, but he knew she was anything but. Emma, the child ghost that he had conjured to bring Ava to him, stared at him in her pint-sized fury.

"Don't worry about it," Rodriguez said, trying to wave away Andy's question. "Thank you for answering the question I had. Go on home."

"After that?" Andy couldn't believe that the captain was being so blasé about something flying a good eight feet toward his head.

"It's nothing," the captain said. He was trying to usher Andy out as Emma passed through the door, giving a giggle that was audible to both men.

"Your nothing sounds like a kid," Andy said. "Are you haunted or something?" Andy had spoken the words before he had realized it.

"Not usually, no," Rodriguez said. He paused, his hand on the knob of the office door, and looked at Andy. "You believe in ghosts?"

"I don't know," Andy said with a non-committal shrug. "My beliefs have been changing a lot this past year."

"Since Riley?" It still pained Rodriguez to say her name. She had been a good cop.

"Yeah." Andy nodded solemnly. "Since Riley died."

"Is that why you took the extra shift guarding the television show?" Rodriguez had pulled his hand away from the doorknob, the shattered coffee pot forgotten. Halleran had been closed off since the accident that had killed his partner. This was the first time Rodriguez had even heard him mention her name since then.

"What do you mean?" Andy asked.

"Were you looking for them to prove the afterlife for you?" Rodriguez clasped his hands behind his back, his mind running in different directions at this turn of events.

"For the most part, I took the shift because it was something Cade would have done," Andy said. "She always worked overtime and holidays to let the guys with families go home to them. Or the women," he was swift to add, knowing she would have punched him for the omission had she been standing there with him. "Figured I didn't have any plans, so I would take the shift." He wasn't about to have his boss think he believed in ghosts or any such nonsense.

Rodriguez nodded and then opened the door for Andy. "Well, have a good night, Halleran. Get some rest. And don't let Raynor rattle you. He'll be gone soon enough."

Andy nodded and left the office, closing the door behind him. He went back to his desk in the now-empty office. Grabbing his jacket off the back of his chair, he noticed a side drawer of his desk was ajar. He opened the drawer and saw a file folder that was thick, its top tab dog-eared and crinkled. He knew he hadn't put that file there. Glancing at the captain's office, he saw the blinds were still closed. Good.

He pulled out the file and opened it. He wasn't sure what he had been expecting to see, but the photo of a corpse was not it. He looked at the next page and saw another corpse. It then dawned on him what he was looking at. The file of papers that Naveen had been sending the captain from the coroner's office. How had that file gotten into his desk?

He flipped it closed and looked over at the office again. The blinds were still closed, as was the door. He could hear shattered glass being swept up. Andy didn't hesitate. He slipped on his jacket and left with the file neatly under his arm.

CHAPTER 19

Notes, Part 2

"You disappeared pretty quick last night," Will remarked as Cadence entered the office.

"I needed some time to think," Cadence replied. "Works better if I can just pace around and talk to myself sometimes."

"Did you come up with anything?" He dropped his blue and white high-top clad feet, which had been up on his desk, to the floor.

"Maybe," Cade said. "I mean, just like before, it's a lot of if this, then that kind of guesses. This is probably the most frustrated I have ever felt about solving a case."

"So maybe if we deep dive it together, we can come up with something," Will said, rising from his chair as Cadence dropped into hers. "I know you said you did that with Snow and Whitfield. But maybe fresh eyes and ears could help?"

"Okay," Cadence said, giving a shrug of her shoulders. "I don't see how that could hurt. You've read the file by now, right?"

"Yep!"

"And you've seen the notes," Cadence said with a gesture to the wall. "So, let's do this. You talk it out to me. Maybe you caught something I didn't or have new insight."

"Sweet," Will said. "Oh, gotcha a gift." He went to his desk and pulled a bag out of the filing drawer there, which was empty since he hadn't done much yet to have files. He placed the bag on her desk with a grin. "You're going to love this, but this is just part one. Be right back with part two."

Cadence couldn't help but chuckle at his enthusiasm. She opened the bag and looked inside.

"Uh, Will?" She looked from the bag to him with an eyebrow lifted in doubt. "I don't knit or crochet," she said, pulling a few balls of yarn from the bag.

"No." He laughed. "But instead of pinning things to the wall and drawing on it with marker, I figured you needed a better solution." He had moved to a closet door on the same wall as the entrance door. Cade didn't recall ever seeing a closet door before.

Will disappeared inside the closet for a moment and came out with two large items. He pushed one and pulled the other. Two large corkboards on casters made their way across the room with his help.

"Trust me, I never mistook you for the arts and crafts type," Will said with a smile. "I just figured that we could put these babies away when we aren't using them. That way, no one can come in and mess with your notes. Plus, you get to be like all the cool detectives on TV connecting the pieces of a case together with yarn."

"I like the way you think, kid," Cadence said with a slight smile. She made a gesture for him to go ahead and start moving the notes she had pinned to the wall onto the corkboard. "Talk away."

"Okay, so hear me out," Will said as he started taking things off the wall. He pinned several of the notes to the corkboards before he began talking. "Oh, hey, toss me the blue yarn."

Cadence obliged and tossed the ball of blue yarn across to him. She watched him tie one end of the yarn to a pin on the far side of one corkboard and then tie it off to a pin on the end of the corkboard closest to her. He let the ball fall to the ground for now, and Cadence watched it roll for a moment, imagining how much her cat Darwin would have loved playing with it.

"We are actually going to get to a point where you talk, right?" Cadence asked, sarcasm mixed with humor in her voice.

"I wanted this whole thing to be a surprise, so I didn't set it up earlier. Give me a minute," Will said.

At length, he got everything pinned up where he wanted it, which was a different setup than the one Cadence had laid out. Will turned and grabbed a yellow ball of yarn and pocketed a green ball into his jeans.

"I would make a joke," Cadence said. "Several, in fact, but your age makes it seem a little perverted and weird. So, carry on."

Will lifted an eyebrow at her comment, shook his head, then turned back to the boards. He took both the yellow and green balls and tied them both to the pin in the note that said "Shaldoxz."

"We know Wolf is working for Shaldoxz, and Shaldoxz is working with Wolf," Will said, looping both strands around the pin in the note for Wolf. "Wolf gave the occult group a ritual to do that brought out a chaos entity at Lexington Hills where Ramon worked and where your group of ghost hunter friends had been investigating." Will took the green strand only and looped it around pins for the occult group, ritual, Lexington Hills.

"Right," Cadence said with a nod but didn't inject any further.

Grabbing red yarn, Will continued, tying it off to begin at the pin for Whitfield. "After a mishap with the first NHD Agent, Whitfield came to you guys to help you out, claiming to be from the NHD. He told you how you had to work with breathers in order to undo the ritual and vanquish the demon. This event, either on purpose or by accident, strengthened your relationship with the ghost-hunting group."

"With most of them anyway," Cadence said. "Lauren was not our fan for quite a while."

Will waved her words away. "Shush, I'm working. Now, things were normal for a while until the case with the old lady who didn't know she was dead. Your ghostie group was working on that. How did they get called in on that, exactly?"

"I don't know," Cadence said with a shrug. "We had one of the watchers keeping track of them. They hadn't gone out as a group in a while. When they did, we were contacted. It was a good thing, too, because that house wasn't in our files as haunted."

"Might not be important, but you might want to find out," Will said. "Just to check off that box. Moving on, you guys are able to move her on. It looks like the humans cleared the ghost, so they get a 'job well done' by the house's current owners, and we move on."

"We also had the dorm case going on at that time, too," Cadence said, to which Will threw up one hand.

"Just hold your horses," Will said. "I'm doing this my way, right?"

Cadence nodded and made a gesture for him to continue.

"Thank you," Will said. "Now, because your breathers did such a good job with the old lady, the wife who lives in that house recommends them to one of her friends, who also happens to be having trouble with a ghost. So, Robin calls on your friends to come and help her and her daughter, Ava.

"Now we know from Sam that Wolf was the one to raise Emma from the dead, and inadvertently the slave who was tied to Emma, Sarah," Will said, working the green yarn back up to Wolf and then to notes for Sarah and Emma. "Sam said that Wolf definitely wanted something from Ava, and he was using the child ghost to try to get at her."

As Will stepped back for a moment, Cadence could see how he was setting it up. The ghosts were above the blue line, the mortals were below it. The locations were in the middle since they spanned a kind of border between the living and dead. Cade was also impressed that Will had taken the ongoing issues seriously and had read back on the cases.

"Now we switch back to the dorm case where your brother was the monitor," Will said after taking a moment to catch his breath. "The trouble there started, in theory, just like the old woman's had. Construction and remodeling of the house. But this time, instead of just upsetting the spirits there, it brought up a ghost that had never been there before. One who wasn't even dead, it turned out."

Cadence nodded but otherwise kept silent. She was intrigued by the way he was putting it together.

"You and Snow investigate and discover everything about Overton, who was once a priest or follower of this Shaldoxz. Now, through all of this, Whitfield is also at your side. Nervous and high-strung, according to you and Snow, but smart. According to him, Overton called Wolf to help him when they had your breather former partner tied up in the basement of the dorm house. Wolf basically told him that it sucks to be him; he has to clean up his own mess and books it out of there. Meanwhile, Overton does the unexpected. He lets his stolen body die and drags you to hell in a handbasket or urn, as it may be."

Cadence shuddered at the memory of that. She still hated it. Not because of the pain and torture, but because she had been caught off guard so easily by him. That she had been the proverbial damsel in need of a rescue. It still stuck in her craw.

"So, we know Wolf was connected to Overton. We know Overton, in his original life, had been a disciple of Shaldoxz, and from the way Wolf spoke, it seems Wolf outranked Overton," Will said. "Would you agree?"

Cadence nodded in the affirmative to Will, who had looked back at her to gauge her response.

"Okay, good. Snow and Sam get you back, but on the way back, they notice the portal seems to be closing. They get through at the last minute, like in movies, where they wait until the last second to diffuse the bomb. Whitfield, whom we have established as a non-human, was part of the ritual side to close the portal, locking Overton away again. The new urn was left in the care of your ghost-hunting group."

"And it is still there," Cadence said.

Will nodded. "Good," he said. "Now we get to Barrington, and this one is the real doozy. No one could have predicted the box thing that the lady brought in that trapped Snow. That ended up being a stroke of luck for the bad guys. Since your ghost group was working on both cases, it was easy for Wolf to find out, likely through calls to the production company, when the prison investigation was to be filmed. That made it easy for him to tell Emma to step up her shenanigans. This was done, I believe, to deliberately split the group.

"Now, Lauren had already made no bones about not liking the prison, not wanting to do that investigation, and Sam was attached to Lauren at that point. So that made one set for the family case: one human, one ghost. That left you, Snow, Whitfield, Derrick, and Aiden. Aiden is a little more sensitive than I think you guys give him credit for, to be honest. He knew the prison was full of bad juju, so he volunteered to take on that investigation. You and Snow agreed that since it was the more dangerous of the two cases, that you two should take the prison as well. That left Whitfield with Sam to cover the family case. Derrick and Aiden decided it would be best not to leave Lauren alone, or probably something along those lines. So, Derrick goes with Lauren. Whitfield casually blows off his assignment and is unreachable that night."

"I have to say I'm impressed, kid," Cadence said, looking at the board with its strands of yarn going here and there like someone had thrown streamers at the board. "You learned the cases well."

"I'm glad you said that because this is the part where you think I'm crazy," Will said, holding up a finger. He continued before Cadence had a chance to speak. "And probably get pissed at me, too," he added with a shrug. "I know you talked to Snow about your suspicions about Whitfield. If he is Shaldoxz or just working for him."

"Yeah, you know because you were there," Cadence said.

"Glad to see age hasn't dimmed your mind," he said with a grin. If she kept calling him kid, he would start making cracks about her age. "Number one, I think Shaldoxz is a made-up thing. A name taken in honor of or to poke fun at a different entity. I was with you on the Whitfield thing until the farmhouse yesterday."

"What changed your mind?" Cadence canted her head in curiosity. She had caught the age barb but let it go, as she was far more interested in what he was saying.

"Two things, and I will go with the less obvious first," Will said. "The stone circle."

"How is the stone circle the less obvious?" Cadence questioned. "It's a pretty damned obvious thing to me."

"Hold on, I'll get there," Will said in a tone of patience, as if he were trying to calm a child. "You said that this circle might be the end point of a portal that you and Snow discovered in the rec room of Barrington Prison, right?"

"Yes," Cadence said.

"Okay, good," Will said. "And it's in your report that Pruitt and his goons were doing everything they could to keep you away from that room."

"Yeah," Cadence said again, not sure where Will was going now.

"And you said that Pruitt was sending spirits from the prison through the portal to inhabit new bodies."

"Yes," Cadence said again with a nod.

"Sending spirits from the prison through the portal to inhabit new bodies on a piece of land known for pain and blood and nothing good, and that has a very old non-human on it."

"Oh shit," Cadence said.

"Okay, good, you're seeing it, I think," Will said. "Now, what was the non-human's name?"

"X'Haldzos," Cadence said.

"Write it down," Will said. He then went to his desk, took a sticky note from there, and began writing on it. "Done?" he asked as he finished.

"Yes," Cadence said, brow furrowed as her mind worked.

Will brought over his note, which read "Shaldoxz," and put it beside her note saying "X'Haldzos." Will began crossing out the letters that the names had in common until all the letters were crossed out.

"What we have here," Will said, "is an anagram. Someone rearranged the letters of a non-human's name to pretend to be something he's not."

"Son of a bitch," Cadence said, her voice a murmur as she stared at the letters on the two notes. "So even if we leave Whitfield out of it, this is starting to look like Shaldoxz, whoever that is, is simply pretending to be a non-human."

"I don't know," Will said, his expression and tone thoughtful. "It's possible that one is a henchman of the other."

"Henchman?" Cadence looked over at Will. One eyebrow was lifted, and the corner of her mouth was crooked up in a half smile. "This isn't a comic book, Will."

"No, it's not," Will agreed. "Which is why you need to take it more seriously. Dude, look: People in positions of power have henchmen. Whether they choose to use that term or call it something else, it doesn't change the job description."

Cadence frowned in thought and leaned back in her chair, looking from the corkboards to the notes on her desk. "So," she began, "if the non-human in the house at Scarecrow Farms is the boss, Shaldoxz is the underling?"

"Okay, let me try to put this another way," Will said, thinking. "Did you ever see *Clash of the Titans*?"

"The old movie with Harry Hamlin or the remake they did a few years ago?" Cadence replied.

"They remade it?" Will looked surprised and offended. "You can't remake perfection. Harryhausen is a master..." He trailed off and shook his head. "You know what? Never mind, that isn't the point. I'm talking about the Harry Hamlin one."

"Sure, go ahead," Cadence said, wondering where the hell he was going with this.

"Zeus rules the roost in heaven, right?" Will said and only continued once Cadence had nodded. "Right, so when Calibos fucked up by hunting the Pegusi to near extinction, Zeus turned him into a monster. He didn't flat out kill him because A) he wanted him to suffer, and B) Calibos's mom was Thetis, a goddess. He didn't want any more trouble since Hera was always pissed at him for playing hide the sausage with any and probably all of the ladies in Greece."

"Will, I—" Cadence said, but he cut her off.

"I'm getting there, I promise," Will said. "Thetis had her hands tied, though. She couldn't go against Zeus. My ultimate point is that the resident boogieman at Scarecrow Farms is Thetis. Shaldoxz is Calibos, Wolf is Queen Cassiopeia, administering the curse that Calibos laid out after his transformation. Wolf's underlings are no different than the guards who had to tie up and burn Andromeda's suitors when they failed the riddle." Will stopped, looking pleased with himself.

"But again, this is being based on a lot of ifs, ands, and buts," Cadence said.

"That's why we need to test it out," Will said.

"How do we do that?" Cadence wasn't sure about Will's proposal now.

"Take Whitfield with us," Will said.

"What?!" Cadence was on her feet in an instant. "Are you insane?"

"That's your best comeback?" Will said, rolling his eyes. "Look, non-humans take all kinds of forms and have their own agendas, not all of them evil. Just because Whitfield is a non-human doesn't mean he's bad. It just means he's been lying to you, but he could be doing that for self-preservation. People tend to have certain prejudices with non-humans."

Cadence sighed and sat back down. She leaned forward and put her elbows on her desk, using her hands to rub her temples. "This is a lot to take in, Will."

"I know," Will said. "And I know you're still kinda new, so you're still getting used to all of this."

Cadence gave a sour chuckle. "The kid is reminding me I'm new."

"I've been on this side for about thirty years," Will said. "You've barely even been here a year. So yeah, you're new. And stop giving me shit about my age. If I'd lived, I would have been 46 by now, so I would be older than you."

"Point taken," Cadence conceded with a nod.

"Good," Will said with a nod. "We've got to get moving. It's going to be a busy day."

"Okay," Cadence said. "Put away the corkboards. We need to do research on the Scarecrow Farms non-human. What it wants, why it's there, if it can leave. I'll have to check with Snow about getting Whitfield back on the team, or at least getting him to come out to the field with us. I think getting him to face that thing on the second floor will go a long way to proving your theory. I also need to talk to Aiden. We should probably also talk to Roland again at Barrington Hills."

"Why the prison?" Will asked.

"Roland doesn't know where the portal goes," Cadence said. "But if we can somehow maneuver things so it opens and one of us can go through, we can prove that, too."

"That's not such a great plan, Cade," Will said. "If it doesn't go where you think it does, you could be in for a world of hurt."

"Good point," she said. "Dammit, I wish this was more of a certain thing."

"Look, some of this stuff you can do on your own, like talking to Aiden," Will said. "I want to spend some time at the drawing board. If that thing at the farm gets rowdy, I want us both to have stuff to take him down."

CHAPTER 20

One Busy Night

"Hi Bonnie," Cadence said in a cheerful greeting to the secretary outside of Snow's office.

"Detective Riley," the older woman said with a bright smile. "How are you, dear?" She took her horn-rimmed glasses off and let them fall to her chest, held there like a necklace by the pearled string attached to each arm of the frame.

"I'm good, thanks," Cadence said with a nod. "I was wondering if you could help me with something."

"Me?" Her light grey eyebrows lifted, showcasing the wrinkles on her forehead.

"Yeah, I know Snow is probably busy, and you more than likely know this," Cadence said. "No need to bother him. If I needed to do some research into non-human names, where would I go? Do we have a library or a mug-shot book or something?"

"Oh, no, nothing like that," Bonnie said. "Well, nothing for officers on this level, at any rate. But I know you and your partner are different." Bonnie pursed her lips for a moment, thinking. She glanced back to the door of Snow's office, which was still closed. This seemed to make her mind up. She opened her top drawer and rummaged a little until she came up with what looked like an ornate old-style key.

"You are the only one I am giving it to," Bonnie said, her voice hushed to a conspiratorial whisper as she handed the key to Cadence. "Not anyone else. No one else sees what is in there, and you have that key back to me within 24 hours."

"Thank you, Bonnie," Cadence said.

"Don't thank me just yet," Bonnie said, her voice still quiet. "Be careful. If they even get a whiff of you not belonging there, they will defend themselves. And you can't take anything out of there, either. It's not a lending library."

"Who's they?" Cadence was now concerned, as she hadn't intended on research being a contact sport.

"Never you mind," Bonnie said, putting her cheery smile on once more. "Just believe that you belong in there, and there won't be any trouble." Bonnie made a shooing motion with her hands.

"Bonnie, thank you," Cadence said, "but where do I use this?"

Bonnie pointed across from her desk. Cadence turned, but all she saw was the wall that was usually there. She looked back to Bonnie, puzzled, but the older woman just kept pointing insistently at the wall. Cadence crept closer and moved to one side of the couch that was in Bonnie's waiting area. Something out of the corner of her eyes caught her attention, and she moved away some leaves of the large potted plant.

There, in the wall, was a simple keyhole. No ornate plate around, not even any sign of a door. Just the keyhole. Cadence was dubious but inserted the key. A sudden bright light forced her to shut her eyes. When she opened them again, she was no longer in the waiting room in front of Snow's office. Instead, she found herself in a library larger than she had ever seen before.

The room was made of stone and contained shelf upon shelf of tomes as far as Cadence could see. Yellow-white orbs of light hung over a few people gathered around a table. Some were reading, others were writing. Something toward the back seemed to be hovering in the air. Cadence took one step, shoving the key into her front pocket, reminding herself that she belonged there.

Before she could take a second step, a winged grey being flew in front of her. It was short and humanoid, but it had horns and leathery wings. It looked like it was made of stone, but Cadence had never known stone to move like that. The only word that came to mind for Cadence was "gargoyle."

"General topic of research." The mouth never moved; the voice was in her head. She was beginning to dislike that feeling.

"Non-Human beings," Cadence said.

"Follow me," the being intoned as it flew over to a circle that glowed red to the left of where she was standing.

She crossed into the circle and found herself in a different part of the library. The stone here looked older, and there were no orbs of light that she could see, save for the one now above her head. A different kind of gargoyle flew in front of her; its leathery wings had leathery feathers and its face was more angular.

"Earthbound or planebound?" it asked.

"Earthbound," Cade said, concentrating on her answers only. The last thing she wanted was to trip some weird security device down here.

The round eyes that it narrowed at her looked odd in the sharp angles of its face. "Stay." It then flew off.

Cadence tried to calm herself as she watched the gargoyle fly off. "I belong here," she kept chanting over and over in her head. Footsteps caught her attention in the otherwise quiet room, and she looked over to see someone approaching from where the gargoyle had disappeared.

A bald man who looked a little older than Cadence stepped into the light. His skin was dark, but not as dark as Croft's, but his heritage was unmistakable, as he dressed a great deal like Croft, or Thoth, as she had to keep reminding herself.

"Seshat wishes you welcome, Cadence Riley," the man said, his accented voice smooth and quiet.

Cadence furrowed her brow. "You know who I am?"

The man smiled, and the expression eased the seriousness from his face. "Seshat knows and passed the knowledge to me."

"How does this Seshat know who I am?" This was beginning to irk Cadence. She hated it when people knew who she was, and she had no idea about them.

She was also certain that if these people knew who she was, then Snow and Bonnie had just set her up. She had no idea what the joke was going to be, but she was wary that she was the butt of it.

The man smiled again. "I am Wep-em-nefret, and Seshat knows you because she is wife to Thoth."

Thoth. Croft. Cadence had no idea that he had a wife. Then again, up until a little while ago, she hadn't known he was an Egyptian god either.

"What knowledge do you seek, Cadence Riley?" He was still cordial and smiling as he asked the question.

"I'm looking for information on X'haldzos," Cade said, figuring getting the information was more important than any possible joke being played on her.

"Follow me, please," Wep-em-nefret said. He led her down a corridor, then turned into an alcove on the right. He gestured for her to have a seat on the pillowed stone bench on the wall. Once she was settled, he pressed a button surrounded by an ornate scrollwork plate. Part of the wall slid aside, and the table behind the partition moved forward with something on it.

"Are you kidding me?" Cadence said, looking from the table to Wep in disbelief.

"Is something wrong?" Wep-em-nefret asked.

"You have a laptop." It was less a question and more of a statement. The computer sat on the table, its monitor glowing in the darkness of the alcove.

"It is far more efficient than dusty old books." The dark-skinned man smiled.

"You guys are hysterical," Cadence said without laughter, shaking her head.

Wep-em-nefret chuckled. "Read well. There are no notes. Only you will take this knowledge with you." He tapped his temple with his pointer finger for emphasis.

"Memorize what I need. Got it," she said with a nod.

"It was good to meet you, Cadence Riley," he said. "Gods willing, we will meet again."

The mortal world was dark by the time Cadence left the library of Seshat. The windows of Aiden's apartment showed the inky sky outside, the black shadows of nearby buildings, and lights setting windows aglow. The apartment was empty. She hadn't bothered consulting a clock or her television to look in on Aiden to find out where he might be. She had just teleported, as her mind had been preoccupied with going over and over the information she had learned.

Her contemplation of the night beyond the window was broken by keys jangling outside, followed by one of the locks turning. Another sound of jangling and the lock on the doorknob turned and opened. Aiden walked in with a bag from a fast-food place and a matching cup with a straw sticking out of it. Cadence was mildly jealous as the takeout food smelled good.

Aiden gave the door a light shove with his foot, and it closed behind him. He tossed his keys on the kitchen bar and headed for the couch. Once he had the TV on and his shoes off, he pulled out his aluminum foil-wrapped burger. Cadence frowned. Usually, he put out the felt shapes so she could let him know she was there.

"I guess he figures no one is visiting tonight," she said with a sigh. If Snow were here, she would have had him start messing with the TV. Snow was excellent at manipulating electrical devices. Cadence could do it to an extent, but not as well and not with much ease. She shrugged to herself and decided to let him eat before letting him know she was there.

At length, he got up to throw away his trash, and that was when Cadence did her thing. She waited until he was in the kitchen, then knocked the remote control for the TV off the couch. When Aiden came back and saw the remote on the floor, he looked confused, and Cadence couldn't help but grin.

Aiden put the remote back on the couch, then pulled his felt shapes out of his jeans pocket and put them on the couch. Cade debated just knocking off the remote again, but knew she had more important things to do than play around with the living. She flicked the green clover off the couch. Aiden waited to see if the white snowflake would follow suit, but it didn't.

"What is up with Snow not being around?" Aiden asked the question as he grabbed both felt shapes and pocketed them. "Hang on. I'll get the box."

Cadence felt the box was cheating, but she also knew it saved time. This way, she didn't have to wait for him to go to sleep and visit him in his dreams. She hated doing that. It felt like an invasion of privacy to her. That and a small part of her feared she would walk right into a dream that was more X-rated, and she had no desire to see that.

Aiden had gone to the back room where he had his equipment stored and his computers running. He came back with the spirit box and turned it on. The sound of intense static filled the room as the device made its bandwidth sweeps.

"Cadence," Aiden said. "What's up?"

"Oh, a whole lot," Cade said, her voice coming through the machine in a staccato manner. "We haven't been able to catch up since the prison. How are you feeling? I saw him grab you." She knew he would demure or try to change the subject if she wasn't point blank with the question.

"A little sore, but nothing weird," Aiden said. "I'm good. Where's Snow? I noticed he hasn't been around since the prison. Did that box thing hurt him?"

"Yeah," Cadence said after a moment of thinking about the best way to answer. "But he's fine now. Even got a promotion. I have a new partner now."

"Oh?" Aiden was a bit surprised at this, but then again, he had no idea how it really worked on that side. "Does the new partner have a name?"

"Let's just leave the new partner as the new partner for now," Cadence said. "I think at this point, the less information bleed we have would be best. Did you get the woman to agree to not air the footage?"

"She is going to be hella hard to convince," Aiden said, sitting down on the sofa.

"I know I don't have to stress this," Cadence said, "but try."

"I'm on it," Aiden said, his voice sounding tired. "Are you with us on the Scarecrow Farms case?"

"Of course," Cadence said. "Don't let Lauren get brave and try to go upstairs unless Sam tells her she can. She was right not to go yesterday."

"Did you go upstairs?" Aiden was curious since he hadn't seen anything more dangerous than the state of the building's disrepair up there. Well, that and the noise, but he wanted confirmation.

"Yeah, I did," Cadence said. "There's a big ugly up there near where the roof is blown out. I've got to compare a few notes to see how we can best deal with it."

"Okay," Aiden said, making a mental note to try to keep people out of the second story. "What's the story with the stone circle in the field?"

"Possibly a portal," Cadence said. "That's my working theory right now, anyway."

"A portal to where?" Aiden lifted an eyebrow in curiosity as he directed the question to the circular device he held.

"Not sure yet," Cadence said, evading the answer she thought was correct. She didn't want to scare him by saying that it might be connected to Barrington Prison.

A knock sounded on Aiden's door, and he turned off the spirit box quickly. "Just a sec," he yelled toward the door. "Just a sec, Cade," he said in a whisper. Aiden walked over to his door and opened it.

"Hi," Teeny said. She was dressed in jeans and a heavy jacket, buttoned to ward off the cold outside. "I hope you don't mind. Liam is sleeping, and I am starting to go stir-crazy at the hospital. I thought I might come spend time with you. If you weren't doing anything."

Aiden smiled a little despite himself. "Sure," he said. "Come on in."

Teeny entered and glanced at Aiden's hand. "Is your apartment haunted?" she asked with a laugh.

"Huh?" Aiden looked and saw that he was still holding the spirit box. That reminded him that Cade was still there. *Shit,* he thought. "Oh! No," he chuckled. "I was just changing out the batteries so they are fresh when we go to the Farm." He closed the door behind her.

"Good idea." Teeny nodded.

"Give me just a sec to put this away," Aiden said. "Make yourself at home in the meantime."

Aiden walked down the hall and turned into the back bedroom that made his office. Cadence had followed, which had been his hope. He set out the clover, which she was quick to knock off his desk. She was irritated at having their pow-wow interrupted.

"Cade, I'm sorry. I wasn't thinking," he said, his voice barely a whisper. "I can't turn this on with her here. Come back later. We still need to talk. Meanwhile, I'll work on getting her to relent on the footage." He put the spirit box away in its case as he spoke.

Cadence rolled her eyes. He had been thinking alright, just not with his brain. She let out a frustrated sigh that he couldn't hear but teleported home.

The apartment was empty, and Cadence wasn't quite sure how she felt about that. She had gotten used to Sam being around when he wasn't with Lauren, but he had been spending more and more time with her as he got more into his role as her guardian. Ramon's presence was always welcome, and she found that she missed him when he was gone. That was something she hadn't felt with any of her mortal lovers. She enjoyed their company when she was with them, sure, but she hadn't felt their absence in such a way. It was almost painful, like part of her wasn't there.

She walked over to her couch and flopped down on it, kicking off her shoes and socks. The silvery scars on her feet made her pause for a moment. They had healed. Ramon had made sure of that. They were constant reminders to her, however, of being the one thing she had never wanted to be. The damsel in distress. It still angered her, not so much the torture that Overton had wrought on her, but the fact that he had caught her off guard to capture her in the first place. The bottoms of her feet were just silver. All scar tissue of her spirit since they had taken the worst of the heat and fire.

"Asshole," she said out loud. "Never again."

"Didn't anyone tell you that you should never say never?" Ramon said as he came in. He gave her a smile, then saw that she was looking at her feet. "Are they bothering you?"

"Just emotionally," Cadence said. "You patched me up too well for them to still be bothering me otherwise." She smiled at him as he crossed the room and sat down beside her.

"So, what's new with your caseload?" Ramon slid an arm around her as he asked this.

"No new cases per se, but some new information," Cade said.

"Like what?" Ramon always had an interest in her cases. If nothing else, it gave him a heads-up as to how damaging it might be to her.

Cadence opened her mouth, but a knock on her door stopped her. She got up and crossed the room, opening the door.

"Is this an inconvenient time?" Snow was standing in the hallway between their two apartments. "Bonnie said you had come to see me."

"Not an inconvenient time at all, Ozzie," Cadence said with a grin, knowing her nickname for him annoyed him to no end.

He grimaced at the name but stepped inside, letting Cadence close the door behind him. "What did you need to see me about?" Snow gave a nod to Ramon as he asked the question of Cadence.

"Nope, we're not starting with business," Cadence said. She wrapped her arms around Snow and held him close for a moment, smiling as he hugged her back. "I've missed my friend too much to start with business."

"This is a nice way to end the day," Snow said. "I'm sorry I've not been around more these past few days. Taking over Alistair's spot has been exhausting."

Cadence looked surprised. "You're still calling him that?"

"Yes, and you should, too," Snow said. "Or Croft, at the very least. It shouldn't be known who he really was. Or is."

Cadence made a zipper motion over her pressed-together lips with a nod. "Mum's the word, got it." Cadence slipped back into her spot on the sofa beside Ramon, and Snow moved to occupy one of the two armchairs that were on either side of the sofa.

"I will admit, curiosity over why you came to see me today brought me over," Snow said. "As well as a desire to catch up."

"Oh, it's been a lot," Cadence said. "We're still not sure if Aiden is going to get Teeny's help regarding the video evidence from the prison. The case they have now could be tied into the prison, too. There is a non-human involved there that has taken up residence in the second story of the house and quite a few other spirits there as well."

"Forgive me, my attention fixated on your statement that their current case could tie into the prison," Snow said. "How is that possible?"

Cadence pulled her phone from the inside pocket of her blazer. She brought up the pictures she had taken. "That stone circle," she began, "is on the property of Scarecrow Farms in one of the unused fields. Well, I guess they're all unused at this point. There's blood on that central stone, like it was used for ritual work or sacrifices."

"Cadence, I still don't see…" Snow trailed off as he got to the picture that she had taken from the vantage point that reminded her of the view from the prison side of the portal when it had opened. "Ah, never mind, I do see."

"You see it, too, then?" Cadence felt vindicated, Snow's words giving her some confirmation that she might not be crazy.

"I do, yes," Snow said with a nod. "We might both be wrong, but I can see why you would think it is connected. What are the odds, though? That this new case would be connected to the prison case?"

"What were the odds that the little girl case would be connected to the Irene Woods case?" Cadence said, countering his argument.

"That was a tenuous connection at best," Snow said, trying to minimize it.

"But it was a connection," Cadence said. "You should come to the office tomorrow. Will and I have been putting our heads together on this, and we've come up with some interesting things."

"Like what?" Snow was glad that the two were working well together, but he was becoming concerned that they were thinking a little too outside the box.

"Like we might want to bring Whitfield back into things, at least temporarily," Cadence said.

"Now I know you've lost your senses," Snow said.

"Didn't you say he was dangerous?" Ramon frowned. He knew she had to do her job, and he couldn't keep her from danger, but this alarmed him.

"Just bear with me, okay?" Cadence looked between them both. "The name of the non-human at the house is an obvious anagram of Shaldoxz. We have our suspicions about Whitfield, but we do know he is non-human and not who he says he is. Taking him there to see how he reacts to this thing and how it reacts to him might prove something, one way or another."

Both Ramon and Snow sat in silence as they considered her words.

"Just be careful, please," Ramon said after a minute. "I love you, but patching you up isn't my favorite thing to do."

"I'll come down to your office tomorrow," Snow said, taking a few more moments than Ramon to respond. "The three of us will talk about what theories you have and what we can do about them. I'm not going to lie; it will need to be a very convincing argument for me to go along with putting Whitfield back on the team."

"I know," Cadence said with a nod. "I wouldn't expect anything less from you."

Snow rose with a smile and a nod. "I'll see you tomorrow, then," he said.

"Sounds good," Cade said.

Snow crossed the room and let himself out. That left Ramon and Cadence on the couch, enjoying a closeness that, a year ago, Cadence would have found unthinkable.

"So, you don't like patching me up, huh," Cadence teased as the door closed behind Snow, and she turned to look at Ramon. "That's a shame. You've gotten really good at it this year."

Ramon laughed. "You've not given me much choice but to get good at it," he said. Then the smile faded, and a thoughtful look replaced it. "You might laugh at me, but I will swear that there is love at first sight. From the moment I saw you walk into Lexington when you were young and breathing, I loved you. And I still do, Cadence Riley."

Cadence smiled, an uncharacteristic warmth filling her. "As weird as it is for me to say this, I agree. I know you saw me years before I ever saw you, but when you appeared in the lobby that first time..." she trailed off, thinking of how to phrase it. "I'm not good at this: relationships, love, words. I know I fought it for a while, arguing with Snow when he teased me about you. But I am so grateful that I have you. That you love me because I know I'm not easy to love most of the time." Cade gave a small laugh. "In fact, one ex told me I was as easy to love as a defensive porcupine is to snuggle. But I do love you, Ramon. So much."

Ramon reached behind Cadence, taking her hair down from its usual ponytail, letting it spill over her shoulders. He savored the moment, knowing that her showing her more vulnerable side was an extraordinary occurrence. He let the silence grow around them as he moved in to kiss her.

"I didn't come over to argue about this," Teeny said.

Aiden ran a hand through his hair. "I know, I know. Sorry," he said. "It's just important."

"Why is it so important, though?" Teeny couldn't understand why Aiden was so gung-ho about burying the footage they had gotten in the prison of the ghost they captured in the box and the things Liam's camera had caught. "You keep saying it's important, but you won't explain to me why."

Aiden sighed and leaned back on the couch a bit. "I can't tell you. It's annoying, I know. But I'm sitting on things, too. All I can tell you is that if this video got out, it would be bad."

"Aiden, I'm sorry," Teeny said with a shake of her head. "This is a television show. Good footage like this has never happened before on any show. Hell, on any investigation I know of. With Liam laid up and production on hold, this footage is even more important. If Russell knew what was on those tapes, he'd already have them in a safe deposit box somewhere."

"And I'm thankful that you didn't tell him," Aiden said. "But did you ever wonder why no shows, no other investigations have gotten the kind of footage you got?"

"Because we're awesome, and they're not?" Teeny knew it was a lame excuse, but she had never stopped to think about that in her excitement.

"You're smart, Teeny," Aiden said. "I know that, but you need to think. What happens if you prove beyond a shadow of a doubt that an afterlife does exist?"

Teeny frowned as she thought. "It would probably put a bunch of religions in a tight spot. But it would also prove that paranormal investigation is a legitimate form of science."

Aiden shook his head. "You're seeing it from a scientific viewpoint alone. Factor in the human equation. There would be fewer mysteries in the world as we know it. The knowledge could have a bad effect on some people. And others might take life for granted if they have proof that it continues."

Teeny opened her mouth, then closed it for a moment. "I hadn't thought about that," she said at length. "You do have a good argument, but Aiden, try to see my perspective. Someone someday is going to get footage like this, proof like this. They won't hide it from the world."

"Why not? I did," Aiden said.

"Bullshit," Teeny said, but the look on Aiden's face made her doubt herself. "You have footage like that, and you sat on it?"

"Yes," Aiden said.

"Why would you do that?" Teeny couldn't believe that he wouldn't jump at the chance to put proof up on the internet, to be the name associated with proof of existence after death.

"I'm pretty sure I just covered my reasons," he said, not wanting to go into detail. He wanted to trust her, but he just couldn't bring himself to do it yet.

"What footage did you get?" Part of Teeny knew he wouldn't answer, but she had to ask.

"I'm not telling you," he said with a chuckle. He then held up a hand to stop her as she opened her mouth. "I'm not showing you, either."

A knock at Aiden's door brought the discussion to an abrupt close as they both turned in the door's direction.

"Grand Central Station tonight," Aiden said with a sigh as he got up. When he opened the door, he was surprised to see Andy Halleran on the other side.

"Yes, I looked up your address," Andy said as he walked in. He stopped short when he saw Teeny on the couch. "Ah shit. Sorry, man, I didn't know you had company."

"Phones are a great invention," Aiden said. "Pretty sure you had my number without having to look it up."

"I was just leaving, anyway," Teeny said, getting up from the couch. "I should be getting back to the hospital."

"How is Liam doing?" Andy asked.

"He's healing, and he's on good meds that make him not feel the pain," Teeny said. She was irritated that her conversation had been interrupted, but maybe it was for the best. She and Aiden just seemed to be going around in circles on the issue of the footage, which seemed to be all he would talk about.

"When he gets lucid, give him my best," Andy said.

"I will. Thank you, Detective." Teeny gave both a nod and left.

Aiden looked over at Andy as the door closed. "Okay, what's so important?"

Andy could tell Aiden was annoyed, but he was there now. No use in trying to go back. "I could use a sounding board, and you are the closest thing to a non-cop friend I have."

Aiden sighed and turned, heading for his kitchen. "And you need this sounding board to not be a cop," Aiden said. He opened the fridge and grabbed two beers, letting the fridge swing shut on its own. He walked back after opening both bottles and gestured for Andy to have a seat on the couch. He followed him there with the bottles and handed one to Andy as he sat down.

"You got it," Andy said. "Thanks," he added, taking the cold brown glass bottle from Aiden.

"Right, shoot," Aiden said as he crossed one leg over the other and took a drink.

"I would say this is hypothetical, but I won't bullshit you," Andy said. "I got ahold of some information the other day that I don't know what to do with." He rubbed his free hand on his pants leg, a habit he had when he was agitated. "Do you remember when you guys first came to me asking for help on Cade's behalf?"

"Yeah, she wanted you to look into some missing persons' files because of the whole college dorm thing," Aiden said with a nod. He remembered the knots in his stomach as they knocked on Andy's door for the first time, getting ready to tell him that ghosts were real, they had proof, and his dead partner wanted to talk to him. He had been sure they were all going to get arrested or thrown in a looney bin.

"Right," Andy said. "Well, Naveen, the head coroner, he told me that he had been accumulating a file of corpses with that mark Cade told us about."

"Really?" Aiden couldn't keep the surprise from his voice. "I'm surprised that the cops were able to keep something like that under wraps."

"It is surprising, right?" Andy said. "It's even more surprising to find out that Naveen had been sending all of this information over to my captain."

"Naveen told you that?" Aiden was glad he hadn't taken a drink because his reaction would have been a spit-take.

"Yep," Andy said. "I asked my captain about it not long after that whole disaster at the dorm. He said he didn't know anything about it. I found out the other day that he lied."

"How did you find out?" Aiden took a sip of his beer after asking the question.

"Oh, that's a fun answer," Andy said, sarcasm heavy in his voice. "The file was just sitting in my desk. I had just come from Rodriguez's office, so I know he didn't put it there. And I'll be damned if there isn't a ghost or something in his office."

"What makes you say that?" This evening was turning out to be extraordinary for Aiden.

"I was sitting across his desk from him," Andy said. "The door to the office was closed. His coffee pot, not the whole machine but just the glass pot, flew from the machine, which was a good three feet behind me. It went over my head and smashed against the wall behind him. I swear it only missed him by inches."

"Jeez," Aiden said after giving a low whistle. "How did he react?"

"Like nothing had happened," Andy said, rubbing his pants leg again. "I mean, I know about ghosts and that would still freak me out. It did freak me out," Andy corrected himself. "He acted like it was nothing out of the normal. He ushered me out of the office, though, and that's when I found the file."

"You think he was hiding the file?" Aiden's curiosity was piqued. "Or do you think maybe someone else had it? Or maybe Naveen left it for you?"

Andy shook his head. "No, Naveen had all his info on the computer at the morgue. And before you suggest it, no, he didn't print it all up. Some of these papers and pictures showed their age. Now maybe someone else had the file, that's possible. But Aiden, if my captain was hiding this for some reason, what does that say?"

"You really think he was hiding it from you?" Aiden finished his beer and set the empty bottle down on his coffee table.

"All I can say for certain is that when I asked him, he said he knew nothing about it, and it seemed like he couldn't change the topic fast enough," Andy said. "He also tried to talk me out of taking the extra detail at the prison, and then the whole thing in his office with the coffee pot."

"I can see why you wouldn't want to go to anyone on the force with this," Aiden said. "Do you have the file with you?"

"Not on me tonight, no," Andy said. "It's at home."

"Bring it by the shop tomorrow? Between all of us, we might be able to get some insight into it," Aiden said. He wasn't about to volunteer that Cadence's brother was always around Lauren, so he could call Cadence in on it, too.

"I'll see what I can do," Andy said with a nod. "And I'm sorry again. I didn't mean to interrupt your date."

"Date?" Aiden laughed. "Bro, I wish. It was more an arguing session."

"I don't know, man," Andy said. "Those were some looks she was giving you as she left."

"Annoyed looks more than likely." Aiden laughed again. "We're arguing over the prison footage."

"Oh. Air it or hide it?" Andy guessed.

"You got it," Aiden said. "And I'm sure you can guess which side she is on and which side I am on."

"Yeah, I think I can," Andy said with a sigh. "Let me tell you, as a friend, though, she was checking you out."

Aiden laughed and shook his head. "Nah, bro, you're more her style. She and Liam even had a spat about it after you went back out to your car after introductions that night at the prison."

It was Andy's turn to laugh. "Well, that sucks for her, then. I've got someone."

Aiden picked up his empty bottle and held it up. "A belated toast, then," he said. "To friends, crossed stars, and weird shit."

"Amen, man," Andy said, and clinked his bottle against Aiden's.

CHAPTER 21

Of Teams and Players

Snow sat on the edge of Will's desk in Will and Cadence's office, his mouth agape. Will had just finished giving his presentation on the corkboard, explaining everything that they had put together so far. Cadence was sitting in her chair behind her desk, her face showing how proud she was of her new partner.

"So," Will said to break the silence that had been extending since he finished, "what do you think?"

Snow's eyes went over the corkboards, going through the yarn line connections and thinking about what had been said. At length, he stood and shook his head. "I think this is amazing work."

"Now, after seeing this, what do you think about asking Whitfield to rejoin us?" Cadence wasn't sure if she was hoping for a yes or a no. Both options presented possible dangers. It was, however, the best way to find out a few things with certainty.

Snow paused before answering, weighing his words. "I think this idea you have about bringing Whitfield with you is a double-edged sword."

"How so?" Cadence knew her own reason for agreeing with Snow, but she wanted to hear his reasons. She also didn't want to be the one shutting down Will after he had worked so hard on this.

"Let's consider first that you are right straight down the line and that Whitfield is working for Shaldoxz or whatever that other creature's name is at the farm," Snow said, his British accent filling the room. "Taking him to the farm where that creature is, where that portal is, could be dangerous. If he can command that creature against you, what's to stop him from doing so? If that portal does go to the prison, what's to stop him from opening it and having the few remaining spirits at Barrington come through?"

"You're on point with the dangers," Cadence said. "But as you said, it's double-edged. You're pointing out the bad. What if he's ambivalent? You've said yourself that just because an entity is a non-human, it doesn't mean they are evil. What if he was trying to help and just got scared?"

"The bottom line," Will said, "is that we need to find out either way. It's great to sit here and give what ifs all day. But it will be better for us to know for sure than to let him just go skulking off into the sunset to do whatever."

"I will admit, you have a point," Snow said. He pressed his lips together, his ice-blue eyes aimed at the floor as he thought. "Fine. I will see what I can do about getting Whitfield back here for the time being. Do you know how much time you have until they go back out to the farm for a proper investigation?"

"No," Cadence said with a sigh. "My time talking with Aiden last night was interrupted, and I couldn't get back to him. I hope to get more today. Will, didn't you say you were going to spend yesterday at the drawing board on new inventions for this case?"

"Not only for this case, but hopefully all cases. As they are needed, of course," Will said. He walked over to his desk and grabbed his satchel from his seat. "Cadence, come on over here."

Cadence lifted an eyebrow, looking wary at the invitation, but she marched herself over to his desk.

"Here," Will said, handing her a small pouch. "I was only able to create five for each of us. I'll work on more later. That's the downside of having to spend energy to make things permanent. It takes a while to get an inventory going."

Cade took the pouch, and Snow left his perch on the desk to come over to her to see what she had. Opening the pouch, she poured its contents into her free hand. Five silver jacks filled her palm.

"I know this will do something amazing," Cadence said. "But right now, all I can think of is that we don't have time to be playing with toys."

"You're right on the first part, at least," Will said. "But you should know, Cadence, that you are never too old to play with toys."

"Mr. McKinney," Snow said, his tone one of warning, "I don't have time for games."

"Another point I would argue," Will said, "but now is not the time. They look like a child's set of jacks, yes. The trick is that when these bad boys hit a non-human, they will inject liquid into the thing that will burn away spirit essence from the inside. Just make sure that you hit who you intend to hit with these. They will hurt any non-human. Including ones on our side, if there are any."

"What if a breather gets in the way of your intended target?" It was Snow who asked the question, even though Cade had also been wondering.

"It won't hurt them," Will said. "Passes right through them since we're on just a little bit of a different plane of existence."

"Are they dangerous to us?" This time it was Cadence who asked.

"Nope, only to non-humans." Will grinned a little.

"Got it," Cadence said. She was careful putting the jacks back into the pouch and tied it onto the belt loop of her pants.

"Sweet," Will said. "Did your research turn up anything?"

"Research?" Snow asked, having not known of a place to research on this side of the veil.

"A little, yes," Cadence said with a nod. "It turns out there were two non-human creatures that were on the property of Scarecrow Farms. Not long after Chalmers bought the land, the reports of the sightings of one of them increased, and the other decreased."

"Do you think one of them killed the other?" Will was the one asking the question.

"Well, we know which one stayed," Snow said.

"Yeah, X'haldzos stayed," Cadence said. "But remember Derrick's research. There was supposedly a goat-like one that lived in the well, too. I found out that it is possible for two non-human creatures to be tied to the same general area. It's also possible for one to get big enough or strong enough to kick the other out. Thus, releasing it from its tether and setting it free to roam the world until it finds a new place to go."

"You're postulating that this goat-like creature has been freed by the X'haldzos creature?" Snow commented.

"That thing was pretty big," Will said. "Is it possible X'haldzos ate the goat?"

"Maybe," Cade said. "But it is also possible it got free. Again, we're working off possibilities here, not definite facts. From what I read, a freed non-human has two possible courses of action. One, to roam until it finds a place to be again. Two, to find a way back to its home, to retake it."

"Cadence, where did you find this information?" Snow was quite curious as he asked this.

Cadence blinked at Snow; she was a bit surprised that he didn't know about the library. "Umm… ask Croft."

"I can't, Cadence. He's gone to Council," Snow said.

"Okay, well, ask Bonnie, then," Cadence said. "And for that matter, ask the woman out. For God's sake, the two of you make googly eyes at each other enough. You pushed me and Ramon together despite my misgivings about relationships."

"Perhaps soon," Snow said and held up a hand to forestall her retort. "I am rather busy at the moment, Cadence."

"Getting back to my research, then," Cadence said, shrugging. "There wasn't a lot on X'haldzos, and there was even less on the other creature. X'haldzos is bad news. He is right up Shaldoxz's alley with the blood and pain and chaos. An interesting point of note is that the two share the same sigil. That leads me to believe that whoever is doing all of this is working for the big guy in the house."

Cadence paused as her phone rang. "Hello?"

Will sat in his chair and kicked his feet up on his desk. Meanwhile, Snow moved over to the corkboard to study it again.

"Oh, hey, Sam," Cadence said. "Oh? Yeah. We'll be there in a minute." She hung up her phone and looked at Will. "Looks like there is a meeting at Lauren's shop."

"Man, I just got comfortable," he said but smiled as he got up.

"I'll let you two get to it," Snow said. "You've done some impressive work in the last few days. I look forward to seeing more from you both. Oh, and tell Sam I said hello," he added with a smile to Cadence.

"What's up, Sam?" Cadence asked as they entered the New Age store owned by Lauren. She walked over and gave her brother a hug. She then moved aside so that her brother and her partner could high-five each other in greeting.

"They're having a meeting before the store opens for the day," Sam said in response. "According to Lauren, Aiden is bringing Andy, who has some info from the dorm case."

"The dorm case?" Cadence couldn't hide her surprise. She glanced over at the table and lifted an eyebrow as she saw Derrick. "He doesn't look great."

Cadence was right. Derrick looked pale and exhausted. He was sitting at the table, one hand cradling a cup of coffee, the other hand holding his head.

"Lauren has already read him the riot act," Sam said. "She is ordering him to bed after this. If he doesn't get sleep, she's going to kick him out of the group until he graduates."

"Good." Cadence nodded. "I know he is close to graduating, but if it comes down to school or caseload, school comes first."

"Yes, Mom," Sam said with a grin.

Cadence flipped her brother off but didn't reply any further to him. Instead, she turned her attention to her partner. "Hey, Will, you should think about what kind of symbol you think would be good for you."

"Symbol?" Will asked.

"Aiden has these little felt symbols he uses that we can knock off the table when we are around," Cadence said, explaining. "He uses a green clover for me. We need something for him to use for you."

"Darth Vader," Will said without hesitation.

"I'll see what I can do," Cadence said, chuckling at Will's response.

"I still feel like a fifth wheel," Will said. "You and Sam have your things. You guys have a relationship with these breathers. I'm just here."

"You aren't a fifth wheel, I promise," Cade said. "We're just still scrambling with the fallout from the last case and trying to catch up on this one. Trust me. You're doing great."

"Is that praise I hear from the person who wanted nothing to do with me?" Will said, grinning as he asked the question.

"Don't push your luck," Cadence said. Although she sounded gruff, Will could see a grin tugging at the corners of her lips.

The door to the shop opened, and both Aiden and Andy entered at the same time. Aiden locked it behind them, then made sure the sign on the door was still flipped to the "Closed" side. He then followed the detective to the back table.

"Dude, you don't look so good," Andy said in greeting to Derrick.

"I've been told," Derrick said, giving Lauren a pointed look. "Multiple times."

Andy gave a slight grunt in answer and let the thick manila folder he had fall to the table. He sat down next to Aiden, giving the man a concerned look about Derrick but letting the matter be.

"Derrick," Lauren said. "I'm going to say this one more time in front of everyone, then I will let it drop. I know you have a hell of a class load and that this is your final semester. If your classes and the cases here start making it so that you are all work and no sleep, there is a problem. I will not hesitate to kick your butt out of this group until you have graduated. You've worked too hard on your degree to let yourself get strung out by a hobby."

"I hear you," Derrick said as he lifted his head enough to look at Lauren. "I understand."

"I'm serious," Lauren said. "After this, just go home and get some rest."

"You're on," Derrick said with a nod and took a sip of his coffee.

"So, what's up, Detective?" Lauren said, turning her attention to him now that her den mothering was out of the way

"Okay," Andy started, rubbing his legs through his pants before setting them on top of the file folder. "I already told some of this to Aiden. I went to the coroner during the whole dorm debacle. Naveen told me that he had seen the symbol that Riley had told us about. It had been on several victims over several years. He had even compiled a file on it and sent it over to my captain."

"How were the police able to keep knowledge of a serial killer secret?" It was Lauren who asked.

"We didn't know," Andy replied, giving a shrug. "Naveen sent the file directly to my captain. My captain sat on it. In fact, after the whole dorm house thing where you guys saved my ass, I asked him about it point blank. He said he had never heard of any cult-like murders with weird symbols taking place in our area. He thought maybe it was something I had dreamed while I was knocked out. Up until a couple of nights ago, I had no other recourse than to just leave it alone."

"Is that what the file is?" It was Derrick who asked this time, and it was obvious he wanted to crack open the file and start researching.

"Oh, wait, this gets better," Aiden said.

Andy nodded to Aiden in agreement before picking up his story again. "It does, yes. A couple of nights ago, I was getting ready to leave the precinct. Captain

Rodriguez called me into his office. He had some lingering questions about what happened at Barrington." Andy wasn't going to go into Raynor; that was his problem. "As we're sitting there talking, the glass pot from the coffee machine he has in his office flies over my head. It misses him by inches, breaking against the wall behind him. He acts like nothing happened and rushes me out of his office. I get back to my desk, and one of my drawers is ajar, and this file is in there."

"That is strange," Lauren said.

"Is the precinct haunted?" Derrick couldn't help but ask the question.

"Not to my knowledge, no," Andy said. "And yes, this is the file about the corpses found with that symbol or that were killed in a ritualistic manner. Some of these might not have anything to do with what you guys were looking for. I don't even know if you are still looking for it. But given the circumstances around it, I thought you guys might want a peek. Careful though, it's not for the squeamish."

Derrick pulled the file toward him and flipped it open. Lauren kept her eyes trained anywhere but on the pictures of dead bodies as Derrick filtered through the information.

"Has your captain been asking about his missing file?" It was Aiden who asked.

"Nope," Andy said with a shake of his head. "Not yet."

"That's odd," Lauren said. "You would think if he went to all the trouble of hiding it that he would rain down holy hell if it went missing."

"You would think," Andy said as he sighed. "Then again, I think he has been a little busy with whatever is throwing things at him."

"Did it happen again?" Aiden looked over from the photos that Derrick was pouring through to look at Andy as he asked the question.

"Yeah," Andy said, nodding. "Yesterday, I was at my desk filling out some paperwork. All of a sudden, this little statue he keeps on his desk comes sailing through the window into the department. Forgot to tell you that little gem last night."

"Knowing the captain, he probably got mad at some bureaucracy and threw it himself," Cadence said, chuckling. "The man can have a temper."

"You're sure he didn't throw it himself?" It was Lauren who voiced the question.

"He was out at lunch," Andy said. "The office was empty. Keller and I both checked it out."

"Maybe after we finish up Scarecrow Farms, we can check out the police department," Derrick said with a tired grin. The grin quickly faded as he flipped to the next picture. "Oh shit."

"What?" the three breathers asked in unison.

"Oh no, I forgot," Cadence said, her tone somber.

Aiden didn't grieve for Bethany Saxon anymore. He had gotten to say goodbye to her. Cadence had helped see to that. He had even begun to feel that he could start moving on with his life and stop blaming himself for her murder. Seeing the picture of her corpse, naked and sewn back together after her autopsy, was too much for him, however.

"Excuse me," he said and rose from the table. He made his way to the small bathroom that Lauren had in the back of the store. He flipped on the light and fan as he entered it, then closed and locked the door.

"What was the about?" Andy asked, echoing the looks of confusion on Will and Sam's faces.

Derrick moved on to the next picture, in part because he didn't want to see Bethany like that, either. He kept his lips pressed together. He knew the story, but it wasn't his to tell.

"That was Bethany Saxon," Lauren said, pitching her voice so that it was quiet. "She had been a part of this group. The day she was murdered was the day that her boyfriend was going to propose to her. He was late picking her up from work because of a hold up at the jewelers where he was picking up her ring. They say that while she was waiting for him is when she was taken and killed."

"Ah," Andy said, his voice as quiet as Lauren's. "I see. Aiden's the boyfriend in question and has blamed himself."

"Yeah," Derrick said, his own answer a breathed word.

"It's taken him a long time to come back from it," Lauren said. "Not that I'm anyone who can throw stones."

"Your bathroom isn't as soundproof as you think it is," Aiden said as he came back out. He had washed his face. It was still damp, and drops of water were darkening the color of his shirt in places. "Either that or you weren't as quiet as you thought you were being."

"Sorry, Aiden," Andy said. "I had no idea."

"No worries, bro. There's no way you could have known," Aiden said, sitting back down. "I'm fine. It just threw me for a loop to see that in there."

"I can imagine," Andy said. "Lauren, do you have a copier here?"

"Yes," Lauren said with a nod.

"I'm about to do something that will get me fired if the wrong person or people find out about it," Andy said. "But I have to get this file back, and I think the information it has might prove useful to our Casper friends."

"You want me to copy the file and keep it somewhere safe," Lauren said, guessing at what he was going to ask.

"You are a smart woman," Andy said, nodding.

"Here," Derrick said. "I'll do it. Lauren isn't going to want anything to do with half of these pictures." The college student rose and went into the back office, and before long, the sound of a copier humming could be heard.

"You said when you began that Aiden already knew some of the story," Lauren said. "How did he come to know it?"

"I barged in on a date between him and the little lady from the TV show," Andy said.

"A date!" Lauren looked at Aiden with a wide smile on her face.

"Aiden had a date with Teeny?" Derrick called from the back room.

"I did not have a date with Teeny!" Aiden exclaimed it in frustration and loud enough that Derrick could hear it in the back. "She came over unexpectedly to talk about the fate of the footage from Barrington. It was pretty much just a big old arguing session. It ended when Andy showed up."

"So, a date," Lauren said with a smile and a one-shouldered shrug.

Aiden rolled his eyes and shook his head, sighing in frustration. "You guys are all awful. That's all I'm gonna say."

"Hey, it's about time you got back on that horse, right?" Lauren said, poking fun at him.

"Lauren, I love you," Aiden said. "But you are the last person to be talking about horses and getting back on them."

"I know," Lauren said. "I'm still not letting you live this down, though."

Aiden looked at Andy with a sour expression. "You just had to mention Teeny being at my place, didn't you?"

Andy spread his hands in front of him in a defensive manner. "Dude, I had no idea it was going to set this off."

Derrick walked out of the back office with the file and a separate set of papers. "Damn, I missed making fun of Aiden, didn't I?"

"I'm sure there's plenty of time left," Andy said as he stood up and took the file folder. "Thanks for this. I may hit you up to look over it again if anything comes up."

"No problem," Derrick said. "I'm going to take some time to go over this in more detail later after we finish our current case. And, of course, after I get some sleep." He added the last sentence as Lauren gave him a stern look of warning.

"Sounds good," Andy said. "I've got to get going."

"Can I ask a favor of you, Detective?" It was Lauren who spoke as they all rose.

"What is it?" Andy replied.

"Can you follow Derrick home? I just want to make sure he gets there in one piece," Lauren said, casting a concerned look at her friend.

"Sure thing," Andy said with a smile.

CHAPTER 22

The Farmhouse at Night

Aiden was in charge. Of that, there was no doubt. He, Lauren, and Derrick were joined by Teeny as they sat around the table in the back of Lauren's shop. *The Dead Show* van was parked out front with all of her and Liam's equipment in it. The sign at the front of the shop was flipped to "Closed" and the door was locked. Cadence, Will, and Sam hovered around the breathing quartet, listening to Aiden's speech as he declared as much.

"Before we get into anything else," Aiden said, "if you have a problem with me being in charge, let me know. I don't want what happened at the prison to happen tonight. Not to mention what is at the farm is stronger, according to Lauren. We don't need to be going around without a plan."

"I don't have a problem," Lauren said, shaking her head.

"Me either," Derrick and Teeny both said in unison.

"Okay," Aiden said. "Then let's get on with the planning. Teeny, what do you need to film today before we get to the farm?"

"I want to film an interview with Derrick about his research on the farm," Teeny said. "I also want to do one with Lauren about what she saw and felt when we were there during the daytime. I..." She stopped in the middle of her sentence, her eyes fixed on the door. "Oh no, what's he doing here?"

A knock sounded on the glass door of the shop, and they all turned and looked. Russell was at the door, smiling and waving.

"What the hell does this clown think he is going to do?" Sam asked.

"Maybe he can scare the non-human into behaving with his sheer amount of sleaze," Cadence said with a shrug.

"I thought he left town?" Derrick asked, obviously very puzzled at this turn of events.

Aiden grumbled. Lauren knew she heard a few words that started with the letter F in those grumblings. Ignoring Aiden, she moved to the door and unlocked it.

"Hey, you weren't starting without me, were you?" Russell asked as he stepped into the shop, moving past Lauren and heading to the back table.

"Russell." Teeny greeted him, plastering on a fake smile and trying to hide her shock and dismay at his presence. "What are you doing here? I thought you were still tied up in California." She rose and gave him a hug.

"I wasn't about to leave you here with these amateurs to get this show in the can," the producer answered. "No offense," he added, though it was clear he didn't care one iota if he gave offense or not.

"Russell, why don't you go sit with Liam? Make sure he isn't alone." Teeny was trying to get him to go away. Over the last week, she had formed a friendship with this trio. She didn't want him coming in here and ruining it.

"He's so drugged up he can't see straight, and you know it," Russell said. "You need me more than he does right now."

"We have it all pretty well in hand," Teeny said.

"Nonsense," Russell said. He waved away the notion that she and three no-name investigators could handle the filming of a television show. "I'm your producer. I'm here to produce."

"What do you think you are going to produce?" The words were out of Derrick's mouth before he could stop them.

"The television show, of course," Russell said.

"You weren't doing that during Barrington," Aiden said.

"Yes, and we see how well that went with you lot involved," Russell said.

Aiden jumped to his feet, prompting Lauren to do so as well, interposing herself between the two of them.

"Hey," she said, pitching her voice to be heard over the beginning of what Aiden was saying. "Aiden, sit down. He's needling you. Mr. Nieves, if you can't be nice, I will ask you to leave the store."

"It's not operating hours," Russell said, smiling.

"That's right," Lauren said, returning the smile. "So, the police will have even more reason to trespass you from my property. This is a private meeting. Nowhere in our contract did it stipulate that you were going to be joining us in the investigation."

"*The Dead Show* is two investigators," Russell said with a shrug. "Since Liam is unable to be here, I am taking his place. Ow!" Russell put a hand to his forehead.

Will stood beside Russell and had a thin stick in his hand. The stick was collapsible and had been in a holster on his utility belt until a minute ago. Now, in his hands, it looked like it had an electric charge to it and was at its full length.

"What?" Will asked, looking innocent as the stick returned to normal, and he began collapsing it in on itself once more. "Like you guys didn't want to do that?" Sam and Cadence had been looking at him in shock and a mix of amusement and disapproval.

"I know I wanted to," Sam said.

Cadence just shook her head and let it go. Now she knew what Snow had felt when she had allowed her temper to spur her actions.

"Problem?" Lauren asked. She had seen a light anomaly near Russell right before he reacted, and she could only imagine what had just happened.

Aiden just smirked.

"Russell, you are never there for the actual taping of the show," Teeny said. "You are going to slow us down and be in our way. Hell, we're already using up time to talk to you. I could be filming an interview right now."

"With Liam in the hospital," Russell said to Teeny, "you are my star. I need to protect you and this show."

Teeny took a deep breath and looked at Aiden, who shrugged in response. She then looked back to Russell.

"I'll relieve you of that responsibility. My contract is up in two months. I won't be renewing it. *The Dead Show* dies when I leave. You and Liam can work something else out. That's between the two of you. But I'm not coming back. This is effectively my last episode."

"Go, Teeny," Cadence said, her voice low.

Russell's jaw was on the floor. "You can't be serious," he said at length. "You've been under so much stress with the show and Liam's accident. You're not thinking clearly."

"Oh, I am so serious." Teeny laughed, even though it wasn't funny.

"It's just the shock of everything that's happened," Russell reiterated. "Once you get back home, you'll feel better, and everything will go back to normal."

"You aren't listening to me, Russell," Teeny said. "I'm done. This is the last episode, and you are not helping us in any way, shape, or form. I will get the equipment that is yours or the property of the production company back to you. As previously agreed to, Aiden and I will edit the Barrington Prison episode and get that to you. We will do the same for this show. That will be it."

Russell stood, his body stiff and his movements slow, as if he were in a daze. "Fine," he said. He then turned on his heel and walked to the door. Aiden rose, and his long legs took him past Russell in a heartbeat, beating him to the door. He unlocked it for the producer and held it open.

"Goodbye, Mr. Nieves," Aiden said.

Russell stopped, opened his mouth to say something, then closed it again. He walked out without another word.

Aiden closed and locked the door behind him. He stood at the door to make sure that Russell had driven off without messing with their cars. He returned to the table to find Derrick and Lauren had gone to the back room and were making coffee. Teeny was standing beside the table.

"Do not make me regret that," Teeny said.

"That was you agreeing to not air the footage that shows the ghosts, right?" Aiden had to ask; he didn't want to assume.

"Yes," Teeny replied with a nod and a small smile.

"Thank you," Aiden said with a smile as a huge sense of relief washed over him.

"Snow will be relieved to hear that," Cadence said.

Teeny climbed on top of the chair she had been sitting on, and Aiden chuckled.

"What are you doing?" Aiden asked.

"This," she said and leaned over, kissing him.

Aiden was shocked, and it took a moment for him to respond. After that moment, he started kissing her back, wrapping his arms around her small frame. They broke the kiss when Lauren cleared her throat, and she and Derrick set down coffee mugs on the table.

"Thought I heard horses," Lauren said, her voice quiet, but Aiden heard her nonetheless.

"Like I said," Teeny said to Aiden, "don't make me regret this." She climbed back down from her chair and then sat in it. "So, let's get this game plan going."

The white skeleton of the farmhouse looked more imposing than before. It sat amid the wild, tall grass in the yellow-orange light of the winter afternoon. The rumbling engines of both vans cut off almost in unison as the vehicles parked in the side yard at the back of the house. It was late afternoon, but already the sun was inching ever closer to the line of treetops at the back of the property. Derrick and Aiden got out of Aiden's van while Lauren and Teeny got out of *The Dead Show* van.

Aiden wasted no time in moving to the back of the van and throwing open its doors. Derrick waited for the women to join him before ambling to the back of the van as well.

"Okay, we'll do a quick piece on camera for Teeny before we lose all of the light," Aiden said. "Then we're going to do three separate vigils. The house first, then the shed, and then the circle."

"Yes," they answered in unison. They had already been over the plan at the shop before they left. They all knew that no one was allowed to go off alone after what had happened to Liam. Aiden had been adamant that he didn't want to spend more than a few hours here tonight.

"Derrick, you and Teeny go set up for her intro. Lauren and I will get the rest of the equipment ready to go," Aiden said.

"I don't think I have ever seen him this wound up before," Cadence said. The ghosts had ridden along with the breathers from the store.

"He's not always like this? This intense?" Will looked at Cadence as he asked the question.

"No, he's an even-tempered guy most of the time," Cadence said. "Derrick is always the 'laid-back, hey, this is fun' person. Lauren tends to be the stricter one."

"I guess what happened at the prison changed his outlook," Sam said.

"So, it would seem," Cadence said. "Will, why don't you take point on Teeny and Derrick, make sure nothing goes haywire over there, okay?"

"Sure thing," Will said with a nod. He was over by the breathers in an instant as they set up their shot at the front of the house.

"How are you adjusting?" Sam asked his sister as they oversaw Lauren and Aiden setting up.

"What, to Will?" Cadence looked at her brother as she answered his question with a question and then shrugged. "He's fine. I mean, he's not Snow. He's not Andy. But I think he's going to be great. He just needs to get used to doing this. He has fantastic ideas. He comes up with all these gadgets. I think I'm going to start calling Q from *James Bond*." She added the last with a grin.

"I thought the age difference might have been an issue," Sam said.

"I'm not going to lie; it was at first," Cadence admitted, shrugging. "But then again, anyone who knows me knows I wasn't going to be happy with anyone they sent in at first. Change and I don't get along. Add to that the fact that he looks like he can't drive, let alone shave. Yeah, I was judgmental and bitchy with him. But he's earned my trust, Sam."

"And that's high praise coming from you." Sam smiled.

Whitfield joined them, popping in beside them. He looked harried and confused.

"Snow said you guys needed me for a case?" Whitfield asked as he came over to them. He looked around, taking in where they were, and he paled. "Why are we *here*?"

Cadence lifted a brow, noticing the emphasis on the last word. "I never thought I would say this, and I'm not going for the pun here, but you look like you saw a ghost."

Whitfield looked back at Cadence. "No, I… I'm fine. Just confused. And this place looks a little scarier than anything I've seen."

"Oh, weird, it sounded like you knew where we are. Well, we can use your expertise," Cadence said. She had filled Sam in on their plan to bring Whitfield back. To see how he reacted to this place. "There's a non-human, big ugly thing, living on the second floor of the farmhouse there. And the added fun of a ritual circle in one of the back fields in case we thought we might get bored."

Whitfield chuckled and relaxed just a touch. Cadence was her usual joking self. The weirdness he had felt a few days ago from her must have just been due to the changing situation in the office. At least, that was what he hoped.

"Is there a plan?" Whitfield asked.

"Aiden has a plan," Cadence said. "I'm just not sure if any of the ghosts, non-humans, or anything else that is here will follow it. Right now, they are having Teeny film an intro to this place. They are using footage from this investigation for an episode of the television show. They plan on doing the house first, then the shed, then the circle."

"Do we have a plan?" Whitfield asked, casting a glance over at the house.

"Try to make sure everyone comes out of this in one piece," Cadence said.

"Okay, then," Whitfield said.

Derrick and Teeny trudged back over through the tall grass with the camera they had been using. Derrick strapped the tripod back into its place in the van and nodded to Aiden. For his part, Aiden handed each of them a camcorder and the bag it went in.

"Each bag has two flashlights, an audio recorder, an EMF reader, and batteries," Aiden said. "Right now, I have the spirit box on me."

"Okay," Teeny sighed, her apprehensiveness obvious. "Let's get this episode in the can so we can all get on with our lives."

The group of breathers and ghosts together made their way into the house. The more solid ones of the group made sure to avoid the spongy spots of wood on the rotting back porch. Derrick held the flashlight in the growing twilight as Aiden pulled the keys out of his pocket and opened the door to the kitchen.

"We're entering the kitchen, which is the room at the very back of the house," Teeny said, her camera already on and recording.

"Oh, Will," Cadence said, a thought occurring to her.

"What's up?" Will looked over at Cadence.

"Aiden has a thing on him called a spirit box. It will pick up our voices, so don't talk at all. Not even to me. Not even in a whisper, if you can help it at all," Cadence said. She had forgotten to warn him about the device prior. She had been so used to being with Snow and his hatred of that instrument. It just now hit her that Will wouldn't know to zip his lips during one of those sessions.

"Got it," Will said, giving a nod and a thumbs up.

"Due to the floors rotting out we're not going into this next area," Teeny said. She moved to the edge of the kitchen by the alcove and tilted her camera to see the room and the bathroom. "This is where the last resident murdered his wife. From the police reports at the time, she was leaving the bathroom when he shot her with his rifle. She was the first to die that day, but not the last." She panned down to show the hole in the floor, so viewers could see why they weren't trying to traverse the area. She then turned and headed back to the trio, giving them a nod.

The group had waited for her to show this to her camera. After she had it, they all left the kitchen and made their way along the hall. They passed by both the staircase that went up and the door to the basement as they made their way into the living room.

"Aiden," Teeny said, panning her camera to the man. "Would you like to explain to the viewers why we aren't going up the stairs we just passed?"

Aiden wasn't thrilled about being on camera again, but he knew it couldn't be helped. "The wood on the stairs is a little too soft for my liking. Rot has taken hold, more so near the top of the stairs. There is a huge hole in the roof that has been letting in rain and snow for God knows how long. I don't want anyone hurt, so we're not going up there."

"Normally, on *The Dead Show,* we don't shun a little danger," Teeny said. "But that proved to be foolish when Liam last investigated. So, we're going to be cautious tonight. This place has been abandoned for a long time and has a lot of decay."

They sat down on the floor of the living room and began setting up. Aiden pulled out the spirit box and set it on the floor in between all of them. After a moment,

Lauren had her camcorder in one hand and her audio recorder in the other. Derrick had his camera sitting on the floor beside him, aimed at the spirit box. In one of his hands, he had the EMF detector; in the other was a thermal imaging still camera. Teeny recorded nonstop as they all pulled their things out of their bags. Their flashlights provided meager light in the darkness of the house, so her camera was filming in Night Vision mode.

They sat in silence for a moment as Lauren closed her eyes and centered herself. The moldy, dusty smell of the remains of the carpet they sat on filled their noses. Sam was standing right behind Lauren, extending his own aura around her to protect her, and his eyes were open. He was watching for any little abnormality that might try to take advantage of his charge in her vulnerable state.

"I am calling out to the human spirits in this house," Lauren said, her voice strong in the silence around them. "We are not here to hurt you. We want to communicate with you. We want to help you if we can. Please come forward."

Will and Cadence were opposite Sam and Lauren, keeping watch over the room and the breathers in it. Whitfield was a little to the left of them, nearer to the alcove entrance. He kept looking up anxiously. Teeny had her camera trained on Lauren. Aiden and Derrick were looking around, straining their ears for any sound that might indicate a presence answering Lauren's call.

"Ronnie or Renee Phillips, are you here?" she asked. Thanks to Sam, she knew they were still around. However, she would maintain that she got the information about their names from the articles that Derrick had dug up about the incident.

Sam felt the shift first, a heaviness that felt like it was pressing down on them from upstairs. Ronnie's small head peeked around the doorway, his eyes round as saucers. Sam offered the boy a smile and a nod.

"What are you letting them do?" Ronnie yelped.

Cadence motioned to the boy to lower his voice as the kid ran toward Sam.

"I'm not gonna be quiet, lady! What she's doing is bad," Ronnie said in defiance to Cadence.

"Someone's here," Lauren said. "A young soul. Ronnie… I think this is Ronnie."

"You've got to stop them. You're making it angry," Ronnie said, pointing upstairs.

"Ronnie," Lauren said. "We're going to turn on a device that can make it so that we can hear your voice. I can sense you're upset. Tell us what we can do to help you move on from this terrible place."

On cue, Aiden turned on the spirit box in front of him. The house filled with the sound of static.

"Stop!" Ronnie yelled, and he himself stopped when he heard his voice echoing back to him in a staccato, static-laden version of itself. His eyes got big again, and he clapped a hand over his mouth. He looked at Cadence in sudden understanding of why she had been trying to shush him.

"Stop what, Ronnie?" Derrick asked.

"Why are you so frightened?" Lauren asked, able to sense how the spirit was feeling. "Are you in danger?"

Ronnie looked between Sam and Cadence. He was trying to figure out how he could make them all go away without having that thing pick up his voice again.

That thought was shoved out of his head, however, when a deep, growl-like laughter came from the spirit box on the floor. Will looked at Cadence and opened his mouth, but she put a finger to her lips, reminding him to be quiet.

Sam held up one finger to the child and mouthed "One word" to him.

"Shed," Ronnie said. His word reverberated in the static filling the room.

Without warning, the house shook, and bits of plaster rained down from the ceiling.

"What the hell?" Derrick said, looking around them. His flashlight danced one way, then the other, as he tried to see what might have caused that.

"Run!" Ronnie screamed before disappearing.

"Lauren," Aiden said. "I think we should take the dead kid's advice." Another sound of burbling, growling laughter came from the spirit box, and Aiden turned it off without waiting for whatever was laughing to finish.

Wind began to rise within the walls of the house, and Derrick wrinkled his nose.

"Ugh, what is that smell?" Derrick asked, pulling the turtleneck of his shirt up over his nose in an effort to hide from the stench.

"That's what we smelled upstairs when we were here before," Aiden said.

"Except it's stronger this time," Teeny grumbled, and she gagged.

There was a sound like something heavy was being dragged across the wood floor upstairs. Bits of plaster from the ceiling began to rain down on them like artificial snow.

"Let's go." Lauren had stood and gotten her things together.

"Do we go upstairs to try to stop that thing, or do we go with them?" Will looked between Cadence and Sam as he asked the question.

"We go with them," Cadence said. She looked around for a moment. "Where the hell did Whitfield go?"

"I'm here," Whitfield said, appearing beside them. His right hand had a good grip on his left arm above the shoulder. "I went upstairs to take a look at the non-human you said was up there."

"Found it, huh?" Cadence could hear the sarcasm in her voice, but she didn't care. "How bad are you hurt?"

"We should do this outside," Sam said, urging them to follow the breathers, who were already in the kitchen.

The house shook once more in time with another sliding thump from the second floor. The breathers wasted no time leaving the house and heading back to the vans with the ghosts hot on their heels.

"Show me the arm, Whitfield," Cadence said once they were out of the house.

"What happened?" Sam and Will both asked the question at the same time.

"I was stupid," Whitfield said. "I got brave and stupid. I went up there to try to talk with it, to reason with it. That one isn't going to be reasoned with." He lowered his hand and revealed a tear in his long-sleeved shirt.

Silvery blood was soaking the fabric around the tear and spilling from the flesh within.

"Sam," Cadence said. "Can you suggest to Lauren that they take five and catch their breath for a few, watch what happens with the house?"

"I'll try," Sam said. He nodded to his sister and then moved to Lauren.

"Did it bite you? Scratch you?" Cadence was trying to get Whitfield to be more open about what had happened upstairs. A part of her wondered if he had perhaps done it to himself to throw suspicion off since he had disappeared without a word.

"Scratched," Whitfield said. "It's got nasty claws. We've got to get them out of here. This place is not safe for anyone. Us or them."

Cadence ripped off the bottom half of his sleeve and wrapped the fabric around his wound, tying it tight. "I'm getting that impression," she said. "But they're obligated to do this investigation. No turning back just yet. It's up to us to keep them safe."

Whitfield looked at his now bandaged arm and then at Cadence. "Thanks. There are some things we are going to have to talk about later."

"You think?" The words were out of Cadence's mouth before she could stop them.

Whitfield paled again. Cade's words confirmed to him that she knew something was up—that he couldn't hide any longer.

"Guys," Will said, "they're moving again." Will had drifted away from Cadence and Whitfield to give the two room to talk. He had stayed close enough to keep an eye on them, however, in case Whitfield decided to try his luck against Cadence. Will was betting on his partner to hand Whitfield his ass if that happened. He just wanted to be close enough to see it happen.

Sure enough, the breathers were beginning to head away from the parked vans and make their way through the tall grass toward the shed.

"Come on," Cade said. "Are you good enough to keep going for now?" He had helped her in the beginning. She was holding tight to his earlier good deeds with them to get her through this. She kept reminding herself that he was neutral and that he had helped them quite a lot before. He was the one who had given her that first dagger.

Whitfield nodded, pressing his lips together in determination and pain, and moved to follow.

Aiden had the key to the shed in his hand. Derrick was shining his flashlight so that Aiden could see what he was doing as he attempted to unlock the shed. The key turned, and Aiden pulled on the padlock. It fell off, and Aiden let it land in the grass at his feet. The thump when it hit the ground was audible.

"That's the first challenge," Aiden said in a murmuring voice. He took a deep breath and seemed to hold it as he pulled on the door.

There was a grudging creak of the hinges. The tall, tangled grass pulled at the door as Aiden pulled it open, but it did open this time.

"I guess the termites decided to stop holding hands this time," Derrick said.

"No kidding," Teeny said, chuckling.

Aiden switched his camera from night vision to normal and put the camera's light on. He then took his flashlight from where he had tucked it into his belt and switched it on, illuminating the shed.

The camera panned left, revealing a huge wooden tool bench running the five-foot length from the door to the wall. It looked old and handmade. Rusted coffee cans held tools that were in a smidgen better shape than the cans they lived in. A handful of dirty glass mason jars, all left open, held nails and screws of various sizes. There were splatters and stains of darker brown mixed in with the rust and dirt.

An antique cultivator sat against the side wall, the wheel of blades facing into the shed instead of the wall. Above it, the wall was lined with hooks that kept a number of handheld farming implements off the ground. The back wall had another workbench. This one had a built-in vise at one end.

"This doesn't look like a fun house for a torturer or anything," Cadence commented in a sour tone. She was standing in the middle of the shed, looking around as Aiden passed the light and his camera over the area.

"Where are they?" Sam said, looking around.

"Who?" Whitfield asked the question as he stood outside.

"The kids," Sam said, looking over at Whitfield as he answered. "Ronnie and Renee."

"Lauren, Teeny, this is where the kids were killed by their dad," Aiden said. "Why don't you two go in and see if you can get anything? Keep lights on. I don't want either of you walking into something sharp and rusty, and there is a ton of that in there. Derrick and I will stay out here while you two try to make contact."

"I thought you didn't want to split up," Lauren said as Teeny walked fearlessly into the shed.

"We will be three feet away," Derrick said. "If that. This isn't splitting up. This is being on the other side of a door from each other."

"And no one is alone," Aiden said.

"We're here," Ronnie and a little girl that had to be his sister emerged from beneath the tool bench. Ronnie was holding the little girl's hand.

While Ronnie looked at Sam and the others in apprehension, the girl, who was maybe five or so, looked outright terrified. She kept tugging on her brother's hand to go back to their hiding spot beneath the tool bench.

"You two stay with them," Will said to Sam and Cadence. "We'll stay out here with the guys."

"Be careful," Cadence said, her eyes on Will as she said it.

"We will," Whitfield said. "You, too."

"Be careful," Aiden said to Lauren. "Just yell if there's trouble." They nodded to each other, and then Aiden closed the door.

"Now what, boss man?" Derrick asked as they took a few steps away from the shed.

"Now I call to see if we can get that back-up we were hoping for," Aiden said. "I'd feel a lot better if he were here."

"Back-up?" Derrick looked at Aiden in curiosity for a moment, then nodded. "Oh, I gotcha."

Aiden nodded to Derrick, lifting the phone to his ear after dialing a number.

Lauren had her flashlight in one hand as she set the camcorder she had down on the bench. This sent the spirit of the little girl scurrying to the other side of her brother to avoid the mortal woman. Lauren flipped the screen over so they could see it from their side of the camera.

"Is that good?" Lauren said, asking Teeny.

"Looks perfect," Teeny said with a nod and a smile. "I don't want to get in your way while you do your thing, so what works for you?"

"There's not a ton of room in here," Lauren said. "Not a lot of options for you to go anywhere." She added the last with a chuckle.

"You told us to come to the shed. Here we are," Lauren said. She was addressing the spirit she hoped was in the shed with them.

"Why did you tell them to come here?" Sam asked, looking at Ronnie.

"It's safer than the house," Ronnie said with a shrug. "I wanted to get them out of the house and away from the thing that lives there."

Renee began tugging on her brother's sleeve. "Hide, we need to hide," she said, her voice an agitated whisper. "She's bringing him."

"Who?" Ronnie and Sam both asked the question in unison.

"Daddy," Renee said, tears welling up in her eyes.

"It's okay," Sam said, kneeling on the ground beside the kids. "He can't hurt you. I'll protect you."

"So will I," Cadence said. "My brother and I aren't going to let anything more happen to you two." She mentioned that Sam was her brother in the hopes that it might calm the girl down—that she would see another set of spirit siblings there, ready to fight for them. For a split second, Cadence's play seemed to work. Then a breeze picked up inside the shed, and Cade's house of cards fell. The girl let out a frightened squeal and dove back under the bench.

Lauren felt the familiar pull on her senses. Part of her screamed against it, not wanting to see anything else awful that happened here. Another part of her knew that the children's story had to be heard by someone.

"With what I saw in the house the other day when we were here, I know that the wife was killed by a rifle in that downstairs bathroom," Lauren said. "I saw it happen. I saw the blood."

Teeny trained her camera on the psychic as she spoke. She noted a couple of light anomalies close to the tool bench, one zipping under the tool bench as a soft cry was heard.

"The husband then came into the children's bedroom, which was the room off of the living room in the house," Lauren said. She remembered the shadow man coming into the room and shooting at the children. "The children escaped out of the window by the fireplace and came here."

Lauren was rocking back and forth on her feet a little as she spoke. Teeny started to reach out to steady her, but then stopped, as she wasn't sure whether touching the older woman would interrupt her visions.

"The children are here," Lauren said. "Ronnie and Renee. They hid under the tool bench to escape their father. He knew their hiding place, though."

In her mind's eye, she could see the shadow man that had been the children's father enter the shed. Warm afternoon light streamed in behind him in the vision. A growl could be heard coming from him, which elicited whimpers and cries from the girl. He turned, and the thundering cracks from the rifle shots sent birds in the nearby trees flying.

The spirit of the little girl left the tool bench and moved to Ronnie, who had moved closer to Sam. Sam hugged the children tightly while Cadence put herself between them and the door. Lauren had been saying what she was seeing. The memory of it had terrified the children, which was understandable. What Cadence didn't understand was why there was a breeze inside the shed when it had been a calm night outside. The shed was close enough to the trees that if it had been windy outside, she would have heard the leaves rustling.

In Lauren's vision, the shadow man became less dark. He crumpled to the earthen floor of the shed. He let out a howl of anger and grief as he came to his senses now that the non-human influence had left him. He picked up the bloody form of his daughter, a gory red hole now marring her pink sundress. He put her back down, anguish in his voice as he cried and protested what had just happened. He reached out toward the corpse of his son, but half of the child's head was gone. It was splattered against the leg of the tool bench and the wall.

Lauren staggered back from the visceral scene, closing her eyes against it, but it lingered in her mind. Closing her eyes only brought everything into sharper focus. She could hear the pained denials of the father even louder. She could see the gore in more detail. She could smell the blood, and she could taste bile as her gorge rose because of it all.

Sam felt Lauren's distress, and he had to disengage himself from the children in order to go to her. Teeny reached out at the same time, seeing the trouble Lauren was having. Both touched her simultaneously. The shock of the physical and spiritual touch at the same time drove the vision from her head and the strength from her legs. Lauren fell to her knees, dry heaving and crying.

"Lauren?" It was Aiden's voice from outside.

Renee ran past Cadence to the door and grabbed the latch on the door.

Teeny crouched down next to Lauren. "What can I do to help?"

Sam was standing next to Lauren, extending his aura to surround Lauren.

"Lauren?" Aiden said again. The door was wiggling as he pulled on it from outside, but it wasn't opening.

"She doesn't like letting people in here," Ronnie said to Cadence with a shrug as he looked at her.

Renee was using all the spiritual might in her tiny form to hold the door closed.

"This must be what happened the other day," Cadence said in a murmur. She moved to the child and put a comforting hand on her back. "Renee, it's okay. They aren't going to hurt you. They want to make sure their friend is all right."

Renee frowned at Cadence but relented, letting go of the latch. The door swung open, and Aiden ran in. Derrick stayed by the door, holding it open since the shed was at capacity.

"I'm okay." Lauren's voice was shaky. "I just had another one of those visions. I made the mistake of closing my eyes, and it got so strong I could smell the blood."

"Are you sure you're okay?" Aiden was frowning. If she had fallen just a few more inches to the side, the blades of the cultivator would have caught her. He wasn't going to point that out, however.

"Yeah," Lauren said. Teeny and Aiden helped her up, and Sam stayed with her, trying to help her steady herself once more.

"Would you two like to stop running from the bad spirits that are here?" Cadence said, looking at the children.

"Can we?" Renee said, looking up at Cadence as she asked the question. It was the first time she had addressed anyone other than her brother.

Lauren began recounting her vision to Aiden and to Teeny's camera, trying to keep the descriptions as PG as possible for the show. She knew someone had to be the voice for the children, to say what had happened. Someone had to be a voice for the father, too, who had been so consumed with grief after the inhuman spirit had released its hold on him.

"I happen to know a super nice lady. She would love to help the two of you get settled in a safe, happy place," Cadence said. She was hoping to distract the children from Lauren's words.

"Are there toys there?" Ronnie said, moving to stand beside his sister.

"If there aren't, we will bring you some," Will said as he entered the shed. "You just let us know."

The three breathers were leaving the shed with Sam in tow. Cadence looked at the two children with a smile, then back at Will.

"Are you and Whitfield okay if I take a couple of minutes to get these two to Bethany?" Cadence knew her priority was here. However, she couldn't just leave the kids there to face their deaths and their fear of where they were over and over again. They'd already been in that hell for over forty years.

"We're good," Will said with a nod.

"Come on," Cadence said to the kids, and each of them took a hand. "Bethany is kind of like an angel. She will take good care of you guys." With that, Cadence teleported herself and the young siblings to Bethany's office.

CHAPTER 23

All Hell Breaking Loose

"**E**verything okay?" Cadence asked Will and Whitfield as she reappeared beside them.

"Is Bethany taking care of the kids?" Whitfield asked the question as Will gave her a thumbs up.

"Yeah, I walked them right in to her office," Cadence said. "I'm just glad she was free. Why are we back at the house?"

They were all back in the living room of the house. Aiden was at the door to the basement, which was open, and he was shining his flashlight down. Sam was still encompassing Lauren in his aura, trying to keep her safe.

"Andy?" Aiden said, calling down.

Cadence snapped her attention to the doorway. "What happened? Why is he down there?"

"Aiden called him while you guys were in the shed," Will said. "He was curious why the detective hadn't shown up yet."

"Except he had shown up when we were all at the shed," Whitfield said, taking over the answer. "Andy came into the house thinking they would be in here. He's now stuck downstairs."

"Yeah, yeah, I'm here," came Andy's irritated voice from the basement.

"Why is he… never mind, stay here," Cadence said and disappeared from the living room. She reappeared in the basement next to Andy.

The light from Aiden's flashlight was shining down on him in the dark. The beam of light was weak and chasing away just the shadows closest to the detective. The light also revealed that the weak steps that Derrick and Lauren had noted the other day had broken under Andy. There were two steps left at the top and the bottom step on the floor of the basement. Everything else had broken off and fallen in large splintery shards to the floor.

The gap between the two parts of the stairs was too big for Andy to jump.

"Are you hurt?" Aiden said as he called down to Andy.

"My pride, more than anything," Andy said in retort. "Please tell me you guys have a rope or something."

"On it," Derrick said.

"Teeny go with him, please," Aiden said, still adamant about no one going anywhere alone.

"Yep," Teeny chirped in reply and moved to catch up with Derrick.

"What happened, bro?" Aiden kept his camera trained on Andy. "Other than the obvious answer of the stairs giving way. Why did you come in here?"

Andy sighed, still sounding annoyed. "When I got here, I thought I heard voices in here. It wasn't a long shot to think you guys would still be poking around in the house. So, I came in the back. I called out, and I could have sworn I heard you calling me from the basement. I was on the stairs when you called my phone. I guess staying still on the steps to answer the call was too much, and down I went."

"I wondered what the crash was," Aiden said. "Now I know. Are you sure you're not hurt? Bleeding? Broken bones?"

"Naw, man, I'm good," Andy said. "Bumps and bruises, nothing that won't heal up quick."

"Guess it's a good thing I called when I did," Aiden said.

"You should have called them when you got here, dumb ass," Cadence said, shaking her head. She knew he couldn't hear her, but she still had to say it. She then teleported back up to the living room.

Derrick and Teeny ran back in, and Derrick handed Aiden a coiled, bright orange extension cord. "No rope, sorry," he said.

"Checked my van, too, same thing," Teeny said. "It's all electronics and cords, no mountain climbing gear."

"Okay, we'll have to make this work," Aiden said.

A light breeze began to pick up in the living room. It brought with it that same stench of rotting meat and hot garbage.

"Quickly," Lauren said, covering her nose and mouth from the smell.

A sliding sound and then a thump came from right above them near the stairs.

"No pressure," Aiden said with a grumble.

"What was that thump?" Andy was asking the question as he watched Aiden uncoil the cord.

"Oh, you know, ghosts," Teeny replied, trying to sound nonchalant.

"I am guessing that they are not the good kind," Andy grumbled.

Teeny took Aiden's camera from where he had placed it on the floor. That way, she could film while Aiden concentrated on rescuing Detective Halleran from the basement. "I'm not sure where you're tying that off," she said. She was looking around the room for something to use as an anchor.

"Tie it around that oven in the kitchen. It's old, should weigh a good bit," Aiden said.

"Teeny and I can go sit on it, too," Lauren said. "My weight can add to it, and Teeny can just keep me company. That way, no one is alone."

Aiden frowned, but nodded. "You two tie it off as tight as you can," he instructed. "Derrick and I will help Andy up."

"And this is where climbing a rope in gym class comes in handy," Andy said from below them.

There was another thump from upstairs, this time louder. The banister of the steps to the second floor shook from the vibration. Lauren and Teeny hurried to the kitchen with the plug end of the extension cord. Sam went with them.

"Will, go with them, too. That way, if anything happens, you can help, if need be," Whitfield said. "I'll stay with Cade."

Cadence gave Whitfield a quizzical look as Will left them.

"I thought you might feel better if it wasn't me assigned to your brother this time." Whitfield said with a shrug.

Cadence realized that Whitfield wasn't wrong. She did feel better that he was with her, where she could keep an eye on him.

Another thump shook the house, this time sounding like it was on the stairs. The stairs creaked as if under a great deal of weight in response. Whitfield moved, placing himself between the main stairs and the stairs that descended into the basement. Cadence frowned. She had gotten used to thinking that Whitfield might be one of the bad guys. This white knight effort he was making was challenging that thought process.

"Look out below," Aiden called. He then began dropping the cord down into the basement. Foot by foot, it descended until Andy caught the large end of it in his hands. He guided the cord down further until he could get his feet on the bottom plug.

"Right there," Andy said. "It's tied off, right?" The last thing he wanted was to fall on his ass again.

"Ladies, are we good?" It was Derrick who called the question out. There was an immediate thump on the stairs in answer. The smell intensified, and Derrick coughed, his lungs and nose objecting to the odor.

"Good to go," Teeny said, yelling back to them.

"Come on up, Andy," Aiden said. His eyes were beginning to water from the stench.

Both Aiden and Derrick had a strong hold on the cord as it went taut under Andy's weight. Derrick and Aiden each braced a foot against either side of the door frame. Andy was swift to climb. He was just a couple of feet from being able to grab on to the top steps when something grabbed him from below. He paused for just a second, long enough to look down.

"Get me the hell out of here," Andy said, bellowing.

"Be right back," Cadence said to Whitfield, hearing the tone of fear in Andy's voice.

Teleporting to the basement, Cadence understood why Andy had the tone he did. The spirit, if that's what it was, was visible to him. To say it was grotesquely twisted was an understatement. It had elongated arms and legs that twisted over and back on themselves. Each limb had far more joints than it should have. Its wrinkled, leathery gray face had red eyes and a mouth that was gaping open wider than one would think possible. There were no teeth or tongue visible, just an impossible black void behind those cracked, dry gray lips. Its hands were wrapped around one of Andy's calves, brittle nails breaking as it tried to claw through the man's jeans.

There were no quips to get the thing's attention, no name-calling. Cadence had one of the jacks that Will had made in her hand. She didn't risk a throw. Instead, she slammed it into the creature's side and was quick to skip back. The thing screamed and released Andy's leg to claw at the small item lodged in it.

Andy wasted no time as it released him and scrambled the rest of the way up the cord. Derrick and Aiden held out their hands to him. He used their help to get onto the floor and away from the dark gaping maw of the basement. Cadence teleported up, away from whatever was in the basement. She felt a little tension ease from her as she saw Andy safe, the other two men helping him steady himself. Aiden yanked the rest of the cord back up, and Cade shuddered as the end of it passed through her leg.

The door to the basement slammed shut as the thing downstairs continued to howl.

"You guys are done in the house, right?" Andy sounded hopeful as he asked the question.

"Yep," Aiden said. He grabbed the cord and didn't even bother coiling it. "Derrick, see if they need help getting the cord loose."

Derrick nodded and ran ahead, skirting the stairs up as much as he could. The stench was almost overpowering.

"What is that?" Andy asked as the smell registered as his adrenaline began to come down. He covered his nose with his arm. "I didn't smell that when I came in."

As if on cue, there was another thump, but this one didn't come from the stairs. This one was on their level, and it came from the small hallway and nook where the bathroom was.

"Are you seeing that?" Andy's eyes were locked on the dark doorway, where five cat-like glowing yellow eyes were watching them.

"Yeah," Aiden said, almost breathless. He picked up the camera Derrick had left on the floor and took a shot of it. He knew that the eyes could be debunked as lights from outside.

"Can we go now? I'm done being in here," Andy said.

"Yeah, let's go," Aiden said. He put his hand on Andy's shoulder and gave him a gentle nudge toward the kitchen.

Both men hustled, moving into the kitchen at a jog. Teeny was just beginning to coil the cord that Aiden was carrying the other end of.

"Gotta go," Aiden said. "Out, now."

"Get her out, Sam," Cadence said. "It's down here."

Sam didn't look or ask for an explanation. He conveyed the urgency to Lauren, and everyone left the house at a run.

Andy's sedan was parked behind Teeny's *The Dead Show* van. The back of Aiden's van was open. That was where they all stopped running in order to catch their breath. They were also trying to see if anything came from the house after them.

"What was that? What happened?" Teeny was looking at Aiden and Andy for answers since they were the ones who had given the orders to leave.

"Before tonight, I never would have gone on record saying a house was haunted," Andy said. "But that house is."

"Are you saying you believe in ghosts now, Detective?" It was Teeny who asked as the other three knew Andy believed in ghosts. Her camera was still rolling and pointed at him.

"Yep, yes, definitely," Andy said, nodding.

"Should we even stay to do the circle?" Derrick asked.

"We have to," Lauren said with a resigned sigh. "Russell will be apoplectic if we skip anything."

"She's right," Teeny said. "But we can be brief."

They were almost through the tree line to the field that held the stone circle when, without warning, Aiden held out a hand to stop Lauren from moving forward. He clicked off his flashlight and motioned for the others behind him to do the same. When he crouched down, the rest of the breathers followed suit. The spirits remained standing, and Aiden kept his camera recording. He was pointing the device through the tree line, filming the stone circle.

"What is it?" Lauren said, her voice a quiet whisper in the night.

Aiden pointed to the viewscreen on his camera. Something moved in the stone circle beyond the trees. A dark, solid figure was moving through the outer stones and heading for the center.

"That's too solid a figure to be a ghost," Aiden said, his voice as hushed as Lauren's was. "That's got to be a person. We're not alone," he said, adding the last with a look over his shoulder at Andy.

"This place isn't a secret," Andy said, also whispering. "It's abandoned with a bad reputation. That makes it a paradise to some people."

"So, are we just going to wait until they do whatever it is they are going to do and leave?" Teeny asked. "Or should we go down and confront them?"

Cadence frowned. "I don't like this," she said.

"I'm tempted to make a crack about you not liking anything," Whitfield said. His expression was serious. "But in this case, I think you're right." Whitfield seemed less like his wired, anxious self. He was far more grim than usual, his eyes set darkly on the circle and the figure within it.

"Will, are you and Sam good with them if we go to the circle?" Cadence said, looking at the two teens.

"We're good. They seem pretty well-behaved right now," Will said with a grin.

"Just be careful, sis," Sam said with a nod.

"You, too," Cadence said.

Cadence and Whitfield teleported down to the outside of the stone perimeter, behind the man at the center stone.

"Did Snow have time to tell you about the runes?" Cadence said, looking at Whitfield.

"No, but he didn't have to," Whitfield said.

"Well, that's something I didn't expect," Cadence said.

"What?" Whitfield looked at Cadence with curiosity. "For me to have knowledge about this place?"

"For you to share it," Cadence said.

"Since when have I not shared information with you or Snow?" Whitfield knelt to examine one of the stones on the ring's inward-facing side.

Cadence followed him into the stone circle. "I'm thinking a couple of weeks ago is a great example of that," she said. "Or when you trashed my notes," she added, making the accusation.

Whitfield was still for a moment, then rose and turned to face her. "I'm sorry about that, Cade. I really am. There's more going on than you know."

"Well, this is one hell of an interesting turn of events," a voice said from the center of the circle.

Cadence turned to see who was talking, as the voice seemed familiar. As she recognized Captain Rodriguez, her jaw dropped. "What is he doing here?" She was speaking more to herself than to Whitfield.

"I'm here to help keep a bargain," Rodriguez said. "I will say that it is good to see you, Riley. You've been missed. Even if you have been stepping on my plans from time to time."

Cadence froze, her eyes glued to her former captain in shock. "Wait, you can see me?" Her mind was whirling, trying to keep up with the jarring new situation.

"You're smarter than that," Rodriguez chided her.

Suddenly, things fell into place for Cadence. What Andy had said about the captain not reacting to a ghost attacking him. Sam saying that the guy who had been interested in Ava had recognized him and seemed familiar. Why Wolf would cut a loyal underling loose after attacking a cop.

"You're Wolf," Cadence said with a frown.

Captain Rodriguez nodded. "Correct on the first try, if a little slow to start."

"Well, since I've caught you in the mood to chat, I have questions," Cadence said. "Why did you split the investigative group between the family and the prison?"

"You know, Riley," Wolf said, taking a few steps toward her, "that was always a strength of yours I admired. Cut through whatever personal questions you might want to ask and get right down to the bones of the matter."

"So, let's get down to the bones." She crossed her arms in front of her chest. Her tone was terse, her body so tense she almost felt like she was vibrating.

"You know your biggest flaw, though?" Rodriguez said, continuing toward her.

"I'm sure you'll tell me." She sighed.

"Always thinking you have the upper hand in a situation." With his answer, Wolf snapped his fingers, and Cadence realized her mistake. The vibration feeling wasn't because she was tense. It was because the circle had been powering up, getting ready to come to life at his command. Whatever he had been doing at the center of the circle while she and Whitfield had been talking had begun powering it.

Aiden and the others had watched the black-clad figure put a sack on the center stone and stab it. Will and Sam were both trying to see what was on the viewfinder as well. The zoomed-in image was better than their sight. Sam wasn't about to leave Lauren to go protect his sister. He knew where his duties were. He also had every faith that his sister could handle whatever was going on down there. Will had promised Cadence he would stay with Sam. So, they all watched as the man sheathed the knife where the sheath was clipped to his belt. He then began speaking as he walked away from the center stone.

"Is he reciting a ritual?" Teeny asked the question in a hushed whisper.

"I don't know," Lauren said with a frown.

"Well, there's no one down there," Teeny said.

"Aiden, can you zoom in closer on him?" Andy asked, moving closer to the camera to get a better view.

Aiden zoomed in as close as he could. The camera was in night vision mode, and they were a ways off. Therefore, the closer the picture zoomed, the less detail it seemed to have. That didn't matter to Andy. Andy knew who he was looking at. The body, the carriage of the man, even the body language.

"Shit, stay here," Andy said, and began barreling through the last few trees and into the field. As he lost the cover of the trees, the circle seemed to come to life. A pale blue force was emanating from the stones on the outer ring of the circle.

"I didn't see anyone else down there before," Teeny said.

Aiden had still been zoomed in on the man in the circle. "What are you talking about?"

Lauren, Aiden, and Derrick looked to where Teeny was pointing. Aiden knew the woman all too well, though the male ghost with her he didn't know. Was he the new partner, maybe? The fact that they could see Cadence and the other man with their own eyes made his heart skip a beat.

"You guys stay here. Andy shouldn't be alone," Aiden said.

"The hell with that," Lauren said, grabbing his arm. "You and I both know who that is. None of us are staying put." She felt Sam's alarm as the young man realized his sister was visible and vulnerable. She also felt his relief when she said they were all going.

"She's right," Derrick said. "We're not leaving them."

"Okay, I'll ask, who are they?" Teeny asked the question as they all followed Andy out into the field.

"Long story," Aiden shot back, turning his head to answer her over his shoulder. "Catch up!"

Rodriguez caught movement out of the corner of his eyes. He turned his head and saw Detective Halleran barreling across the field toward him. A hundred feet or so behind was the paranormal investigation group and the small woman from the TV show.

"Well," Wolf said, giving a toothy smile to Cadence and Whitfield, "this is about to get very interesting."

"Go home, Rodriguez," Whitfield said. "This isn't the time."

Cadence lifted an eyebrow and turned to face Whitfield. "So, it is you. Shaldoxz."

"Yes," Wolf answered. "He is Shaldoxz."

"There's a yes and no answer that goes with that," Whitfield said.

"What?" Both Rodriguez and Cadence asked in unison.

Andy skidded to a halt at the edge of the circle. "Captain," he called out. "What the hell?"

Rodriguez looked over at Andy and shrugged. "This is going to put a hell of a crimp in one of our careers."

"Andy, stay out of this," Cadence said, trying to keep him safe. She then did a double take as she realized that he could see her.

"I would listen to Riley if I were you, Halleran. And you might want to tell that to your other friends, too," Rodriguez said, pointing to the others running up behind Andy. He then turned and began making his way back to the center stone as if he hadn't a care in the world.

"Does this portal go to the prison?" Cadence asked, turning to Whitfield for answers. He seemed more inclined to talk right now than Wolf did.

"It's more complicated than that," Whitfield said.

"You know me well enough to know I hate that answer," Cade said.

"You're thinking of it in too narrow a term. This isn't just a door. It's a phone," Whitfield said. "Depending on the runes activated, the intentions of the one running it, and the sacrifice used, it can go several different places."

"That makes sense," Will said from the other side of the circle.

"Stay out there," Whitfield said to both Will and Sam. "This field will fry you if you try to cross."

"To answer your question, Riley, yes, I'm opening the portal to the prison," Rodriguez said.

"Gonna be pretty disappointing for you, then," Cadence said with a note of smugness to her voice. "Pruitt's not there to run your show anymore."

That made Wolf stop and turn around.

"He's gone where?" Rodriguez asked, turning to face Cadence once more.

"A place you sure as hell can't reach him," Cade replied.

"Who is Pruitt?" Andy asked, feeling like he was playing a game of catch-up.

"Ghost at the prison," Aiden answered, his voice quiet. He knew Teeny was beside him, filming this whole thing. He also knew that Cadence and her friend were both visible and audible. The two of them were going to have a lot to discuss. If they got out of this alive, that was.

"That's not a tone I expect from you, Riley," Rodriguez said.

"Yeah, well, you aren't my boss anymore," Cadence said. "And I lose a lot of respect for a person when I find out they're the bad guy."

"Bad guy?" The look of surprise on Wolf's face was genuine.

"Yeah, bad guy," Cade said, crossing her arms over her chest once more. "Did your IQ take a nosedive after

I died or something?" She ignored the vibration of her cell phone ringing in her pocket.

"Cadence," Whitfield said, shaking his head. "This isn't black and white."

"Riley, I am not a bad guy." Rodriguez chuckled.

"Okay, putting aside everything else I can tie to you," Cadence said. "Let's start with this little party trick here." She gestured to the center stone for emphasis. "You're smuggling the spirits of prisoners out of the prison and using them to possess bodies like Overton did with Caulfield."

"Riley, you, of all people, should see what I'm doing as a good thing," Wolf said. Then a thought occurred to him, and he looked at Whitfield. "She doesn't know, does she?"

"You're not getting what you're after tonight, Wolf," Whitfield said. "Just let it go. Bring down the circle."

"You've had her trust all of this time, but you've never told her?" Rodriguez was beginning to get angry at Shaldoxz. He couldn't fathom why the non-human was trying to hide his identity and intentions from Riley.

Birds exploded from the treetops behind them. Their caws of protest at being startled followed them as they flew off. There was a loud snap of wood, and something crashed in the small forest. Everyone, breather and ghost alike, turned toward the tree line.

"Open the circle," Whitfield said, his voice a sharp command. Whitfield's body transformed. Gone was the mild-mannered, unassuming, and harried middle-aged man with wild hair. That visage was replaced by a new one.

Whitfield was not a form kept in shadows, as Rodriguez was used to seeing him, either. He changed into something no one had seen in well over a hundred years. Whitfield, Shaldoxz, whatever his real name was, looked like he was half man, half goat. The legs were those of a goat, complete with fur. The torso and arms were that of a man. The neck changed near the head. The head itself was a goat-like form, complete with strange brown eyes, a muzzle, and horns.

"What the hell?" It was almost a unanimous saying that went up from everyone except Rodriguez and Cadence.

"Your plans," Wolf began.

"Will wait," came Whitfield's voice from the strange mouth. "Open the circle. These people need safety."

Rodriguez looked at Shaldoxz with uncertainty.

"Do it," Whitfield said, the bellowing of the order sounding more animalistic the louder the voice got.

Rodriguez turned to do as Shaldoxz asked. Just then, the non-human from the second floor of the farmhouse crashed through the tree line. Its huge body didn't stop when there were no more trees in front of it. The tarry, slick blackness of its skin glistened in the moonlight, and it was visible to everyone as it was using so much energy. The five yellow eyes all blinked at different intervals as it galloped toward the circle.

Rodriguez saw what was coming at them and ran the last few paces to the center stone. "Scatter," he yelled, wanting the rest of them to get out of harm's way. The non-human was too fast, though.

It took it just a few more galloping leaps to reach the circle. Sam stood in between the creature and Lauren, whom the thing had been making a beeline for. Her power made her the juiciest morsel on the field. X'Haldzos took no notice of Sam, but the force of his being sent the young guardian flying. Sam stopped only when his body slammed against the energy field of the circle.

Sam shrieked in agony as Cadence yelled his name. She took one step toward her brother. Whitfield's hand caught her arm in a strong grip. She would never have guessed at such strength from the entity she had once thought of mild-mannered. He shook his head at her as he held her still. She looked back at her brother once more, watching as he vaporized into ash. His echoing scream hung in the air for a moment more.

"Sam!" Cadence screamed. The sound of her heart breaking was evident as she dropped to her knees.

"Lauren," Aiden yelled.

The energy of the force field fell.

The shock of Sam and his protective energy being torn from her had caused the psychic to fall to her knees. The non-human wasted no time in grabbing her up in its taloned fingers and squeezing. The snap of her ribs was audible. It threw her with all of its might toward the center of the circle. Its aim was true. Lauren's head cracked like a melon on the center stone. Rodriguez backed away at a run, tripping over one of the outer stones as he did.

Will was throwing his jacks, trying to stop the thing, trying to get it to pay attention to him. The toys were ineffective against the entity, however, and just bounced off its skin. When Will ran out of jacks, he ran into the circle and grabbed the pouch off Cadence's belt. Cadence was still staring at the place in the air where her brother had been, her mind numb.

Whitfield shook Cade's arm. "Cadence," he yelled, having morphed back into the form she knew.

She looked at Whitfield, her expression blank for a moment. Then her eyes burned with anger, and she ripped her arm from his grip. She ran out of the circle to Will, sliding to a stop beside him.

"The jacks should have worked," Will said in disbelief.

"Get them out of here, Andy," Cadence said in a yell. Aiden and Derrick went to see if they could help Lauren, despite both men knowing it was a lost cause.

"Oh my God," Teeny said, her voice small and quiet. Her eyes focused on the blood pouring down the center stone from Lauren's broken head.

The creature let out a bellow and used one talon to flick Lauren's corpse from the stone. The circle hummed to life once more. The portal opened, and the creature issued a rumble. White light poured from the tear in the planes of existence, forcing everyone else to look away. The light disappeared, and it took with it X'Haldzos.

Andy had his cell phone out of his pocket. 9-1-1 had already answered. Rodriguez was nowhere to be seen. Aiden and Derrick were kneeling beside Lauren's crumpled body. Aiden was crying. Derrick was numb. Teeny was standing behind Aiden, her hand on his back, trying to console him as best she could in the moment.

Whitfield walked over to Cadence. "Before you start," he said, holding up his hands as if to shield himself from the unrelenting fury in her eyes. "This was never meant to happen. I'll come with you and explain everything."

"I don't care what you had meant to happen," Cadence said, her voice quiet but shaking.

"Just go back, dude," Will said. He put his hand on Cadence's shoulder in support. "You don't have any friends here right now."

Whitfield looked between Cadence and Will, then nodded and disappeared.

Not So Happily Ever After

Whitfield, Snow, and Ramon were in the office that Cadence and Will shared when the two of them returned. An ambulance had come to the field and collected Lauren's body. Whatever had happened when the non-human left the field through the portal, it had rendered Will and Cadence invisible to the breathers again. Something that had been remarked upon by Teeny and Andy.

As they arrived at their office, Cadence took one look at the faces of the three men and nodded. "So, you know," she said, her voice flat.

"Cadence, I'm so sorry," Snow said. "I know what he meant to you."

"We all know," Ramon said. He took a few steps toward her, but Cadence held up her hand to stop him.

"Not right now," she said.

Ramon took a step back. He had seen her depressed. He had seen her angry. The level of fury that was evident on her face he had never seen from her before.

Cadence swung her head to look at Whitfield, and to his credit, he met her gaze and didn't flinch. "I know you want vengeance," Whitfield said.

"Right now, what I want doesn't even matter," she said, beginning the tirade she had been building in her head. She turned, beginning to walk toward Whitfield. "Right now, what I want is to rip your head off and shove it so far up your ass that your horns pop out of your neck. But that's not going to help the situation."

"Wolf was right," Whitfield said. "You are good at putting aside the personal to get to what matters." He knew bringing up her old captain was a dangerous thing to do. However, he didn't see how it would make his situation any worse.

"Wolf?" Snow asked only that single word, looking between Cadence and Whitfield.

"Oh, he didn't tell you that?" Cadence looked at Snow as she asked the question. "Wolf was there, live and in person. And he's my freaking Captain."

"The one you said goodbye to at the precinct after you died?" Snow couldn't believe it. The grief-stricken police captain he had seen not a year ago was a major player in everything they had been dealing with.

"Oh yeah, that's the one," Cadence said, turning her attention back to Whitfield.

"I didn't know until after Lexington that you had been his officer," Whitfield said.

"Would it have made any difference?" It was Snow who asked the question, which surprised Cadence.

"No," Whitfield answered with a shake of his head.

"Captain Rodriguez said you had plans," Cade said. "What are your plans? He seemed to think they were based on good intentions. And I'll be honest. He never struck me as a particularly heinous person until tonight. But then again, you had me fooled until this past investigation, too. So, I guess I'm not as good a judge of character as I thought."

"I know I'm the new guy," Will interjected, "but I will say that his test came up grey, remember? Grey is not evil. Grey is neutral."

"If you want an explanation, Cadence, please sit down," Whitfield said with a sigh. "You are peppering me with questions and threats. That isn't going to get us anywhere, as much as I know you want it to."

Cadence gave Whitfield a hard look. She was angry. She was grieving. So, as usual, she was channeling her grief into anger because it was easier for her to deal with. Sam had once called her a Happy-Fun-Ball-of-Rage when she was upset. It referenced an old Saturday Night Live skit they had both loved.

"Do not taunt Angry Rage Cadence," Sam would say, teasing her.

That memory took a bit of the wind out of the sails of her anger, and she went to her desk and sat in her chair. Ramon moved to stand behind her, using a gentle touch to rub her shoulders. Snow sat in the chair at Will's desk, and Will sat cross-legged on the floor in front of his desk.

"There has been a lot of misinformation about what's going on," Whitfield began. "Some of it I put out there. Some of it you guys assumed, or others assumed, and I just never bothered to correct it. You guys chasing your tails a little gave me breathing space. None of that matters now.

"Yes, I'm non-human. Will, that was clever, however it was that you tested me. I don't have a name of my own. So, I scrambled the name of the non-human at Scarecrow Farms since that's where I came from. I was there first. X'Haldzos was drawn to that area by the amount of blood and pain that was centered there a few centuries ago. He is what made that land bad, what cursed that house. He drove me out of my home. And he is now a bigger problem to you than I ever could be."

"Can we put a pin in the X'Haldzos topic and get back to what the captain was talking about with your plans?" Cadence had been quiet as she listened to Whitfield. However, her brain kept circling back to that comment made by the man she now knew was Wolf.

"Your former captain has an incredible gift, as you've now seen. His innate ability to interact with our world is rare among breathers. The plan that he was talking about was a lie. Well, not a lie, but not something I am involved in. He thought that he was working for me on a plan that would have good spirits like you possess bodies of the less savory. Kicking their souls out to be chained and used as weapons of fear to keep people in line. He wanted to decrease crime, decrease the evil in the world."

"We know about the movement of spirits who want to be considered gods by the breathers." Snow crossed his arms in front of his chest as he spoke. "That they want to possess people to live again and to chain non-humans to use them as instruments of fear against the breathers. So, if you were lying to Wolf about that being your reason, what were you, in fact, doing?"

"I was trying to keep X'Haldzos in place. He may have kicked me out of my home, but I didn't necessarily want him to move on. Unfortunately, in order to keep a creature of blood and pain sated, I had to do some creative maneuvering."

"Creative maneuvering?" Cadence shouted. "You authorized and participated in the murder of people. Overton's patients, the students at the dorm, Bethany Saxon. "

"I never claimed to be good, Cadence," Whitfield retorted, shouting back at Cadence as he was fed up with her interruptions. "I caused pain and bloodshed in order to keep the bigger danger from getting loose. That's not me trying to be a hero. That's me being fucking practical. The runes on the sacrifices channeled the pain and blood to it, so it didn't have to go hunt. That way, it didn't go blight anyplace else. But I kept the sacrifices moderated so that it didn't get too strong."

"I fail to see how the college massacre was moderation," Snow said. "Or the massacre that Overton had planned for his party when he was dealt with."

"Overton was a mistake," Whitfield said. "One that I helped them deal with. I helped them imprison him. When he got out and took over that college kid, that massacre was all him. The minute I found out, I made sure he was aware ... of my displeasure."

"The summoning ritual at Lexington?" Ramon asked the question, and Cadence was not only surprised that he spoke up but at the anger simmering in his voice.

"I gave it to Wolf," Whitfield nodded. "When the group he had do it bungled it, I sent Banks to you to help clean it up. When she failed, I came myself. And that's where one lie began to snowball into more as Croft attached me to your team."

"Let me see if I've got this straight." Cadence sighed. "Croft didn't know who you were when he assigned you to us. You've been orchestrating all these murders under a fake name: Shaldoxz. You have been doing all of this to keep the real demon, and yes, I'm using that word for it, at the farmhouse. Overton was an overzealous maniac that you tried to keep in check and helped to imprison when he got out of hand. And you lied to the captain about what you were doing, so he would turn a blind eye and help hide the crimes."

"In a nutshell," Whitfield said with a shrug.

"How did you and the captain even become a team?" Cadence tapped her thumb on the desk as she stared at the wood there. She couldn't look at Whitfield right now. Her brain was too busy puzzling through all of this to deal with the pain and anger his face brought.

"He saw me when he was young," Whitfield said. "I hadn't encountered any breather with the strength of his ability. I was curious about what he could do with it. I helped him hone it. As he chose his life's work, it was a great opportunity for me. I then had a tool at my disposal to help hide the truth of those murders. And his cult, as you call it, is something he believes is doing bad for good reasons. And while that's true, the reasons aren't the ones he thinks they are.

"But now X'Haldzos is free," Whitfield continued. He turned to face Cadence and leveled his gaze at her. "So, I ask you, Cadence. Do you want your revenge on me? Or do you want me to help you take revenge on the non-human that has been the cause of all of this?"

Cadence was silent for a moment, thinking. At length, she brought her jade eyes up to meet Whitfield's gaze.

"I don't want revenge," she said, her voice like ice. "I want this to end."

Book Club Questions

1. What did you suspect about Croft? Were you right?

2. Did the turn with Russell and Teeny surprise you? Why or why not?

3. What are your thoughts on Snow's situation?

4. What are your thoughts on Will?

5. Are you looking forward to seeing more of Will and his inventions?

6. Did Whitfield surprise you?

7. What do you think will happen now that the non-human at the farm is no longer there?

8. What do you think is going to happen with the paranormal group now?

9. Do you think Cadence and her new partner make a
   good match? Why or why not?

10. What are your predictions for book 5 in The Life
    After Series? How do you think the characters will
    move forward?

Author Bio

Growing up in a haunted house and having a father who loved horror set the stage for Amanda's creative life. This Urban Fantasy author has been writing since her teen years, blending horror, fantasy, and the paranormal. Amanda balances her day job, her writing, her family, and helps her husband run a board game group and YouTube channel, Tabletop Misfits. Local to Southwest Florida and a total geek, you can often find her conventions, either as a vendor or an attendee.

Cadence and all the others will return in *The Life After Series, Book 5: Dead Man's War*

iden had opened the store. It had felt like the right thing to do. At the very least, there might be some sales, so there would be less he would have to box up to send back to vendors or to put in storage. Some people had come up to the shop to light candles and lay flowers in front of the window in memory of Lauren.

The bell over the door chimed, and Aiden looked up to see Tom from Pho-Q walking in. He stopped, seeing Aiden behind the counter, and shook his head.

"So, the story in the paper was true?" Tom asked.

"Yeah, it's true," Aiden said with a sigh. It was not the first time he had given that answer today.

"Damn," Tom said, shaking his head in dismay. "I'm sorry, man. Anything we can do for you guys?"

"Nah," Aiden said. "I'm going to be working on closing up the shop."

"Why not keep it open?" Tom asked with a shrug. "Can't hurt to have a place with this kind of stock at your fingertips with the kind of stuff you guys get up to. Or are you and Derrick not continuing with it?"

"He and I really haven't talked much since this morning," Aiden said. "I assume he'll come in when he gets up. Unless he has homework or something."

"Well, you guys come by when you get hungry," Tom said. "The food's on us."

"Thanks, bro," Aiden said.

Tom nodded and headed out. He held the door open for a woman coming in with flowers. Aiden directed her to put them outside with the candles and other flowers that people had been leaving. He recognized the woman as someone who had been a regular customer of Lauren's. Once she had left the shop and put her flowers in with the growing memorial, Aiden bent over, leaning his elbows on the glass case, and rested his head in his hands. He was beyond exhausted and numb.

The bell chimed again, and Derrick walked in, his backpack slung over his shoulder. He looked like he hadn't slept much, if at all. Aiden walked over to him and gave him a hug. That was an action that took Derrick by surprise, but he hugged his friend back.

"Okay, that was weird," Derrick said. "Cool, but weird."

"Yeah, well, I figured we both could use it," Aiden said with a shrug. "We've got each other." It had been in the back of his mind all day. They had lost Bethany. They had lost Dan, now Lauren. Their little paranormal group was down to him and Derrick. Teeny might join them, but he wasn't even sure there was going to be a group left after the next few days.

Derrick nodded and made his way back to the table they always sat at. "How come you have the store open?"

"I have work to do in here, anyway," Aiden said, answering Derrick. "Figured I would open it up and see if I can offload some of the inventory. And people have been coming in all day."

"I saw the little memorial out front," Derrick said with a nod.

"How are you doing?" Aiden asked.

"I would figure I'm doing better than you. You knew her longer," Derrick said with a shrug.

"Doesn't mean you don't have your own grief," Aiden said. "Last night was bad."

"Yeah," Derrick said, shuddering a little. He just kept hearing Lauren's head hitting the rock. When he closed his eyes, all he could see was her body in the black bag with her head cracked open as they zipped her up.

"I guess the big question is, where do we go from here?" Aiden let Derrick think about that for a moment as he disappeared into the back office. When he returned, he had two cups of coffee in hand. He sat down and passed one cup to Derrick, keeping the other for himself.

"Thanks," Derrick said, taking the offered cup. "And that's a question I was going to ask you."

"I figure any decision about the group comes from both of us," Aiden said. "We're the last two left."

"Do I lose points if I say I'm a little scared after last night?" Derrick looked at Aiden, fearing the man's opinion of him saying that.

"No, bro, not at all. I am, too," Aiden said, much to Derrick's relief. "What happened last night was scary shit."

"Have you heard from them?" Derrick pointed his finger up and swirled it around in the air as he asked the question.

"Not a word," Aiden said. "But given what we saw, I didn't expect to." As an afterthought, he fished the green felt clover out of his pocket and put it on the table. He hadn't thought to put it out before.

"So, you're closing the shop?" Derrick said, looking around. "It's going to be weird not coming here anymore."

"I know," Aiden said with a sigh as he ran a hand through his hair, pushing it back off his face. "I mean, I could keep it open. But I don't know what I would do with it. I'm not a psychic. I'm an audio/video guy."

"Photo studio?" Derrick had always wondered why Aiden didn't have his own studio. He operated based on business cards, online ads, and word of mouth.

"I don't know." Aiden shrugged. "Never really thought of opening one."

"How long is left on the lease?" Derrick asked.

"I have to find it," Aiden said. "I think it's in a file here. I want to say maybe five or six months. I know Lauren was thinking of closing."

"She was?" Derrick couldn't conceal his surprise.

"Yeah," Aiden said, nodding. "With all the cases we were getting, her hours here were getting weird. She said people had been complaining that they didn't know when to come in."

"Which brings us back to the question of if we will be doing any more investigations," Derrick said, leaning back in his chair.

"Yep," Aiden said. "It's a vicious circle, isn't it? I've been going around and around with it all day."

"Come to any conclusions?" Derrick was hoping Aiden had answers.

"Nothing concrete," Aiden said. "I think we both need to think about it. With us being in the papers at Christmas for the college dorm thing, and now with this, who knows? We may not get any more cases. People may be too scared to call us."

"Or they might figure we're really good, and we'll get even more cases," Derrick said.

"Maybe," Aiden said with a slow nod. "I'll be honest. It might be best to table the discussion until we get through the funeral."

Derrick nodded, then looked at his phone as it rang and winced. "Shit, it's my mom. I'll be right back." Derrick grabbed his phone as he got up and answered it. "Hey, mom," he said as he made his way out the door.